DELIGHT IN DISGUISE

Prudence had come to the bathhouse in the fashionable resort of Brighton assured that the Prince Regent himself enjoyed the curative powers of its steambaths and massages.

Now as she lay in the steam room and saw a man's hands come through the holes in a curtain, she forced herself to relax. Surely this was a proper course of treatment, not a source of immoral pleasure.

As those hands slick with soap caressed her shoulders, she felt the tension that had plagued her since she resisted a seducer's kiss begin to ebb. So far, so good, she thought, even as delicious shivers began to run through her. Even when a man's voice gently asked if he might go further, she felt no cause for alarm.

Of course, Prudence had no way of knowing that the voice was not that of an Indian masseur—but that of an English lord with devilishly different designs on her. . . .

Lord Ramsay's Return

Elisabeth Fairchild

A SIGNET BOOK

SIGNET
Published by the Penguin Group
Penguin Books USA Inc., 375 Hudson Street,
New York, New York 10014, U.S.A.
Penguin Books Ltd, 27 Wrights Lane,
London W8 5TZ, England
Penguin Books Australia Ltd, Ringwood,
Victoria, Australia
Penguin Books Canada Ltd, 10 Alcorn Avenue,
Toronto, Ontario, Canada M4V 3B2
Penguin Books (N.Z.) Ltd, 182-190 Wairau Road,
Auckland 10, New Zealand

Penguin Books Ltd, Registered Offices:
Harmondsworth, Middlesex, England

First published by Signet, an imprint of Dutton Signet, a division
of Penguin Books USA Inc.

First Printing, March, 1996
10 9 8 7 6 5 4 3 2 1

To my brother, David, and his wife, Renda,
who have just embarked on an adventure overseas;
and to Anna Marsico (my masseuse),
whose spiritual journey
has been an inspiration to me

ACKNOWLEDGMENT

Special thanks to the Dallas Public Library
for chasing down both editions of
Sake Deen Mahomed's published works.

AUTHOR'S NOTE:

Mahomed's Baths were opened in King's Road, Brighton, in 1786 (on the current site of the Queen's Hotel) by Sake Deen Mahomed, a native of India. The baths offered vapor or Turkish baths, the first in Great Britain, and a "shampooing" service (massage), performed by an attendant through flannel sleeves in a tentlike cover. After a number of successful cures, Mahomed published his methods, along with a list of his clients, several among them noble names. He was eventually appointed "Shampooing Surgeon" to King George IV, who suffered from arthritis and gout. William IV continued the appointment. Mahomed lived to the ripe old age of 102, dying in 1851.

Chapter One

Brighton, England, in the summer of 1818

Had Lady Childe not passed from this world to the next on the first day in July at Sake Deen Mahomed's bathhouse in Brighton, it is likely Charles Ramsay would never have met Miss Prudence Stanhope. It is a certainty he would never have touched her—body, heart, mind, and soul—as intimately as he did without their even having been introduced.

Fate had it that the overburdened heart of Ester Wilke Childe, a woman of enormous girth and tumultuous pulse, who vehemently refused to be bled as her physician advised, chose that sultry afternoon to cease its beating. Like a quivering blancmange the great woman had wedged herself in one of the large, wooden, hot-and-cold tubs in which the patrons of the bathhouse were encouraged to soak.

She appeared to be quite content with this arrangement until with a mildly alarmed voice she clutched her bosom, saying, "Oh my! What's this then?" before keeling face first into the steaming Turkish bath in which she was immersed.

"Lady Childe!" The attendant who came in with fresh towels was suitably alarmed by her posture.

Lady Childe had not the breath within her to respond.

Dismayed, the attendant dragged her head out of the water and cried loudly for assistance, which came running from every corner, indeed from every floor of the bathhouse. It took, in the end, six strong men to lift the respected lady from the confines of the tub.

Lady Childe's passing, in and of itself, would not have thrown Lord Ramsay and Prudence Stanhope together had it not required the assistance of every one of the bathhouse attendants, with Sake Mohamed himself directing the proceedings, to transfer that stout and august lady out of the bath and into a dry place, where she was reverently covered, toweled down, and clothed, even her hair being arranged before a physician was called to view the body, pronounce her deceased, set pennies over her eyes, and cover her face.

It was while this debacle unwound on the floor immediately beneath her, that Prudence Stanhope reached the limits of her lung capacity. With a great gasp she cast open the flap of the tentlike covering beneath which she steeped in a fog of steam, and drank in a mouthful of ordinary air. Gingerly she turned her head, rubbed the sweating ridge of her brow, and in a whisper designed not to aggravate her aching head, complained to her traveling companion, "I feel like an overcooked bag pudding. What keeps the man? I should like to get on with this. Do you think he forgets me?"

Mrs. Moore, an industrious woman who believed with all her heart that idle hands made the devil's mischief, was never to be seen without some article of needlework in her hands. As soon as she finished counting out a row of three knit, two pearl, she agreed. "He does keep you waiting forever. Do you have the headache, my love? Perhaps this shampooer has a concept of time quite foreign to us."

Prudence sighed, stretched her chin, and listened to the eggshell crunch at the base of her neck. Her head felt as if it were filled with the fog of steam in which she had so long surrounded herself. "Quite likely, Mrs. Moore. The gentleman is from India, is he not?"

Mrs. Moore clucked her tongue. "It has less to do with his being from India and more to do with his being a man, I'm thinking. They are no more to be depended upon than children, mark my words."

"Men are not what one might call faithful creatures," Prudence agreed wearily, though given an alternative she would have liked to claim otherwise.

"Isn't it always the same? I shall just go and see if I can light a fire under one of these lazy attendants." Rising briskly from the chair where she had been occupied with her needles and wool, Mrs. Moore went to do just that, without waiting for further agreement from Prudence, whose aching neck and shoulders so completely occupied her attention that she made no other comment than a moan.

"Kismet?"

Charles Ramsay listened as his brother tested the pronunciation of the word with unrestrained sarcasm. Rupert was uneasy with the concept—almost as uneasy as Charles had been when he had first seen the dreadfully scarred stub of all that was left of his younger brother's once perfectly healthy leg. Rue shifted uncomfortably beneath his hands, but he made no complaint as Charles massaged the rock hard muscles of the shoulder that bore so much of Rue's weight when he leaned into his crutch.

"An intriguing idea, isn't it?" Charles murmured.

"Bloody barbaric idea," Rue grumbled. "I believe you have been wrapping that turban too tight about your head. Was war with the French fated? Was the loss of my leg? What about the loss of your fortune? Of all the card games Jack ever lost, was it predestined he should lose the one in which he chose to risk your entire inheritance? Bah! I will not swallow such stuff and nonsense!"

Charles touched his palm to his forehead, just below the band of the headpiece Rue ridiculed. "My head has grown comfortable with both the turban and the idea of kismet, Rue, even when it comes to Jack. Life is a journey. Every fork in the road offers opportunity for choice."

"Jack is a fork in the road?"

Charles laughed. "No. Jack is an obstacle, but obstacles offer opportunity for enlightenment. Every encounter, good or bad, offers up opportunity for growth and understanding."

"If it's growth and understanding Jack's stupidity offers you, you'll soon be big as a house and wiser than Moses."

"Sir!" They were interrupted. A woman filled the doorway, arms akimbo. "How can you keep Miss Stanhope waiting so long?" Her tone was indignant.

Rupert sat up beneath his tent and poked his head out of the flap to stare. "You keep some female waiting, Chaz? I'd no idea!"

"Neither had I," Charles drawled with amused wonder.

The woman who stood brazenly in the doorway, uncowed by the idea she might witness a gentleman in an embarrassing state of undress, was a matronly creature of advancing years, uncertain station, and wilting hair, with the dress and commanding air about her of a female who brooked no nonsense from anyone she believed beneath her in age or station. At the moment she looked greatly offended, and from the pointed narrowing of her eyes, he was the offender.

"For more than half an hour, sir . . ." the woman scolded, head bobbing, the folds in her neck trembling like a turkey wattle. "My mistress, a patient and mannerly young woman, has been cooking in a broth of hot vapor. She is about to faint from breathing steam, her face is quite pink with the stimulation to her circulation, and she would like very much to be decently clad again. Enough is enough. You will attend to her shampooing at once, or I shall have you reported."

Charles Ramsay found the woman's unblushing audacity diverting. He knew that he did not look in the least like an English lord in the turban and flowing Turkish robes he chose to don whenever he and Rupert visited the bathhouse, but that someone might mistake him for an attendant had never crossed his mind.

Beside him, his brother Rupert adjusted his tent-drape more securely about his nether regions. For a moment, equally amused, their eyes met.

"Mustn't keep *Miss* Stanhope waiting," Rupert suggested mildly. "Kismet calls."

That Rupert, of all people, should encourage him to mischief only deepened Charles's amusement. He smothered the beginnings of a grin. Fate and opportunity were not to be ignored when they beckoned so insistently. He bowed obsequiously and gestured toward the door. "You will lead me to your mistress?"

"This way." Haughty in her triumph, the woman set off down the hallway skirt swirling.

"Do not enjoy yourself too much," Rupert cautioned, his eyes sparkling with glee.

Charles could no longer repress a laugh. "Do not stir from this place until I return."

Rupert shrugged and slapped at his stump. "Where am I going to run off to?"

Rash Ramsay, as Charles was known to both friends and enemies alike, needed no further encouragement. He set off without hesitation to see to the shampooing of Miss Stanhope.

Chapter Two

Chilled, Prudence pulled the stifling drape back into place over her head and tried to sit still. Steam bloomed warmly from the spigot at her feet, blurring her vision within the tenting. Once again the air felt thick in her throat. Breathing took almost as much effort as waiting did in this steam tent. She had grown completely unaccustomed to sitting still, waiting for others to wait on her. For the past five years, Prudence Stanhope's life had revolved around quite a different scenario. She, the unattached and penniless relative, had become—since the death of her parents—one who waited on those who waited. She sat with pent energy, her muscles braced. A part of her was poised to jump up in answer to the summons of anyone more worthy, more financially fit, than herself to do little more than sit, steam, sweat, and soak.

She did not know exactly what to expect from the shampooing Dr. Blair had prescribed. She had high hopes that at last she would find relief from the pinching pain in her neck and back. The vapor bath had warmed her all over, warmed her almost to the core of her being. She was drenched with the sweat of that warming in a manner to which she was wholly unaccustomed. The length of linen, wrapped for modesty's sake around her torso, clung to her like a second skin. The sound of her own breathing was louder than usual, the smell of the herbs used in the baths clean and strongly fragrant. If she moved, the fabric of the tentlike draping felt rough against her skin. Her neck sang with a high-pitched pain.

"I prescribe a course of the waters in Brighton," Dr. Blair had declared in a voice that brooked no argument, peering at her from behind the shining lenses of his spectacles, which slid with regularity down the long, narrow slope of his nose to perch on its bulbous end.

"Brighton?" Her cousin Edith's husband, Timothy, the gentleman to whom Prudence was indebted for both the roof over her head, the three meals she ate each day, and the very clothes upon her back, expressed immediate resistance to the idea. "Why Brighton? Will not the waters in Bath or Tunbridge Wells suffice? It is more than twice the distance for Pru to go all the way to Brighton."

Prudence knew why Timothy questioned the physician. The knowing increased the sorrow that weighed heavily on her heart. Two events—the loss of the baby and their mutual loss of self-control—colored everything Tim did or said these days.

The doctor shook his head. "Neither Bath nor the Wells will do. Miss Stanhope requires a treatment they do not offer."

"Sea bathing?" From the very manner in which Tim spat out the words, it was evident how little faith he placed in the new craze for saltwater dousing and drinking.

Dr. Blair had peered down his narrow nose at the gentleman who so rudely challenged his authority. He cared not to have his medical judgement questioned. Of late, certainly since the unfortunate and completely unavoidable miscarriage of Sir Timothy Margrave's unborn son, his every diagnosis had been questioned.

"Sea bathing is not a bad idea, sir," he had said solicitously, "but it is another treatment I had in mind, one safely practiced for over twenty years in Brighton. The Prince of Wales is a known recipient of this highly efficacious Indian remedy, as is the Earl of Essex, the Duchess of Leeds, and Lord and Lady Middleton. However, if you insist that Miss Stanhope must not go to Brighton . . ."

Timothy had been outmaneuvered. "Not at all," he objected. "I have every desire that my cousin should receive the finest of care."

Dr. Blair had nodded. "Of course you do. Rest assured this treatment is just the thing to improve Miss Stanhope's energy and cheerful spirits. The body shampooing, you see, is relaxing to the nervous system and yet stimulating in the extreme to the blood flow."

Prudence had been intrigued. How could something be both relaxing and stimulating at the same time? How curious that it should be an Indian treatment. Prudence had just been reading to her cousin's daughters, Jane and Julia, about India.

Prudence rolled her head back and forth and listened. Eggshell. Her neck sounded like crushed eggshell. In fact, she felt like an egg these days—fragile, brittle, easily broken, and all sticky goo inside.

Prudence started when Mrs. Moore swept back into the room. She was followed by a man. His spicy, foreign scent conjured up images of the faraway places Prudence delighted in reading about, places with names that rang like music: Singapore, Ceylon, Delhi, Hong Kong, Zanzibar, Constantinople.

She had pointed out the tantalizing names to Jane and Julia on the globe. She had read to them of elephants and monkeys, lions, tigers, rhinos, and the cobra snake that could be charmed by the playing of a flute. As their governess, she had filled the girls' heads with the importance of the trade that enabled them to enjoy tea, sugar, rice, cotton, coconuts, cocoa, and cinnamon. She had sent them about the house to find bits of these foreign places in the rosewood, ebony, teak, mahogany, and satinwood furniture they took for granted.

She had refrained from discussing more sensitive topics— sacred cows, karma, reincarnation, Buddha, Confucius, Shiva, Vishnu, and Mohammed. Her own penchant for the romantic and the lure of the unknown kept her up most nights, reading every scrap of material she could get her hands on by guttering candlelight. In the dark stillness between dusk and dawn, it was easier to imagine what would it be like to explore people, places, and ideas so completely different from those she knew. The more she read, the more she felt bound by the familiar green of the English countryside, by globes, maps, music lessons, and by the likelihood that she would never set foot off British soil.

It was disappointing in a way to think that this treatment today, at the hands of a gentleman from India, was the closest Prudence Stanhope would probably ever get to satisfying her longing for adventure. She waited beneath her tent, in breathless anticipation, repressed desires throbbing in her every heartbeat.

"I have found someone at last, Prudence. His name is Chaz." Mrs. Moore spoke too loudly in the expectant silence of the room. Her chair creaked a protest when she sat down and picked up her knitting again.

Click, click, click—the needles counted time, increasing rather than reducing Pru's anxiety.

A whoosh of cool air swirled around her legs as the weight of the tenting was lifted away from her toes. The world had come to her rather than the other way around.

"If you will be so good as to turn off the steam, we shall begin with the feet, madame."

Simple words, spoken in flawless English, with only a hint of something foreign in his inflection and delivery, and yet the effect the shampooer's voice had on Prudence was anything but simple. As if she were a tuning fork just touched and his words the notes of an instrument she had heard but once before, each syllable rang in her ears.

With a strong desire to hear the man more clearly, Prudence bent to turn off the spigot at her feet. The heady blanket of steam subsided, and with it all noise but the clicking of Mrs. Moore's needles, the drip of moisture from her canvas tent, and the sound of her own breathing. That her treatment involved this stranger from a strange land, touching her body, she knew. An unanticipated touching had made her tense to begin with, had it not? How could more touching relax her?

There was a difference of course. Here, she was completely encased, her identity hidden as much as that of the shampooer was hidden from her. This stranger could not see her. He did not know her. His touching would have no personal meaning to either of them—no meaning, no pull, no destructive desire—and yet her heart beat faster faced with this treatment.

Her body anticipated his touch as anxiously as her ears awaited the sound of the stranger's voice. Too long had she fought off her desire, not only for foreign lands, but for the love of a gentleman equally unattainable. She was restless, trapped in the shell of her own inappropriate desires, especially now that she knew they were reciprocated—now that Timothy had breached the bounds of decency and expressed his feelings for her, not only with words, but with his touch.

So tightly wound had Prudence become, that she feared she might shatter beneath the hands of this stranger.

The man knelt. Flannel-gloved hands clasped her ankles. Prudence flinched.

"Relax," he said evenly as he lifted first one foot and then the other to rub briskly at her heels and soles with a pumice stone.

Her feet tingling with the unusual stimulation, Prudence was relieved when the stone was laid aside and a bag of soap, the bag itself made up of some kind of animal skin still furred on the outside, caressed her toes with yet another undeniably stimulating texture. Soap liberally applied, the flannel-gloved hands then made a business of rubbing and prodding at the flesh of her feet with a businesslike thoroughness. Prudence longed to pull away. This was not at all what she had expected.

As if the shampooer read her thoughts, the prodding stopped. He knelt, holding the lathered heel of her foot cupped in the palm of one hand. It was an oddly intimate connection to share with a stranger.

"It would be best if you sought an attitude of repose." His every word resounded in her ears, the voice of a flute so sweet it could charm a snake.

She could not trust this voice. Men, especially charming ones, were not to be trusted.

She laughed mirthlessly. There was not an ounce of repose to be found in her entire being. She was, to the contrary, wound tighter than a music box. "Repose? I have quite forgotten how such an outlook is achieved."

Chapter Three

Rash Ramsay was snared. As though he was a rabbit, an unknown, unseen female had captured him with the lure of her longing. He clasped between his hands the ankle of a young woman whose face he might never recognize were he to meet her unveiled, and found himself yearning to ask a multitude of impertinent questions. He also longed to see more of the figure hidden beneath the waterproof canvas that hung suspended from the ceiling like mosquito netting. He wanted to stroke the delicate arch of this foot, to nibble each exquisite rosy toe, to take full advantage of this unusual encounter. Yet his desire became secondary to the question of how someone so young had lost her ability to relax. What trouble could this inexperienced female have encountered to so weigh her thoughts? As if the answer to that mystery was imbedded in her satiny flesh, his fingers began to ply her skin with an industry and thoroughness that surprised a satisfying moan from her lips. It felt good to touch a woman again, her skin soft and dewy from the baths.

Charles's eyes closed with satisfaction. No matter that this poor creature was strung tight as a bow. No matter that he could not see her, did not know her, might never have answers to the questions her remarks raised, he was ready to make her body sing with a music she had never known before. It had been too long since Rash Ramsay's last encounter with the fair sex, longer still since he had set hands on the skin of an English lass. This shampooing had begun as a lark, but with Miss Stanhope's jaded admission of a complete lack of repose in her life, it became an encounter not so much of the flesh as it was of two like spirits.

She wanted to know how to relax. The wonder of it was, Rash Ramsay could help her. Had her needs been otherwise, he had not the means to assist. He could offer neither money nor land. The title he possessed was meaningless. Despite these insufficiencies, Charles had brought riches with him from overseas. The art of relaxation was one of them. He might not be able to see who this rigid young lady was, but he would have the satisfaction of melting her stiffness like butter beneath his hands.

"Imagine yourself in a favorite place," he suggested, "a safe place where nothing and no one can trouble you."

"Does such a place exist?" she murmured dubiously.

He liked the sound of her voice. It was low and earnest, without the vaguest hint of seductiveness or cajolery. The weight of her matter-of-fact skepticism gave him pause. Perhaps she was right to doubt that such a place existed. He could not, after all, claim that this was a safe place, nor that he was someone who had come with absolutely no intention of troubling her. Her question shifted his intent, reminding him of his own belief that every encounter was an opportunity to know one's self better. Chance had thrown him together with this suffering female for a reason, perhaps to remind him of his own attitude of repose in helping this woman to find hers.

"There is such a place," he said with certainty. "I know without doubt, for I have found it in the midst of chaos."

He had. Despite the fact that he had returned to Great Britain to find his entire fortune gambled away, his sister now wed to the man who had won it, and his youngest sibling just returned from a runaway marriage to Gretna Green, Charles Ramsay believed what he had told Rupert. There were lessons to be learned from every encounter, every hardship. Perhaps more important, he believed completely in the core of peace deep within him. That this tightly strung young woman should question the very existence of such repose bound them together in a way he had never anticipated. He wanted to dispel her doubts.

"I'm sure Miss Stanhope is not at all interested in your opinion," Mrs. Moore said tartly. "Best keep your thoughts to yourself."

"To the contrary, Mrs. Moore," Prudence languidly contradicted her. "I am most intrigued by the man's philosophy. Do go on, sir."

"An attitude of repose lies within each of us," he said. His hands gently persisted in their ministrations to her feet. "Between waking and dreaming it is to be found. The stillness of repose will see you through the direst of circumstances."

The foot in his hands twisted.

The shampooer's thumb found tender, aching spots where Prudence had not thought there was pain. The probing was delicious, almost erotic. Prudence floated in the steady rhythm of hands against her feet, then ankles and calves. She felt warm and heavy, as if she were surrounded in steam again, floating into sensations she had never experienced before.

He stopped the shampooing of her legs at the knees. She had feared he might go higher. She had tensed with the thought, her pulse quickening. Men were not, after all, to be trusted. Neither, for that matter, was she. When the drape fell back down over her toes, she felt betrayed by needless fear.

"Pray, sir, how do I get to this place of peace?" His shadow stood, moved to her side, and reached for the drape once more. The shape of the shadow reminded her of the man she had seen on the beach that morning.

"Put your hands through here," he directed. His voice touched her as much as the cool air that fanned across her breasts and belly as he extended the flannel sleeves that intruded on her canvas tent. She put her arms through the sleeves.

He took each hand as he had her feet, in a manner they had never been taken before. Pumice, not so vigorously applied this time, then the furred bag of soap lathered across her palms, knuckles, and wrists. After which, his slick, flannel-gloved hands seemed bent on familiarizing themselves with her very bone structure. The rippling music of the shampooer's touch worked its way over every finger, every knuckle, every line in her palms. Prudence was floating again. She was the sandy beach, and he the tide from a distant shore, come to shape her.

Charles held a young woman's trusting hand in his and wondered what unseen forces had come together to allow him the privilege of paying homage to these strong, well-shaped, capable fingers.

Was it fate, kismet, or the devil that draped Miss Stanhope's form with tenting material, damply molding it to her breast? Her shapeliness pleased him, stirring his desire.

A lark, begun with just such provocative moments in mind, seemed now—as he massaged her relaxed and unsuspecting hand in his—voyeuristic and juvenile.

This young woman had come to the bathhouse because she longed to be well. Thoughtfully, Charles worked his way across fingers, palm, the throbbing pulse at her wrist, and up the rigidness of first one arm and then the other. The muscles beneath his searching fingers were rock hard. She seemed braced, he thought, as if to catch herself from falling.

What troubled Miss Stanhope? What pushed this creature so close to the brink of her sensibilities that she need fear falling?

The impression that she teetered on the edge of a precipice touched Charles Ramsay. With a show of self-control he shut his eyes to the enticing vision of her breast and concentrated on loosening the tightness beneath his hands.

She had asked him how to find peace. He would tell her what a Turkish masseur had told him.

"Imagine a gate," he began.

A gate? A gate leading where? Prudence longed to throw back the tent flap to look into the eyes of the gentleman who asked such a thing of her in a voice that conjured up images of the distant places she longed to explore.

"Never mind your silly gate, young man, you must do her neck." Mrs. Moore interrupted. "Prudence, you must tell him it is your neck and shoulders that trouble you so."

The work on her arms ceased.

"You may pull your arms in," the voice said.

With a rustling of canvas, Prudence drew in her arms like a turtle. Canvas rustling again, his hands, one of them clutching the soap bag, invaded her turtle-shell tent by way of the sleeves she had just vacated.

Prudence flinched from the invasion, her arms crossing protectively over her bosom. It occurred to her that this Chaz person might take advantage of their circumstances and touch her nakedness. The memory flashed through her mind of the manner in which her cousin had touched her not so long ago. The memory both shamed and aroused her. She pushed it away.

When the shampooer did at last touch her, his soapy flannel hands groping along the back of her neck and shoulders in the manner of a blind man trying to find his way, she shivered violently. Gooseflesh stood up all along her arms.

The hands stopped their slick progress.

"Are you cold?" the man asked. His tone was kind.

"No, not really." Prudence felt foolish.

"You are nervous?" he surmised.

She sighed. "Yes."

"Nervous is not good in the shampooing. One must strive for an attitude—"

"Of repose?" She said the words in exact unison with him. Her prickly attitude was anything but one of repose.

He laughed. She liked the throaty rumble. It was warm and contagious. She laughed along with him—a hedgehog with a sense of humor.

"That is better," he said. "One can approach repose by way of laughter. We will try again."

Simple words, simple in their sentiment. Prudence was affected by the gentle simplicity of this man: his voice, his manner, his touch. She was ready this time as his soapy hands passed slickly over her back and shoulders. She did her best to relax. Perhaps there was no threat in this man or in his touch. He demanded nothing of her but a state of repose.

"Imagine a gate," he said, as he had said once before.

Whatever did he mean?

For an instant his hands hit a spot that made her long to moan. In that instant his hands were the gate he referred to, a sensual gate to a realm in which Prudence floated on the sensation of touch. She tried to catch herself, to stop herself from falling under the spell of her own senses as they were stirred by a stranger's touch.

A gate. He wanted her to imagine a gate.

"What kind of a gate?" she asked.

God, his hands hit the spot again. Bliss. That was what it felt like—pure bliss. Was he trying to seduce her, just as Tim had seduced her, with no more than a touch?

The shampooer leaned into her tent-covered shoulder. His voice, deep and steady, did not sound like the voice of someone who meant to lead her astray. "A gate leading into a garden."

He gave her time to think, time to recover from the head-turning sensation of his hands on her shoulder.

"Can you see it?" There was nothing demanding in the question, only patience—infinite, calming patience.

Prudence saw no gate at all. She was floating on the rain-heavy cloud of his voice, on the steady pulsing rhythm of his hand on her neck. As if by his very insistence, a gate appeared, old, wooden, and half fallen from its hinges.

Surprised, she said, "Yes, I see it."

"Go through the gate and look around."

He was finished with one shoulder. As he spoke, his voice, moving from one ear to the other, accentuated the dizzying impression that Prudence was either floating or falling.

"What do you see?" he asked.

Unwilling to reveal the strange, dreamlike vision that lived in her imagination, she turned the question on her questioner. "What do *you* see in your garden?"

His voice continued to weave a tandem spell with his insistent hands. "I see a lush, tropical place with trees so tall and thick they cover up the sky in places. There are monkeys in my garden, swinging from branch to branch among the trees and birds the colors of precious stones. In the middle of the garden stands a temple, a crumbling ruin covered in ancient stone carvings that have recently been defaced by malicious intruders."

Pru had grown very still listening to him. Her neck and shoulders felt like warm candle wax beneath the relentless pressure of his moving hands. She was the candle and he the flame. She shook the fancy from her head. Her mind was full of odd imaginings today.

He was working on the base of her neck, the exact spot where Timothy had caressed her with kisses. As much as she had feared being touched in that particular spot, the movements of the shampooer's hands were not what she had anticipated. She had expected a touch that took something from her. Strangely, this touching effected just the opposite sensation.

Without realizing she did so, Prudence began to trust this stranger and the intentions of his hands.

"My garden is not so colorful a place," she murmured.

"No?" He did not ask her to elaborate. He did not pressure her in any way. In so doing, she could not deny the part of her that longed to be asked.

It was Mrs. Moore who obliged her—Mrs. Moore whose needles ceased clicking, jarring Prudence into fresh awareness of her presence. "What does your garden look like, love?"

Telling was awkward, but not telling would have proved even more awkward. "It is a kitchen garden," Prudence said uncertainly, "one with a high brick wall."

"Go on." The steady clicking of Mrs. Moore's needles resumed.

Prudence wanted to talk. So different was the garden she had imagined from the one the shampooer had described that she needed an explanation. What she saw troubled and confused her. "It strikes me odd," she blurted, her eyes still closed, the vision still hanging before her. "The garden I see is in serious disrepair."

"How so?" the shampooer asked, his hands never still, his voice never unkind or disbelieving.

"The gate is off its hinges." Her own voice sounded remote, almost as if she stood outside herself, listening. "Weeds and a trailing vine are choking the beds. There are unwanted creatures rustling about in the vegetables. They have been chewing at the carrots and peas. There is a stone fountain with a pale, marble cherub for a centerpiece, but no water runs in it. I do not think anyone has tended this place in years. The only things still flourishing would appear to be a glass house full of exotics: pineapples, limes, lemons, and bananas. The trees are laden with ripe fruit. I have but to reach out to pluck them."

"Take a hoe to the rest of the place, and it will be set right again," Mrs. Moore rasped to the tune of her needles. "Better yet, hire a gardener." She cackled at her own wit.

Prudence was more interested in the shampooer's reaction than Mrs. Moore's. "Why is my garden so different from yours, sir?" she asked.

There was a moment of silence. The hands she had begun to know and trust continued their soothing ministrations to the stiffness in her back. "The garden is a symbol of how you see yourself," he said, his voice like music.

Her first reaction was to reject this nonsense. "I am a garden?" she asked sarcastically, as unhappy with his response as she was with the ache in her back that his hands seemed at once to aggravate and soothe.

"What does a kitchen garden mean to you?" The shampooer's voice was as soothing as his hands.

Prudence closed her eyes and slid into the sensation of his touch. What *did* a kitchen garden mean to her?

"A kitchen garden is a place essential and practical rather than beautifully ornamental like a rose garden. It provides sustenance for an entire household."

"And are you like your garden in those respects?"

The question was not a complicated one, and yet it was unlike any question that Prudence had ever been asked. Was she like a kitchen garden?

He hit a sore spot. "Ow!" she grumbled.

"I beg your pardon," he apologized.

Mrs. Moore's clicking paused. "Why that's you exactly, my

dear. You are essential and practical rather than ornamental. The whole household would have been at sixes and sevens without you during the illness of the children and Mrs. Margrave's confinement. There's no one else looked after them with such love and diligence."

Prudence sighed wearily. "But the garden is not thriving."

"Do *you* thrive at present?" the shampooer asked.

"No, I suppose I do not. Otherwise I would not be here. What of the vine?"

"What do vines represent to you?" He deftly turned the question back on her. What was it Mrs. Moore had called him? Chad? No, Chaz.

She groaned as he hit a knot of pain on the right side of her neck. Tim had kissed her there, kissed her passionately. Chaz politely apologized again, but it was not really this man she required apologies from.

"Vines cling," she said, thinking aloud, concentrating on the question rather than the pain. "They cover anything they can wrap their tendrils around, softening the look of the landscape. They are desirable plants as long as they don't jump their beds. Ow! Ow! That spot hurts."

"I beg your pardon, madame." He moved his hands to a less painful spot. "You were saying vines are desirable?"

"Yes, as long as they stay in their designated beds." Beds! The word gained fresh significance.

Mrs. Moore paused in her clicking. "Vines will choke the life out a garden if allowed to run wild," she said with practical fervor.

Unexpected tears sprang to Prudence's eyes.

The voice of India, of faraway places and foreign philosophy, spoke. "Is there something or someone desirable in your life who clings like this vine? Something that has jumped its designated place, that chokes the life out of you?"

Pru fell silent again, a pensive, thoughtful silence. She glared at the shadows that played across the interior of her fabric tent. Strange how this simple line of questioning, in tandem with the shampooer's touch on her back and shoulders, opened her up somehow, mind and body, and drained out the feeling of tightness, of tension, of lonely despair. The hands on her back seemed to reach deep inside her, body and soul, exposing hidden truths.

"Perhaps there is," she said softly and closed her eyes. Tears that stood poised to fall burned twin tracks down her cheeks.

Chapter Four

Prudence Stanhope strolled out of the warm humidity of Mahomeds Baths with a spring in her step and the image of a garden in her head, a garden that needed a good hoeing. She shook away the thought. Released from the clinging heat of the bathhouse, from probing hands and probing questions, from a disturbing dip into the unknown, the day's dim sunshine felt as friendly as an arm across the vague ache in her shoulders. The breeze that stirred her freshly dressed hair and the ends of the ribbon tied at her throat was a gentle hand tracing patterns on her neck. The sound of the ocean shushing against the rocks beneath was a voice, calling her to dip her toes, as carefree as a child. Was this tranquil moment of contentment the elusive attitude of repose her shampooer had mentioned? Had she, in this instant, captured it like a butterfly in the palm of her hand?

Prudence hesitated a moment on the steps, luxuriating in the feeling. She looked up the hill toward New Steine Street where she had taken rooms, viewing Brighton with fresh appreciation. This thriving city had sprung from the ground, almost overnight, like a colony of mushrooms, pale and perfect, row upon row of cream-colored bow-front houses and shops. There was a strangely unreal impermanence about a place so freshly hatched, just as unreal and impermanent as her current feeling of well being. There was, beneath the fragile surface of this peaceful moment, the core of something ancient and worn within her soul. She wondered if in time that too could realize an attitude of repose. She was glad she had followed the doctor's directions to come here, glad she had followed his prescription for rest and relaxation, but it was all at the expense of one to whom she would rather not be indebted in any way. That truth marred the peace she had gained at the baths this morning.

A strange feeling touched upon her spine and shoulders like an echo of the shampooer's art, like a reminder of another touch she had suffered in the not so distant past. Prudence turned, half expecting to find Timothy there.

Of course he was not, but two gentlemen unknown to her, both of them blessed with hair that glinted in the sun like freshly polished copper, stood on the far side of the street staring! At her? She looked around her to verify the suspicion and realized that the cavalcade that had emerged from the door she had herself exited was probably the reason for their interest.

"Gently, gently!" A gentleman with the face of India and the coat and high white stock of an English businessman backed out of the door first. It was Deen Mahomed himself, shouting his concern to the six robed attendants who followed him, bearing upon their shoulders a heavily laden board, over which was draped a sheet.

Prudence wondered more about which of these attendants had served as her shampooer than she wondered about the large, irregular shape beneath the sheet until a flabby hand swung heavily from the shifting burden, and Mahomed let loose a cry of concern. "Please exercise care, gentlemen!" He personally tucked the hand out of sight again.

"Oh dear!" Prudence and Mrs. Moore said in unison.

"What have we here?" Mrs. Moore muttered.

"Can someone have died?" Prudence did not like to voice the thought, but what other conclusion was there to be drawn, given the evidence? Her sense of peace drifted away like smoke on the wind.

Mahomed nearly backed into them as he continued to direct the gentlemen with their burden.

"Come out of the way, Mrs. Moore," Prudence said sensibly.

Mahomed, hearing, turned to address her. "Miss Stanhope, is it not? Did you grow tired of waiting? We have had a most unsettling morning. Perhaps you will understand why we were so long in attending to you?"

Prudence nodded. "I can see you have been busy. One of your patients?"

"Regrettably, it is so, but it is an uncommon occurrence indeed, an honor of sorts, for this dear lady to begin the journey to her next life from my bathhouse. You will return tomorrow for your treatment?"

Prudence found his supposition that the dead woman began a journey to another life strangely comforting.

"Ester!" A high-pitched wail from the street interrupted any reply she might have made. "Ester! Stop the coach, man. That can be none other than my sister."

Swiftly excusing himself, Sake Deen Mahomed was off to attend to yet another female who was sure to be unhappy with his services today.

With the slamming of a door and a heartfelt wail, a rotund woman burst from the door of a carriage that had pulled up in the street. Prudence could not help but look in the direction of the coach. What captured her attention, and held it, was the face of one of the copper-haired gentlemen, framed for an instant in the bright square the window of the coach made against the darkness of its interior. He was still staring, not at the progress of the deceased as she had first assumed, but at her!

The body of Lady Childe was being carefully hefted into the carriage, along with the highly distressed sister of the deceased. All the while the young man with coppery red hair regarded Prudence intently through the opening of the carriage window. The vehicle lurched forward, carrying away its unhappy passenger and her completely uncaring sister.

The gentleman and his companion, hidden from Prudence for an instant, were revealed more completely. Two almost identical coppery red heads shone sleekly in the sunlight. The shorter of the two gentlemen had turned to watch the progress of Ester Childe. He was worth a stare or two himself. Well-dressed and handsome, his leg was missing below the knee. He leaned into a padded crutch, the stump of his leg balanced on a peg. And yet, he received no more than a cursory glance from Prudence. She was interested in the two-legged gentleman who stood beside him—the gentleman who seemed to have eyes for nothing and no one but her.

He stared unblinking from beneath the dark brim of his hat. Such unwavering perusal was undeniably forward and unsettling. More unnerving still, she would have sworn, though he did not smile, that he looked amused.

His mouth did not give her an impression of humor. It was set in an uncompromising line. His eyebrows—one arched slightly higher than the other—held a trace of amusement.

That a stranger might be amused at her expense tore something within Prudence that she had begun to think mended. Men! She wanted to believe them creatures worthy and dependable, but she had yet to find a specimen one might trust anymore than she had trusted an Indian shampooer this afternoon. Perhaps she had been a fool to trust *him*.

Though the fellow across the street stared—behavior so uncouth any school lad would know better—and though he was burned as brown and rough as a common laborer, still she could not mistake him for anything but a gentleman. His coat was both fashionable and well-cut, as were the full Cossack-style pantaloons he wore in lieu of leggings. The sash rakishly tied at his waist was unusual. Bright blue and purple in color, it was of a complex pattern she was certain must be either Indian or Turkish in origin.

This striking combination of sun-touched coloring and foreign fabric gave her the impression that the gentleman had traveled the far reaches of the globe. His very staring seemed to verify such an assumption, for surely only someone foreign, worldly, or exceptionally rude dared stare at a female with such impunity.

He was tall and held himself erect, if not out of pride, then from something closely akin to it. His hair was fired by the sunlight like sparks in a rising flame. Its redness accentuated the shadowed depths of the eyes that continued, unwavering, to regard her.

Normally, Prudence would have turned her back on such rudeness. Today, her every cell alive and aware and sensitive to sensation, she could not immediately ignore such attention. There was something undeniably arresting in being the object of open scrutiny. Could it be, she wondered, that this man knew the sensual stimulation she had just received? Was it writ so plain on her face, that she had walked the garden of her imagination while she consented to a stranger making free with her body?

Should she care if he did know? Life was all too brief, was it not? The poor lady who had been helped by six grunting men into her sister's carriage for the last time would have agreed with her on its brevity, she was sure.

Prudence lifted her chin and stared back at the stranger for a moment that stretched far too long for her liking. He should have looked away from her chill gaze.

Not this sun-touched curiosity of a man. His narrowed eyes brazenly swept the length of her. His errant eyebrow rose a notch.

"Rude fellow," Prudence murmured indignantly to Mrs. Moore, who stood beside her with her head down, gasping like a fish thrown abruptly from the water.

"Oh dear. Oh my dear, I must apologize. I had no idea."

Prudence was too annoyed with the brazen, faintly amused gaze that followed her every move to pay much attention. "Apologize?" she asked. "Whatever for?"

With a toss of her head she turned her back on the rude gentleman and set off briskly up the hill toward their lodging, her mind returning to the strange conversation she had shared with a shampooer.

Mrs. Moore came pattering after her, huffing a little to keep up with her energetic pace. "My dear Prudence, you will likely be quite angry with me, and I do not know how to go about telling you this in any way in which to avoid that quite justifiable anger, but tell you I must."

Prudence slowed her pace and stopped to look first at her indecipherable companion and then out over the Channel. The water glittered and flashed in the sunlight like a thousand dancing bits of broken mirror. A part of herself was like that today, shiny and shattered and yet incredibly fluid all at the same time. The artful work of the shampooer had made her feel this way. It was fanciful, she was sure, and yet she felt released, like a new chick from its shell by a pair of magic hands.

"Tell me what?" she asked.

Mrs. Moore flapped her hand back in the direction they had come. "That man back there . . ."

"Which man?"

"The one who stared at you just now."

She had all of Prudence's attention.

"What of him?"

Mrs. Moore swallowed hard and stared at her shoes. "He's the one who gave you the shampooing."

Prudence laughed, completely disbelieving. "What?"

"I'm ever so sorry, my dear." Mrs. Moore darted a morose look at her.

"This is not utter nonsense?" Betrayal touched Pru's neck with pain. Embarrassment burned in her shoulders and neck, in every spot where she had been touched by the shampooer. Prudence folded her arms defensively across her chest. Surely no Englishman would dare defame a perfect stranger in such a reprehensible manner!

"I wish it were nonsense, Miss Stanhope, with all my heart. You must believe me. His clothes are different enough, you may be sure, but it's him. There's no mistaking that face." Mrs. Moore resorted to her handkerchief. Tears sprang to her eyes. Her nose required blowing.

Prudence frowned. All sense of repose fled her being. In its place anger flooded. Her frown became a heated glare as she looked back down the street. She had been so completely fooled! She had trusted the man, trusted him completely with her body and with the workings of her mind! It pained her to be duped again, this time by a stranger. To be betrayed twice by young men of rank and fortune who would appear to think nothing of humiliating her with the magic of their touch and their sweet, empty promises left her feeling violated.

The copper-haired gentlemen had turned to walk in the opposite direction, toward the Pavilion.

Rage, like a dragon, uncurled its tail and unfurled its wings. Prudence wanted to swoop down on them, to stop their nonchalant progress away from her.

"However could you mistake him?" she demanded incredulously. Her question was directed to herself as much as it was meant for Mrs. Moore.

The Ramsay brothers turned into East Street.

There, in all his portly glory, a trail of followers like the tail of a comet behind him, they encountered the Prince Regent, come out onto the grounds of the Pavilion for a stroll.

"Kismet?" Rue asked in an undervoice.

Charles nodded. "Most definitely kismet."

The Prince greeted both Ramsays through the archway that led onto the grounds. They were old acquaintances. He asked them if they were on their way to honor him with a call.

Charles responded that that was indeed their mission, but before he could go on with the more important business of mentioning the treasures he had brought back with him from overseas, treasures he hoped the Prince and his set would find desirable enough to pay royally for, a female voice interrupted them, calling stridently, "Sir! You there, sir! Stop a minute. My mistress would have a word with you."

The Prince turned his royal head, his expression grave, to observe the instigator of such an interference to his discourse.

"Who is this creature, gentlemen, who comes running pell-mell after you? What business have you left undone, that she would chase you through town in broad daylight?"

Several of the Prince's entourage chuckled.

"Isn't that the kismet woman?" Rue whispered gleefully in his brother's ear.

The woman who chased after them was none other than Mrs. Moore, looking quite wind-blown and out of breath, her complexion blotched red, her hair more disarrayed than ever. Behind her strode a younger woman, looking radiant by comparison, her complexion rosy with the effort of catching up to them, her dark eyes sparkling with what could be nothing but ire, beneath the dark thundercloud of curling hair piled high on top of her head. Her carriage was so stiff as to be almost regal.

"Is that Miss Stanhope, you dog?" Rue was awestruck.

"I cannot say," Charles said.

"Cannot or will not?"

"I never got a glimpse of her face."

Rue suppressed a chuckle. "Of what *did* you get a glimpse, pray tell?"

Charles wisely refrained from answering. The beautiful woman he knew must be Miss Prudence Stanhope had pinned him with a glare as she advanced. She had large, deep-set eyes—inky blue he could see now for the first time—the color of indigo. They were beautiful eyes, but the stormy look in them at the moment was anything but beautiful. Her utter contempt of him struck like a bolt of lightning. She was angry; beyond angry, she was livid. The power of her ill-feelings for him seemed almost a palpable thing. Disbelief, anger, sadness, hurt, and betrayal moved like clouds through the depths of her eyes. It had never occurred to Charles that his foolish prank could generate such emotion. He felt as if he stared into the face of someone smoldering from a fire he had carelessly lit.

That Miss Stanhope was bent on giving him a public set down seemed a given. Charles feared to do so would besmirch her reputation far more than his. Rash Ramsay was known for the unpredictability of his behavior. This morning's business would bolster his reputation, not ruin it. But word of their unprecedented encounter was sure to ruin whatever reputation this proud young woman might cherish. Charles did not want Miss Prudence Stanhope ruined by this morning's rashness, nor did it serve his current business purposes well to become the latest topic of gossip.

In a gallant attempt to preserve both their futures to the best of his ability, he put a stop to any embarrassing outburst of emotion she seemed quite capable of exhibiting in her current frame of mind, by moving at once to her side, where he took up the resistance of her hand and drew her before the Prince, saying, "Highness, I am honored to present to you a charming

young lady whose acquaintance I have only just had the pleasure of making, Miss Prudence Stanhope."

"Charmed, utterly charmed." The Prince's stays might creak
a little these days when he bent to take a lady's hand, but he
cut a dashing figure all the same. He was always impeccably
dressed, and the high neckcloths and collars that he affected in
order to hide the bulging goiter in his neck gave him a certain
polished formality that was intriguing juxtaposed with his anything but regal smile. That Miss Stanhope was charmed
enough to hold tongue on her closely contained rage came as
no great surprise. What could she do when faced with pleasantries from the future king of England than curtsy and deliver
pleasantries in return?

As Charles had hoped, she was forced to abandon all intent
of taking him to task. Beyond an occasional dagger-sharp look
thrown in his direction, she behaved with admirable decorum,
while her companion looked on with narrowed eyes and
tightly pursed lips. So pretty by contrast were Miss Stanhope's
manners and person, that the Prince, whose head had always
been quick to turn when it came to feminine attractions, was
pleased to include her in an invitation that he directed first to
the Ramsays.

"You must dine with me two days hence," he insisted. "I am
putting together a small table of friends."

The Ramsay brothers accepted the royal invitation with
proper gratitude. Not so, Miss Stanhope. She was angry, and
accepting invitations to dine with the very persons with whom
she was so furious could not suit her sensibilities.

"How very kind, Your Highness, to ask someone you have
only just met in the street," she said with brittle politeness.
"Sadly I must decline."

"Oh, but you cannot refuse me, my dear." The Prince
blessed her with a sunny smile, taking her hand into his with a
touching, humble air. "My table will be shockingly uneven in
ladies and gentlemen if you do not come."

How could anyone refuse invitation twice from a Prince
when he clung to one's hand and would not let it go until one
acquiesced?

Prudence Stanhope could not. Graciously, she recanted her refusal and reclaimed her hand. She even agreed to the Prince's suggestion she need not trouble herself with transportation, for Lord Ramsay would be happy to convey her to the Pavilion.

"Lord Ramsay?" The hint of confusion as she repeated his name was not lost on Charles. It occurred to him that she had no idea what his name was. He swept off his hat and bowed before her.

"At your service, Miss Stanhope."

Storm clouds gathered in the depths of indigo blue. She opened her mouth to object.

"We have much to discuss," Charles reminded her.

After a moment's consideration, while her gaze burned through him, she nodded her head. She would be ready to roast him on the spit of her anger when next they met, of that he was certain.

Chapter Five

Prudence prepared with the utmost care for her second encounter with the Prince Regent, more carefully still for her second encounter with Lord Ramsay, whom she could not think of without every inch of skin he had so inappropriately touched flaming with the memory. To heighten her discomfort in having been so completely taken in by the man, she soon discovered her sham shampooer was known by the odious and highly suggestive nickname Rash. It was the proprietress of the rooms she had taken in New Steine who told her as much. The woman rolled her eyes with disapproval when informed Lord Ramsay's carriage would be calling for Prudence two days hence.

"It is never Rash Ramsay, himself, you mean, miss?" she exclaimed, curiosity writ plain on her face.

"I believe the gentleman's Christian name is Charles, Mrs. Harris," Prudence corrected her.

"Yes. That's the one they call Rash. I have heard he is just returned from India, and that he is often to be seen dressed like a native of that country."

"That's true enough," Mrs. Moore muttered. She had excused her mistaking an English gentleman for a bathhouse attendant because of the gentleman's clothing; a turban that covered every trace of his hair, she had said, and robes that greatly resembled those worn by all of the attendants. Prudence would have found her description of Lord Ramsay too outlandish to credit had she not seen the shadow of the man's turban herself. Why would a nobleman disguise himself in such ludicrous attire? The deceit of the man struck her afresh.

A man called Rash might do anything. He had gone to great lengths to deceive her. Odious man!

Mrs. Harris regarded her with disbelief, as if it were inconceivable that Pru had never heard of the Ramsays. "They are infamous, Miss Stanhope! Every one of the lot has been nicknamed for their sins by the *ton*." She closed her eyes to think. "There's Rakehell, Randy, Rip, and Rue."

"Are they all scoundrels then, to bear such wicked nicknames?" Prudence should have suspected as much after the nasty trick the man had pulled on her. Dear God! The blackguard's hands had been all over her person! Odious, odious man!

"I would suppose they must be." Mrs. Harris looked her up and down as though reassessing her character. "There is a sister, too. She is called something as well, but for the moment the name escapes me. You have truly never heard of them, miss?"

"No," Prudence said thoughtfully. "We are rather secluded from London gossip in Gillingham." Realizing that she was herself judging an entire family based on nothing more than gossip, and finding the idea distasteful, she asked, "Are the Ramsays referred to by these unfortunate nicknames by their friends, or only their enemies?"

Mrs. Harris blinked at her. "I would not know, never having met one. However have *you* come to meet a Ramsay, Miss Stanhope?"

Her reply was anticipated with an excess of interest. Mrs. Moore, who had stopped halfway up the narrow stairs to their rooms, threw a worried look over her shoulder. She had been protesting Prudence's imprudent acceptance of an invitation to the Pavilion for the entire length of their walk back up the hill. Prudence might have agreed with her had Mrs. Moore not been so insistent in her condemnation.

"We should never have chased after the man," she had wailed. "But how was I to know he was a lord, and standing there nattering with none other than the Prince Regent himself? I was struck speechless. None could have been more impressed than me to see you chatting with the nobs as comfortable as you please. And glad I was to see it, too, that you could behave so normally amongst your own kind like that, but however could you agree to dine with the Prince, my dear Miss Stanhope?"

Prudence had grown weary of her never-ending diatribe of negative sentiment and censure.

"How could I refuse?" she asked tersely, her nerves on edge. "Ramsay, the dreadful cad, deserves a fine set down. A set down I intend to give him. Besides, the Prince would not take no for an answer."

"But my dear Miss Stanhope, what are you going to wear? You've nothing suitable in your wardrobe, surely, for an evening in the company of the Prince and his set."

It was with that dilemma in mind that they had returned to the boardinghouse. What *was* she going to wear? And what must she say now to satisfy Mrs. Harris's curiosity as to her relationship with Lord Ramsay, the one called Rash? Mrs. Moore seemed to be holding her breath, waiting to hear as eagerly as Mrs. Harris.

"How did we meet?" She repeated the question, searching for the right combination of words. The truth of the matter made her cheeks burn. Her stomach roiled with anger. Prudence had no intention of telling the whole truth of the matter, and yet she would not lower herself to concocting a lie either. "I was introduced to Lord Ramsay only this morning," she said carefully. "It was at the Prince Regent's suggestion that I accepted the offer of his carriage. He was asked to dine at the Pavilion as well, you see."

Mrs. Harris's eyes fairly popped from her head. "You know the Prince then, miss? I'd no idea."

Prudence nodded and resumed her progress up the stairs. "There's no reason you should have known," she said.

Mrs. Moore rolled her eyes heavenward and stifled a chuckle. "No reason indeed," she hissed when they had safely gained the landing.

The matter of what Prudence would wear to dine with the Prince proved almost as sensitive a question as the ones Mrs.

Harris had posed. There were but five dresses in the wardrobe. They were the best of the castoffs with which cousin Edith had blessed Prudence. Of those five only one was what one might call evening wear, and that one was hardly suitable for dining with the Prince. But as it was all she had, Prudence took it out of the wardrobe and hung it up.

She and Mrs. Moore reflected upon its deficiencies.

"Oh my," Mrs. Moore sighed, so upset she dropped a stitch in her knitting. "What are we to do? That poor frock looks every bit of the three years it has seen wear."

Prudence tipped her head. She had little money in her possession. As a poor relation dependent on her cousin's largess, she was not paid in coin, as if she were a servant. She was paid in food and lodging and the clothes upon her back. She had been given a pocketful of coins for the trip, but not enough for extravagances. She could certainly not afford to have a dress made for the occasion. Determined to see the positive, she pointed out, "The fabric is good, and this shade of blue, though out of fashion this season, is very pretty."

Mrs. Moore nodded. "Your cousin always thought so."

Prudence did not care to be reminded she wore her cousin's clothes. She feared she assumed too much the mantle of Edith's life along with her clothing. She had come to Brighton to change that. Best change the garments as well. "The neckline is outdated, as are the sleeves, but perhaps they may be altered somewhat. This chenille trimming is easily replaced, and the ribbons. With fresh gloves and one of those new gauze shawls I shall be quite respectable."

And so she was after a great deal of seam ripping and restitching. Not fashionable, by a far cry, but presentable. Her finances had been stretched by the purchase of new gloves and a particularly fine Chinese shawl, but the results pleased Prudence. She had no crepe turban, plumed toque, or French satin cap for her head, no coronet of silk flowers, nor an aigrette of pearls. Her meager purse would not stretch so far, but Mrs. Moore took pains with the curling iron, saying kindly, "Your hair you need never be ashamed of, miss." As she pinned and curled and debated over the placement of haircombs, Pru practiced the diatribe with which she intended to put Lord Ramsay in his place for his completely unacceptable behavior.

With her words arranged as carefully as her hair, she flung open the door at the appointed time of his arrival and promptly forgot every word she had memorized.

Rash Ramsay had arrived in what appeared to be formal Indian attire! Dear Lord! He wore a bright blue and gold turban and damask slippers with curling toes! How could an Englishman, especially an odious Englishman, look so completely comfortable, so devastatingly handsome, in such an outlandish outfit?

Ramsay managed.

In explaining how she had mistaken an English lord for a bathhouse attendant, Mrs. Moore had described the appearance of Ramsay at the bathhouse in flowing white robes and a turban. Her words did not do justice to the magnificent apparition standing quietly before Prudence. Buttoned high at the neck, a beautifully tailored tunic of milk white silk brocade was cinched at the waist by a wide, silken sash of brilliant blue and gold. Matching white trousers, cut so baggy they billowed in the breeze, drooped over the deep blue damask slippers with curving, tasseled toes. No one could mistake this vision in the doorway for a bathhouse attendant. The gentleman looked more like a foreign potentate.

Prudence felt like a pigeon standing before a peacock. She drew her shawl a little tighter around the shabbiness of her newly refurbished dress. Was this another prank? The idea made her angry. Did Rash Ramsay garb himself so flamboyantly that he might throw her completely into the shade of his brilliance?

Determined she was neither to be intimidated nor diverted from her planned course of action, no matter how awestruck his appearance left her, Prudence squared her shoulders, sailed past Ramsay before he could offer her his exquisite arm, and strode regally to the steps of his carriage.

Without so much as the courtesy of a response to the cheerful good evening he uttered, she said, "As I am intent there should be no further misunderstanding between us, my lord, I must take this opportunity to properly condemn you for the outrageous manner in which we were first introduced."

She was complimenting herself internally that her words had been delivered with an admirable lack of quavering emotion when a feminine voice inquired from the depths of the carriage, "And what outrageous manner was that?"

Prudence bit her too hasty tongue. With a feeling of alarm she accepted the hand Lord Ramsay held out for her assistance in gaining the height of the body of the coach. She could not continue standing in the street with her mouth open, pretending she had not heard the woman, no matter how much she might wish to. The anger she had hoped to vent and the speech she had so carefully rehearsed collided at the back of her throat. Lord Ramsay's eyes were gleaming with amusement. His eyebrows rose and fell as if to ask silently whether she required assistance in extricating herself from her verbal faux pas.

She glared at him severely. Completely foolish she felt, completely at a loss for the right words.

"I handled the matter with unforgivable rudeness." Ramsay volunteered an answer to the unseen female in his coach.

That was true enough. Prudence stepped into the carriage, her breath catching in her throat as she waited with growing dread for the rest of his explanation. What would this scoundrel say? Ramsay had thus far ignored all the rules that governed gentlemanly behavior. He could ruin her forever with no more than one ill-chosen word. Why did her tongue fail her so completely? Why did she not throw herself from the trap this coach had become? She ought to run from the humiliation this man intended to heap upon her head. She could not speak. She could not run.

She settled herself in the far corner of the carriage and faced the man she had seen earlier, the one with the wooden leg. A lovely, dark-haired female with porcelain fine complexion sat beside him as if she belonged there. Prudence was relieved to see these two wore sensible, ordinary clothing very much like her own.

With a sense of trepidation Prudence waited for Rash Ramsay to finish what he had begun, shaken like the carriage as he followed her in and planted his flowing silks beside her without a trace of awkwardness. The man seemed larger than life, larger and bolder. His eyes met hers without blinking.

"I first caught sight of Miss Stanhope on the steps just outside Mahomed's Baths two days ago."

Pru swallowed hard and closed her eyes, expecting the worst.

"I thought I recognized her from some earlier encounter." His snake-charming voice paused rather significantly.

Her eyes flew open. He could recognize her from only one "earlier encounter," the encounter in which he had played at being her shampooer. And it was her body he would recognize from that exchange, not her face! Did he mean to ridicule her openly in front of the woman who eyed her with such open curiosity? Pru braced herself for the coup de grâce.

The gentleman directly across from her knew the truth as well as she did. With a worried look in Lord Ramsay's direction followed by an uncomfortable clearing of his throat, he disengaged himself from the conversation by pressing his face to the pane of the window, as if completely captivated by the view.

Ramsay continued languidly in his explanation. "I was, I hesitate to admit to you, Grace, inconsiderate enough to stare intently at Miss Stanhope as I tried to place my recollection of her."

"You stared?" Grace repeated. Her tone suggested she was convinced there must be more.

"I did stare—most inconsiderately. Did I not, Miss Stanhope?"

Prudence could not help but stare herself, at Ramsay in his outrageous attire. She felt like a mouse, caught between a Persian cat's paws. Did he mean to play with her before the kill? She hated to agree with the man on any subject when she was so filled with anger and mortification, but she managed to nod and say, "You did," without sounding as if she were spitting the words at him.

"And had you met before?" Grace inquired, little knowing

what consternation rose in Prudence's breast with the question.

"I had never had the pleasure of an introduction to Lord Ramsay." Prudence tried to sound as smooth as Ramsay, though she felt as if every word forced its way through her lips. "I have not yet had the pleasure of an introduction to you, either." She was surprised how collected her voice could sound. "I am Prudence Stanhope. You are?"

"Your manners, Chaz, have always been atrocious." The gentleman across from her tore his attention from the scenery long enough to shake his head sadly at Ramsay. "But since your overseas jaunt they are worse than ever."

"I am changed by my travels," Ramsay admitted.

Rupert Ramsay introduced himself and his new wife, Grace. He offered up her name as if it were a gift. Prudence was impressed by that, but little else. The man was a coward to so completely remove himself from their conversation.

The newly wed Mrs. Ramsay was not easily turned from the topic they had been discussing. "My husband speaks highly of Mahomed's vapor baths and shampooing, Miss Stanhope. Do you find them equally salubrious to your health?"

Charles Ramsay turned his handsomely turbaned head to hear her answer. Prudence could not look at him. She was sure he was eager to be amused yet again at her expense if she were foolish enough to admit she took pleasure or comfort in the outrageously invasive shampooing he had given her.

"I do not feel qualified to offer up an opinion after only three sessions in the baths," she said carefully. "I feel privileged to have been waited upon by Sake Deen Mahomed himself these past few days. It remains to be seen whether the treatments have affected my health, either positively or adversely."

With a nod of his head Rupert Ramsay approved of her answer. She did not turn her head to read his brother's reaction. She would not be able to stop glaring at him if she began.

"I do hope the condition you are treating is not a serious one?" Grace's concern sounded sincere.

Prudence laughed bitterly. *Can one ever be cured of one's distrust of man?* she wanted to ask. *Is distrust and a feeling of betrayal a serious condition?* "My physician feels I suffer from a strain of the nervous system," she said openly, tired of skirting the truth. "It gives me headaches, a disturbing numbness of the hands on occasion, and a stiffness of the neck and back that is quite painful, but certainly not life-threatening. I had . . . have great hopes that the baths will help me to regain an attitude of repose. I have it on excellent authority that all pain is easier to bear if one can but relax." She would like to have spit the words at Ramsay, but restrained herself from an unmannerly display.

Rash Ramsay's gaze never strayed from her face. Tension hung between them like a live thing; Prudence could feel its intensity. Grace noticed it as well. Her gaze zigzagged from Prudence to Ramsay and back again.

"I wish you speedy recovery. What other plans do you have for your time spent here in Brighton?"

"I would like to see the tide pools I have heard mentioned, to see if I might collect a few shells to give to my pupils as going-away gifts."

"Pupils?"

"Yes. I live with my cousin's family, acting as governess for her children, but . . ." She paused. How did one tell strangers that one felt like a potential home wrecker? Such an admission was not at all conducive to securing a suitable new position. Prudence rubbed her temple. Her neck felt very stiff this evening. She pushed away the bothersome thought of the relief the hands of the man beside her had brought to her only the day before.

"I fear I have overstayed my welcome," she said. God knew there was truth enough in that. "I hope to find a new position, either as a governess or as a lady's companion. Do you know anyone who is in need of a female to serve in such a capacity?"

Chapter Six

Any surprise Grace might be experiencing in hearing that her brother-in-law saw fit to escort a governess to dine with the Prince Regent was masked as skillfully as Charles hid his own dismay. Miss Stanhope was a governess? He would never have guessed it was so. Miss Stanhope did not resemble in the least any governess he had met with in his childhood.

"No positions come to mind right away, but I will let you know if I hear of anything promising," Grace said graciously.

Miss Stanhope never looked at him, never so much as turned in his direction, Ramsay noted. She kept all of her attention firmly fixed on either Grace or Rue. He did not mind. He was feeling a trifle conspicuous in the Indian wedding finery the Prince had begged him to wear. Miss Stanhope's wide-eyed awe when she had met him at the door to her boardinghouse had done nothing to relieve his awkwardness. But he was willing to put up with a little awkwardness if it helped his business. Besides, he could study her to his heart's content as long as she was not glaring at him. As familiar as this young woman was to him, feet and hands, shoulders and neck, he was not yet accustomed to the arrangement of her features, the thick cluster of dark brown curls, the expressions that brought to life the curve of her lips, and the interesting manner in which the set of her chin, like the point of a compass, indicated the direction of her feelings.

She was conscious of his interest. He could feel her awareness. He sensed too, her suppressed rage. He must make a point of allowing Miss Stanhope to vent her anger soon. He wanted her to look at him with something other than disgust clouding her gaze.

"I wonder if you would mind sitting for me," Grace said after she had explained that she was a watercolorist.

That got Charles's attention; Miss Stanhope's as well.

"A sitting?" She sounded confused.

"Yes. I would dearly love to paint your portrait."

"Why me?"

Charles almost laughed. Why her? Surely that was obvious. And yet, in studying her attractive profile—the cloud of dark hair, the deep blue eyes, the rigid little chin—he decided Miss Stanhope honestly had no idea why someone should wish to paint her portrait. There was nothing coy in her expression.

His incredulity was voiced by Grace.

"Why? You have a face that cries out to be painted, Miss Stanhope. There is something in your expression that reminds me of the Mona Lisa. You see, I cannot quite decide whether you look sad or amused, unless of course you look at Charles and then your expression is nothing but angry. Do you still hold a grudge against him, Miss Stanhope, for his earlier rudeness?"

"Do not tease our guest, Grace," Charles was moved to say, and at last Miss Stanhope turned stiffly to regard him. "She has every right to be angry with me if she chooses," he said evenly, his eyes never straying from hers.

Her brows rose. Her eyes narrowed warily. He surprised her in justifying her anger, and yet there was a level of skepticism in her gaze that convinced him she would not so easily forgive him.

He wanted her forgiveness. More than that, he wanted her friendship, that she might open her heart and mind to him again, as she had done under his hands in the shampooing that made her so angry with him now.

The carriage hit a rut in the road, throwing them together. His arms went around her to ensure she was not thrown to the floor. Her hands clutched at his tunic. Surprise widened her eyes. She felt it too, he thought, the energy that pulsed between them like something live whenever their flesh met, whenever they so much as brushed up against one another. Swiftly, they righted themselves; swiftly, she looked away and busied herself with reaching for the strap by the door, that she might not chance to fall against him again. He was not so anxious to avoid such repetition.

"Is your turban tight enough?" Rupert asked with a grin as he reached out to straighten its position on his head.

Grace tried not to laugh and failed. "You are very brave, Charles, to wear that outrageous outfit."

Rue came to his defense. "Chaz promised to wear the wedding clothes. He's not one to break a promise."

"You mean to be married?" Miss Stanhope asked with a confused expression, as if such a concept were inconceivable.

"Yes—" He meant to go on, to say "eventually," but she cut him short.

"I should like to meet your intended. I am sure she must be a female of great fortitude, optimism, and courage."

Charles smiled. Her insult was subtle, even funny, but an insult nonetheless. "I trust you will not mind waiting," he said politely. "I have yet to meet a woman so well endowed."

Further gibes were forestalled. They pulled into the portecochere of the Royal Marine Pavilion, and the door was flung open by one of the liveried footmen.

Charles helped Miss Stanhope from the carriage. "Still in a mood to strangle me?" he asked lightly.

"I fear such an activity would ruin my new gloves, sir," she said primly. "We must contrive to work out our differences in a more civilized fashion."

He agreed and held out his arm to her.

The octagonal hall in which Prudence got her first glimpse of the interior of the Marine Pavilion was painted in pink, lilac, and red. The ceiling was constructed in such a manner that it appeared to be tented. But there was no lingering allowed just within the unusual doorway. More guests were arriving at their heels. They were swiftly shown into the entrance hall, which went by in a blur of cool green and gray as hats and gloves were taken from them, and Ramsay took her hand as if it belonged to him. Prudence observed that there was a dragon motif in the wallpaper, but other than that she could remember nothing of the room, only the sliding warmth of Rash Ramsay's silken sleeve beneath her hand.

They were ushered through a wide doorway leading into the heart of the building, an astounding place—an extremely long, low-ceilinged corridor painted a peach pink with a contrasting mural of bamboo and birds in soft shades of blue. Close on the heels of the cool green entryway, the place glowed with warmth, light, pattern, and color. It resembled an intricately painted jewelry box. Prudence could not help but stare, at the walls first, where life-size Mandarin figures clad in real Oriental robes and set in arched wall niches gave the impression a foreign delegation had been stuffed and placed on display. She glanced at Ramsay. Was he to be stuffed as well? The idea amused her. He deserved to be stuffed.

The ceiling drew her attention. Trimmed in an elaborate bamboo fretwork with wooden bells dangling around the base, it sported a crenelated canopy that threw interesting shadows against the walls. The vaulted heights boasted beautifully painted glass skylights, hard to view now against the night sky. The gallery was lit by Chinese lanterns dangling from tall, elaborately carved supports. The lanterns' glow was caught and multiplied in a series of glittering mirrors, trimmed in what looked like more bamboo.

Prudence was dumbstruck. Her hand dropped from Ramsay's arm without her ever being conscious of it. This was a place quite out of the ordinary, a place almost beyond imagination.

"What do you think?" Grace asked.

Prudence liked Grace Ramsay. The woman had a naturalness about her that immediately put one at ease. "I feel I have been transported to another country, without ever having to suffer sea sickness."

Grace laughed. "Well put, Miss Stanhope. Come, I will show you my favorite objet d'art in this room."

Grace took Prudence's hand and led her to the nearest of

eleven doll-like figurines lining the walls. Standing two and a half feet tall on a pedestal, a beautifully detailed old man in an elaborate Oriental court costume with a wise, painted face and what looked like real hair, bobbed his head at her.

"Aren't they charming?" Grace said. "I think the attention to detail in their rendering is absolutely marvelous."

The Ramsay brothers joined them. "It has become a famous game among the female visitors here, to try and set all the heads bobbing at once in a mad dash down the length of the room," Rue said.

Lord Ramsay eyed Prudence speculatively. "Are you in trim enough form to accomplish such a feat, Miss Stanhope?"

Dare he refer to his rather intimate knowledge of the form to which he referred? The flame of unexpressed anger heated Prudence's cheeks.

"I should think you must be quite spry to keep up with your schoolroom charges," he suggested blandly.

Prudence bit back the first retort that came to mind. She would behave with cool composure. "Surely, ladies do not really comport themselves like hoydens, dashing down the room with no other end than to set the heads of these figurines nodding?" She looked to Grace for some sort of reaction.

Grace laughed. She had a pretty laugh, and yet it was difficult to tell just what she thought of such a scheme, either from her expression or based on what she said. "You look spritely enough, Miss Stanhope. Shall we lift up our skirts and make the dash?"

Giggles from two other females who made up the dinner party and a sudden thundering of their slippered feet on the carpeting as they hiked up their skirts and ran, interrupted them. It was clear from the reaction of the gentlemen in the room that this pastime earned their undivided attention. As many bobbing heads might be seen among the guests as among the figurines. Flashing petticoats and the glimpse of fair ankles were perhaps more the point of the exercise than in watching the nodding figurines.

The only gentleman who chose to ignore the romp was Lord Ramsay. He watched her reaction instead.

She dared to look him directly in the eyes. "As I care less to make a fool of myself than I care for someone else to make fool of me, I must decline participation in such sport." There was an answering glimmer in the gray green depths that gave her the impression she had scored a hit.

Grace Ramsay ruined any satisfaction she might have been feeling. "Ah, but if one cannot occasionally play the fool, life becomes a very sober affair, doesn't it, Charles?"

As if to underscore her remark, the Prince Regent chose that very moment to entrust his majestic proportions to a pretty bamboo staircase at the end of the room. Knowing how frail such a wood was, and observant of how ponderous was the descent, for the Prince was currently suffering from the gout and his right leg was bound in a great white bandage, Prudence watched with wide-eyed concern until Lord Ramsay, who seemed to read her mind, relieved her by whispering, "Wrought iron."

Prudence slid a wary look in his direction. She did not trust her escort, certainly not when he dared to wear a turban to dine with the Prince.

"It only looks like bamboo." He nodded his elegantly attired head toward the stairs which bore His Highness safely to ground level with nary a creak. "I was myself concerned the first time I saw him come in by way of those stairs."

Prudence felt stupid and confused. She had expected some sort of subterfuge from Ramsay, not this empathic recognition of her fears. That Ramsay felt compelled to ease her concern was even more baffling. What kind of trick was this? Prudence was too angry with Rash Ramsay, too ready to recite her grievances against him to have her head turned by a kindness that flew in the face of her opinion of him. And yet she could not dismiss his words entirely. They reminded her too much of the voice she had listened to at Mahomed's Baths, a gentle voice she had foolishly come to like and trust. The impression that she had stepped into a world as foreign as the bathhouse, and that Rash Ramsay meant to be her guide, was undeniable.

She had no opportunity to work out her feelings. The

brown-bewigged Prince settled into the specially designed Merlin chair that had been stationed at the base of the stairs and directed his attendant to "wheel him about the room," that he might welcome all of his guests before dinner. He bore down on them, his bandaged leg stiffly preceding him, in the curiously noiseless, wheeled contraption, accompanied by his current mistress, Lady Hertford—who had ousted Lady Jersey, who had in her turn ousted Mrs. Fitzherbert as the Prince's favorite. The woman was in her fifties—she could be no younger—and yet the bloom had not entirely faded on her beauty. Prudence stared at the couple with interest. Here was another oddity in this house full of oddities. Mistresses were not commonly made welcome and public in the manner that the Prince's mistresses were.

From the Prince there was a personal word for everyone, even a governess.

"I am very pleased to see you here, Miss Stanhope. I was not at all sure I had convinced you to come." He reached out to pat her hand, and when Prudence thought he must let her go, he clung to it a little longer. "Do you know that the last young lady I had to convince to join me here was my daughter, Charlotte."

"Your daughter?" Prudence felt compelled to give the Prince's hand a squeeze. The entire nation had mourned Princess Charlotte's unexpected passing in the winter of the previous year, following the difficult stillbirth of a boy who might have one day been king. Rumor had it that the Prince had been nigh inconsolable. Tears welled in Prudence's eyes. Memories of her cousin's equally unproductive delivery, of the abject despair that had affected everyone in the Margrave household as a result, flooded her with the pain that had grown familiar to her, a binding ache that had settled in her neck and shoulders. "I am so sorry if I have provoked painful memories, sire," she said earnestly.

The Prince let go her hand and winced as he shifted the positioning of his leg. When he looked up again, his expression was carefully polite. "She enjoyed herself while she was here. I hope you will as well."

With an air of dismissal he turned to address Lord Ramsay. "Ramsay! You have worn the Indian wedding silks for me, just as you said you would. Turn around. I must see everything." The Prince's voice was a trifle too cheerful.

Lord Ramsay turned for the Prince, pointing out the garments of his costume as he did so. "The coat, sire, is called an achkin, the baggy pantaloons are pyjamas."

"Pyjamas? What a queer word. It rolls off the tongue ever so quaintly. Has the sash a name?"

"Yes. It is a kamar band."

"Marvelous!" His Highness chortled. "Such lovely color! You must tell everyone of your travels ere the night is out. I am told you have brought back a number of rare treasures that I might be interested in acquiring now that I intend to add a touch of India to the exterior of the Pavilion."

Ramsay inclined his head. "I would be pleased, Highness, if you found them to your liking."

The Prince ordered the wheels of his chair set in motion with the lifting of a finger, then stopped the servant who pushed him about and ordered the chair rolled back again. "You must set me straight as well, with regard to Jack's ill-luck at the tables. I had heard the whole of your fortune was gone missing when you returned, and that your sister has married the very man who now holds title to the majority of it."

Prudence was surprised. What was this? Something more shocking than an Indian wedding costume?

Ramsay did not appear to be rattled by the embarrassingly personal nature of the Prince's inquiry. He politely inclined his head, a faint smile lifting his lips. "All too true, Highness. My siblings have, in my absence, kept the gossipmongers merrily prattling."

Prudence clenched her teeth to stop her mouth from falling open.

The Prince laughed. "Much as have my own, sir. We are due weddings. Have you heard? Speaking of which . . ." He ordered his chair turned to face Rupert Ramsay. "Introduce me to this beautiful female you wear upon your arm like a trophy,

Rue. I understand you were convinced to run away to Gretna Green by this rogue, madame."

Grace Ramsay curtsied with a smile and leaned close to the Prince's ear to whisper coyly, "You have it in reverse, Your Highness. It is I did the convincing."

Such an admission brought a roar of appreciative laughter from everyone who overheard the remark.

"We have much to discuss then, madame. I do love a good romance," the Prince said with a laugh.

Prudence blinked in dismay. What rare, rash, and intriguing company had she connected herself with? Fortunes lost? Runaway marriages to Gretna Green?

Ramsay offered his arm to take her in to dinner. "Do you enjoy romance, Miss Stanhope?" he inquired as if such a question were nothing out of the ordinary.

They were passing under the landing of the bamboo stairway when he asked. In the contained space his voice carried. Hers was not the only head to turn in startled response to his question.

She stared at Ramsay, her mind whirling. She could not admit to him that he was, in his wedding attire and turban, the most romantic creature she had ever had the pleasure of despising. She had no choice but to answer his impertinent question. Too many had heard it asked for her to ignore him.

"Surely every female enjoys romance to a certain degree, sir," she managed to utter.

He nodded, his turban a curiously colorful extension of his head. It was incredibly irritating, the way he could look completely amused without smiling. "And surely every gentleman spends the majority of his youth testing the boundaries of a woman's enjoyment."

Someone who had overheard them laughed.

Prudence was unused to provocative statements, publicly announced. "Delicate boundaries, sir, must be tested with delicacy," she said stiffly. "Surely an indelicate man, prone to *rashly* exceeding those boundaries, spends a great deal of his time apologizing for his excess?"

The irritating look of amusement intensified. He recognized her gibe for what it was. "Indeed, a *rash* man"—he placed undue emphasis on the word—"prone to *rash* acts, must spend his time either in apologizing for his excesses in romance, or in being congratulated on his successes."

Chapter Seven

Entered by way of a low, dark, narrow passageway that acoustically channeled Lord Ramsay's provocative repartee to most of the party who followed, the dining hall opened up—a vast space ready to swallow any retort Prudence might have uttered. The room inspired openmouthed awe. So high and unusually decorated was the domed ceiling, all eyes were drawn immediately upward. There, the leaves of a gigantic painted plantain tree against a pale blue sky provided a strange nesting place for an enormous three-dimensional silver dragon—wings spread, tail coiled, red flames snaking from its jaws.

Ramsay was staring at her, enigmatic and mysterious in his strange and beautiful outfit, the turban casting a shadow over eyes that seemed to hold no questions, only answers.

"Remarkable, is she not?"

"She?" Prudence asked incredulously. How dare he assume the dragon was female?

He shrugged, intent on her reaction, no sign of the amusement she was sure he took in her reaction other than one arched brow. "The creature has offspring."

It was true. Suspended from the dragon's silver claws dangled the brilliance of a weighty chandelier loaded with cascading crystal and six, smaller, silver dragons, from whose jaws tinted glass lotus blossoms bloomed, along with the dancing flames of the latest technological marvel, gaslight.

"Are you so familiar with the habits of dragons that you can be sure the male does not instruct its young in proper dragon behavior?"

He appeared to give her view consideration, but in the end he shook his head. "I am quite sure that is left to a governess dragon."

"Are you?" Prudence refused to laugh at this clever dig. She refused to look again at Ramsay in his colorful attire. He was the focus of too many stares. "Well, as a governess I must correct you. In Oriental art the dragon is symbolic of the masculine. It is the tiger that is associated with females."

"And with flames, sharp teeth, and claws, do the two go about tearing one another apart?" he suggested.

She ignored the remark. Something about the dragon puzzled her. She frowned up at it. "Are not winged dragons considered the embodiment of evil in the Middle East? Why in the world would the Prince choose to decorate his dining hall with such an icon? And why would this evil have lotus-blossom flames erupting from the mouths of its offspring? Does not the lotus represent the search for one's soul by way of the body's most basic energies to both Hindu and Buddhist?"

Ramsay was staring at her again, his eyes sparkling. "The lotus means . . ." He paused suggestively both brows raised. ". . . many things—as does the dragon."

The mischief in his expression placed her on the defensive. He looked at her as if she had just broached an inappropriately suggestive topic. She was not at all sure she had a proper grasp of the lotus symbol. She *was* sure she did not want him to tell her the many things the lotus meant.

The room, a blaze of light and color, was too warm for comfort, as was the knowing look Ramsay directed her way. The mystery of an evil dragon poised above the dining table troubled her far less than the undeniable intrigue of an Englishman who dared appear at a formal dinner in Indian wedding silks. Perhaps some distance from Rash Ramsay would clear her thinking. His every remark provoked her. Why did he always broach such sensitive topics? Why did she burn with the embarrassed memory of his hands on her body every time he looked at her? Why had he offered her no apology?

Prudence moved purposefully away from her bothersome escort, to examine the rest of the room. Flanking the walls and windows a number of gasolier lotus lights balanced on the tails of yet more dragons clinging to gold and lapis pedestals. These dragons were almost wingless, the more traditional Chinese creature that symbolized the power of the emperor and good luck. Prudence found herself wanting to discuss with Charles Ramsay the significance of both dragons appearing together. She doubted anyone else in the room knew or cared about the religious significance of dragons and lotus flowers. Did the Prince know the meaning of the objects and icons with which he surrounded himself?

She hazarded a glance in Ramsay's direction.

He was standing, like a visiting rajah, beside one of the ornate dragon-legged Oriental sideboards, chatting with a small group of the guests. As if he felt her gaze, he looked up. He stared at her, unblinking, until the Prince, in his Merlin chair, passed between them.

"Not all is complete," the Prince was explaining to one of the other guests. His face lit with pleasure as he explained what was yet to be done. These were not the features of a man who intentionally hung the embodiment of evil from his ceiling. This was a man who was as captivated as Prudence by the marvels of foreign lands. He dared to lavishly, and without discrimination, fill his Pavilion with whatever caught his fancy, just as he dared to ask a friend to appear at a formal function clad in the wedding costume of a foreign country.

Prudence allowed the spirit of the magnificent room to fill her with its intended grandeur. She made a point of examining more closely the southern end of the room, where the wall and ceiling met in such a manner as to appear to be a tent. It was all the rage in London, she had heard, to decorate ballrooms with fabric so as to give the appearance of a tent, but this was the wall itself, rolling down in a soft curve like drooping fabric.

"Interesting symbols. Would you not agree?"

Lord Ramsay had broken away from the group he chatted with. He stood staring at her, as had become his habit—his knowing gray-green eyes appearing larger and more brilliant, framed as they were by the bright folds of the turban.

Prudence had not really paid much attention to the pattern on the wall. The wall itself was too diverting. Now she examined the tangle of gilded figures that formed an overall pattern on the upper portion of the tenting in black and green and gold.

"The lotus again, and more dragons—wingless dragons." Ramsay said as if he read her mind.

"Good luck dragons," she said softly. "The yang of yin and yang."

His brows rose. She had surprised him again.

Prudence took perverse delight in shocking the man who seemed intent on shocking her. She craned her neck to stare at the wall. "A phoenix as well, and there, Saturn in the midst of more heavenly . . ."

"Bodies?" He finished the sentence she left hanging, his voice on the edge of laughter. "A rare thing, that," he drawled playfully.

Prudence tried to freeze him with contempt. How dare he continue to remind her of their first encounter? How dare he smile at her as if he expected her to share in his amusement? Her breath caught up in her throat. Why did he not take this opportunity to apologize for deceiving her at the bathhouse?

She summoned up the courage to confront him. "There is, sir, something we must discuss," she said. "I will not be put off any longer."

His smile faded. The sparkle died in his eyes. "You wish to take me to task for introducing myself to you in a wholly inappropriate manner."

"Yes, I do. You should never have touched me in the manner that you did."

"No, I should not have touched you as I did." He looked at her keenly, his expression serious. His words seemed weightier than hers.

He could not have taken the wind from her sails any more effectively. "My reputation, sir." She could not leave the words unsaid.

"Yes." He understood.

"The only thing a dependent female may possess of any great value."

"I do understand."

She had expected an argument from him, or abject denial, not this ready admission of guilt. "Do you really?"

"Why should you think otherwise?"

"How can a man who has cultivated a reputation for rashness understand the value of a woman who has cultivated—"

"Prudence?" he interrupted helpfully.

She exhaled heavily. "Can you never be serious, sir? How can I believe a word you say when you refuse to be serious? I feel compromised, my lord, compromised and betrayed."

He frowned. "Betrayed, Miss Stanhope? You trouble me greatly with such an accusation. I have myself been betrayed recently by someone I trusted implicitly. It was never my intention to so wound you."

Her laugh was bitter. "I have no reason to trust anything you say to me after such a beginning as we have had. Was I good sport? Did you enjoy leading me on like a sheep to the slaughter? Your fabrication was, I must admit, as carefully detailed as your outfit this evening. I fell completely prey to the entire fantasy. I even began to believe that the work you had done on my neck and shoulders was genuine."

"Ow!" He winced as if from a slap in the face. "The work on your shoulders was genuine," he said defensively. "Surely you have found that the bath attendants perform largely the same routine. You see, I have visited bathhouses all over India, Turkey, and Persia, and in so doing I have learned some of the technique."

"And the rest? The gate? The garden?"

The clanging of a gong interrupted their increasingly hostile exchange. Lord Ramsay politely offered his arm. "May I take you to your seat?"

She did not want to accept his arm. She wanted to finish her harangue. She wanted him to apologize. Still no apology from this enigmatic man, only probing questions, knowing looks, and a smile that most women might find disarming. To Prudence it was an irritation that she was drawn to this man despite her every intention to the contrary. She felt too often that she was the source of his amusement, and as a serious young woman, used to being taken quite seriously, his jesting only served to wound her.

"Tell me, sir," she said crisply, ignoring his arm, "was the garden you spoke of once—like the decoration in this dining hall—no more than whimsy? Did you construct the entire fantasy as nothing more than an amusement to confound the gullible?"

She did not wait for his answer, for she did not want to hear excuses. She crossed to the table and examined the place cards, searching for her name.

Charles Ramsay followed. He did, in fact, find her place before she did, and stood holding her chair so long she could not refuse it without looking foolish. He leaned into her shoulder as she accepted the chair. "It was not like that. You know it wasn't."

Hearing urgency in his tone, Prudence sank into her chair, certainty shaken.

He sat beside her. "It wasn't," he said emphatically, in an undervoice, his gaze intent. Something indefinable in his eyes made her want to believe him. He forced himself to greet another of the guests who sat down before leaning close to murmur, "I am distressed you should imagine my perfidy so grim."

She plastered a smile on her face for the benefit of the other guests and answered him in similarly diminished tones. "*You* are distressed? Imagine then, *my* distress in that you have *not* seen fit to honor me with an apology for your reprehensible behavior at Mahomed's bathhouse."

"I haven't apologized?" His surprise was nothing more than wide-eyed pretense.

"No, you have not!"

His look of amusement returned. "Dear me. It appears I must apologize for my lack of apologies."

He would not be serious. Indeed, he seemed incapable of it. She would have had trouble taking him seriously, dressed as he was. Prudence knew he meant to make her smile with his nonsensical remark. She was in no mood to be amused. The table was filling. Even whispering, they could not continue their current topic, and *still* he had not apologized properly, with feeling or believable remorse.

Rash Ramsay licked his lips uneasily. Prudence liked to think he looked a trifle concerned. "If you would indulge me in a game of a backgammon after dinner, perhaps I could make amends?" he offered.

Prudence considered his suggestion. "Perhaps," she said with a notable lack of enthusiasm.

He had pushed it too far. She meant to ignore him now. Charles could see such was the case, for even as he opened his mouth to speak to her again, Miss Stanhope made a point of turning to the gentleman seated on her other side. His name was Ponsonby, and he was a well-known philanderer. Prudence spoke to him of the weather. Ponsonby asked if she was the young lady he had earlier heard defending her position on romance.

"I beg your pardon." Charles interrupted their conversation with the intention of rescuing her from Ponsonby.

Prudence turned to him impatiently. "Yes?"

"Have you nothing to say to me, Miss Stanhope?" he murmured softly, so Ponsonby would not hear. "Nothing of the weather, or the food, or our surroundings?"

Her gaze would not meet his. In a polite but dismissive undervoice she said, "There lies too much unsaid between us, sir, for small talk to fill the void."

She would have turned away then, but he held her attention, saying softly, "You speak of an unsung reprimand and an unvoiced apology."

Her gaze met his at last, her eyes very blue.

"We have that yet to settle between us," he said earnestly. "But this is neither the time nor the place, surely you agree?"

Her lips pursed, and her chin rose. "But I do not agree. Surely an apology cannot come too soon." She turned away from him again.

They sat thus, side by side, so close their sleeves kissed, tension binding them together while a great chasm of misunderstanding and bruised feelings yawned between them.

Chagrined that she should first take him to task for bad manners and now punish him by preferring conversation with Ponsonby, Charles refused to let her have the last word. When Prudence placed her napkin in her lap, he surreptitiously swept up the linen square and then bent over, as though to retrieve it from the floor.

"I beg your pardon," he said with undue emphasis.

She turned as he rose. Their heads almost bumped, so close was his face to hers.

"I *do* beg your pardon," he said again, earnestly.

In her surprise, some barrier in her gaze that had kept him distanced fell away. For an instant he felt he could see into her very thoughts. She was pleased with his apology; she liked him the better for it. Her breath quickened. Her lashes swept down too late to cover what her eyes revealed. Before anyone else at the table paid unwanted attention to his remorse and fell to questioning it, he handed her the absconded napkin. "Is this yours?"

She frowned at the napkin, glanced down into her lap, and looked up with a trace of confused disappointment. "Yes. Thank you."

She went back to chattering with Ponsonby, a man who was bound to mistake her intent.

Dissatisfied, Charles found conversation elsewhere himself, but throughout the service of the meal, to be sure his point was taken, and to interrupt Ponsonby's progress, he politely excused himself to Miss Stanhope for one farcical faux pas after another. As the platters of lark pastries and ham in Madeira sauce, sweetbreads Provençal, and woodcock fillets were handed about the table by the guests themselves in the Russian fashion, he had ample opportunity to interrupt with, "Beg pardon . . . do you care for anything? . . . Can I tempt you with these? . . . Forgive my intrusion, but the fish looks particularly appetizing."

In brushing against her shoulder on occasion, it was "I am sorry" and "Please forgive my clumsiness." In jarring her arm so that she tossed a spoonful of peas willy-nilly onto her plate, he said with a laugh, "I had hoped to appease you in quite a different manner."

Each time, their eyes met. Each time, he hoped she understood that his apologies were twofold. Her eyes spoke of understanding, but the tight line of her mouth refused to relent. She did not care to be amused. In every instance she returned to her conversation with platter-faced Ponsonby. It was rather disheartening.

He really must get back to business, rather than waste time trying to ingratiate himself with a young woman who would seem unwilling to forgive. Ramsay abandoned the madness of his apologetic antics and concentrated on promoting the goods he had to sell to any ear that would listen. That had been his initial intention in accepting this evening's invitation, his intent too, in draping himself in Indian trappings. He was, after all, surrounded by potential customers for the goods in which he had invested.

He was just congratulating himself on his success in obtaining promises from four of the dinner guests to come and view his treasures when Miss Stanhope captured his attention by hissing at Ponsonby in a terse undertone, "Sir, the tines of this fork are very sharp. I am distressed that I feel driven to leave you scarred in order to impress upon you my seriousness with regard to the inappropriate disposition of your hand."

Charles turned, instantly assessing the scene. Ponsonby had planted his beefy hand on Miss Stanhope's delectable thigh under partial cover of the tablecloth. The fat sausages of his fingers were under threat of puncture from her hovering fork.

Charles could not resist involving himself in this intriguing contretemps. With admirable nonchalance, and every indication of its being an accident, his shoulder came into jarring contact with Miss Stanhope's.

Ponsonby let loose a yowl that focused all eyes in his direction, but there was a swift end to his noise as two plump, pricked sausages were thrust into his mouth for sucking.

"I *do*, most humbly and from the bottom of my heart, beg pardon," Charles said softly, so that only Miss Stanhope heard.

Prudence turned to regard him as she returned her fork to the table. For the first time that evening she smiled without reservation. Indeed, she seemed in danger of laughing outright. Her shoulders shook with suppressed amusement. "Apology accepted, my lord," she said when given a moment in which to collect herself.

"Excellent," he said, and then he made her eyes go very round in reaching around the back of her chair with his own fork to prod Ponsonby's shoulder. "My good man, I believe you owe the young lady an apology," he said firmly when he had succeeded in getting Ponsonby's attention.

Remarkable, Prudence thought, how one man's touch could distance and revolt one's sensibilities while another man's touch drew and enticed those same senses. Was the difference no more mysterious than that their intent was diametrically opposed? Could one sense intent flowing like water from a man's fingertips? Prudence was not sure how to behave once she had accepted Lord Ramsay's apology. How was she to deal with a gentleman who had run his hands all over her flesh without permission, when he saved her from another who had much the same object in mind?

Anger was not a pretty emotion, but Prudence had grown comfortable with it. She had clung to it. Anger had seemed appropriate given the circumstances. Now that fury's heat no longer warmed her, what was she to feel toward Lord Ramsay?

Unsure of herself, Pru withdrew from conversation and concentrated, first on food, and then, just as rich, on the talk that ebbed and flowed around her. The "little" dinner the Prince had planned served to remind Prudence of how frugal her means had become. There were forty to sit at the table, with course after course of rare delicacies. Everything in the Pavilion seemed excessive to her: the people, the setting, the very food she enjoyed. She was enjoying herself—and yet it seemed a wicked, indulgent sort of enjoyment.

She felt as if she betrayed the self-reliant young woman she had become over the past five years, wallowing now in these undeserved riches.

The tally of what the evening's entertainment had to cost ran through her head as if she were here to keep ledgers. There was too much of it, she decided—too much chatter, food, laughter—too much glittering wealth and light and heat. She found herself dizzied by the excesses into which she had plunged—dizzied, too, by the complete turnaround in her opinion of Rash Ramsay.

She had been convinced he was no more than a wealthy and arrogant young man used to having his way in all things. And yet, as she listened to his exchanges with the other guests, she realized Ramsay was little better off than she in circumstance. The man was struggling to survive his sudden descent into penury. His own brother Jack—a man others referred to in whispers as Rakehell—had betrayed his trust, gambling away in a single hand of cards what was left of the waning Ramsay fortune.

Lord Ramsay might have been a pitiable creature. He was not. This was no crushed and beaten individual. Ramsay had not given up. He seemed to thrive on what he referred to as the challenge change had brought to the journey of his life. His indomitable spirit, his savoir faire, his lighthearted sense of humor each evidenced itself in his every action, in his every word.

Unlike the Prince, who depended on Queen and country to relieve him of the astounding debts he had accrued in the remodeling of the Pavilion, Charles Ramsay had gone overseas to establish trade connections. That much accomplished, he now struggled to establish himself as a businessman among a group of peers who viewed him with eyes widened by the shock of his recent losses—and the thought that there, but for the grace of God, they too might languish. They had trouble, she realized, in getting past that emotional response. As a result, there were few who took him seriously in his new enterprise.

He impressed her. Despite her every desire that she should not find Ramsay appealing, he was. Of all of the men in the room, the Prince himself included, there were none Prudence longed to know more about than Charles Ramsay, whom she had so recently believed a completely depraved and unforgivable creature of contempt. Strange, but his very ability to laugh, to jest with her, to wear an outfit designed to draw all eyes, these things seemed most remarkable. In all that had initially irritated her, she found something undeniably admirable.

Her outlook changed, Prudence could not help but recall the afternoon in which this gentleman had played his devastating practical joke on her in making her believe he was a bathhouse attendant. His voice and his touch had charmed her then, as his fighting spirit charmed her now. She did not want to be charmed. She was, she thought, too easily charmed.

She gave her head a mental shake. No, she did not want to be charmed. There was too much danger in it. Her wits abandoned her when gentlemen charmed her into admiring them.

Chapter Eight

When the men had gone off to smoke and talk of the up-coming races, the women drifted into the oval Saloon to chat of men and children, hairstyles, fashion, and the latest re-decorating plans for the Pavilion.

"A withdrawing room for the ladies is in the process of being painted and carpeted," Lady Hertford explained with the condescending air of one who had reason to know. "The walls are to be carmine red, the carpet two shades of green in a dia-mond pattern, and a green striped silk sultane sofa has been ordered from Bailey and Saunders in London, with draperies and hangings to match."

The thought crossed Pru's mind that no matter how favored a female Lady Hertford might be at the moment as the Prince's fourth acknowledged mistress, the permanence of her situation was precarious. Mistresses could be cast off as easily as the tired decor in a room. That hard truth was worth remem-bering.

"What is a sultane sofa?" she whispered to Grace.

"An ottoman done up in the Turkish style." Grace further lowered her voice to whisper wryly, "It is the sort of furniture one might expect to find in a seraglio." She hinted at the con-nection already lampooned in the London papers by the more biting political cartoonists, between a harem and the Pavilion.

Prudence could not completely disguise her shock. "Grace!" she gasped.

Linking arms companionably with her, Grace drew Pru-dence away from the cluster of women who hung about the door they had just entered, to more closely examine the re-markable panels of Chinese wallpaper.

Grace sighed. "As an artist I cannot deny a certain fascination with the decor here, but I am partial to the more austere beauty of Greek and Roman form. This excess of chinoiserie haphazardly blended with Turkish and Indian design I find rather overwhelming. Do *you* care for it?"

Prudence laughed softly, more comfortable debating the Prince's unusual taste in architectural detail than his equally unusual way of life. "Odd as you may find me, I do. This place transports me to far distant shores. I have only to look around to forget I am in England."

"And have you reason to forget?" Grace asked as if the question were of no real importance, her gaze wandering.

Had she shown more interest, Prudence would have closely guarded her tongue, but with the feeling that any remark she might make was soon forgotten, she responded candidly, "Haven't we all?"

Her voice sounded too wistful.

Grace turned to look at her, brows raised. Too late, Prudence bit down on her tongue.

"I suppose we do," Grace admitted. "I wonder if you will come to trust me enough to tell me yours."

Prudence had trouble meeting her gaze.

"Along those same lines," Grace alarmed her in continuing, "I have in mind a proposition. I wonder, will you answer one question of mine if I promise to answer all questions you have concerning my brother-in-law?"

Prudence blushed. "What makes you think I have any questions with regard to Lord Ramsay?"

"Ah, but my dear, I have been watching your face across the table all evening. I *know* your mind teems with questions. Tell me you do not wish to know more about how Charles lost his entire fortune to my brother. Tell me you are not curious about Charles's sister, who has since married my brother. Perhaps you already know about Charles's travels? And what he plans to do to remake his fortune?"

Prudence was disturbed to think she might be so easily read. She could not deny her curiosity, but neither would she forget that there was a price for its fulfillment. "What is the one question you want answered?"

"You must tell me—for I am certain there is a marvelous story behind the event, and neither Rue nor Charles will breathe a word of it to me—how did you first meet the two of them?"

Prudence had no desire to reveal so much to one whom she knew so little. She smiled stiffly. "I must refuse your kind offer. It would surely be most unfair of me to promise such an exchange when I have so little to tell."

Grace studied her. "You are a miserable liar, Miss Stanhope. Is the truth so scandalous? You intensify my eagerness to get to the bottom of your story. I am disappointed, of course. If you will not trade, I shall be forced to use my most devious methods of extracting information from my husband. Are you quite sure you've no desire for answers?"

Prudence pressed her lips together, thinking. Grace might tell her much that no one else could. It was tempting. But in the end she shook her head. She could not reveal any of the scandalous circumstances under which Rash Ramsay had touched her—intimately touched her. "Your price is too high," she whispered. Slipping her arm from Grace's, she walked away.

Grace was on her heels in an instant, catching her arm again, to search her face in disbelief. Her gaze darted around the room before she whispered urgently, "Charles has never disgraced you, has he? If he has, I shall . . ." She clenched her fists. "I shall . . . Ooh! I don't know what I might do."

Her concern was so genuine, her readiness to do battle so fervent, Prudence laughed. "You've no need to do anything. I am not disgraced." *At least not in the manner you suppose*, she thought. "Really, I am extremely embarrassed more than anything else."

Grace took up her arm again. "I am so very relieved to hear you say so. Not that I would have you embarrassed of course, but of my husband's brothers, I quite like Charles, and would not have liked to have my opinion of him so drastically altered. You see, I have quite made up my mind that he and

Miles, my brother, must get along. Now, in apology for pressuring you to reveal what I will never again trouble you to tell me, I shall freely explain to you precisely how Charles lost his fortune, by way of Jack, an irresponsible gambler if ever there was one, who had been entrusted with his financial affairs while Charles was overseas trying to establish trading rights through the East India Company, a last-gasp effort to prop up their already flagging fortune."

Though he did not smoke or care much for the races, Charles's time away from Miss Prudence Stanhope was well spent. Two more gentlemen promised to drop by for a gander at the things he had brought back from India and the Orient. The Prince continued to evidence interest. He was, he said, thinking about redecorating one or two rooms at the Pavilion in the style of India to harmonize with the new screen of *jalis* tracery he planned to add to its exterior columns along with the new rooftop domes and minarets he proudly displayed plans for.

When the Ramsays made their entrance to the Saloon along with the other gentlemen, Charles's gaze was drawn immediately to Miss Stanhope. Engaged in earnest conversation with Grace, the rosy light of the nearest Chinese lantern warm on her face, Charles was convinced that Miss Stanhope was the most attractive female in the room. The importance of establishing his new business was magnified in his mind.

How did a penniless man go about wooing a penniless maid? No, not maid, governess. Standing in the midst of so much pomp and splendor, so much overbearing evidence of wealth, Charles Ramsay was woefully aware of how little he had to offer a woman, any woman, even a penniless one.

If wealth was what won a woman, was she worth winning?

Charles thrust the dilemma from his mind. He had promised Miss Stanhope a game of tables. Perhaps with their heads bent over the board he might, at last, offer her proper apology.

"Miss Stanhope, the backgammon board awaits us." Removing the turban from his head, he gestured toward the yellow drawing room, where many of the guests were heading toward the card and backgammon tables that had been arranged for their pleasure.

There was something new about the look she turned on him. She was no longer angry with him. That was part of the difference, but not all of it. There was something knowing in the blue depths of her eyes, something that evidenced an unexpected awareness of who he was. Charles had no idea that the look he beheld, unnerving in the eyes of a stranger, was the same one Prudence Stanhope witnessed in his eyes every time she looked at him. Charles wondered what Grace and Miss Stanhope found to talk about. The history of the Ramsays, he would wager.

Miss Stanhope's hand slipped into the crook of his arm, without the stiffness or hesitation to which he had grown accustomed. "Do we play for stakes, my lord? I must warn you, I've no money to wager."

That was a blessing, for neither had he.

"Perhaps we should play for time," he suggested.

"Time?"

"Yes." The appeal of the idea increased even as he offered up an explanation. "Winner takes an hour of loser's time."

"Time? Time for what?" The wariness he was used to witnessing in her eyes returned.

He shrugged. "Time to be spent as winner sees fit."

She was frowning as he settled her in a chair before the board most removed from the others. "For example?"

"For example, if you win the first game, you have me at your command for one hour's time, to invest however you see fit. You might ask me to play patience for an hour, a game I detest. You could use the hour to require me to transport you somewhere, or act as escort, or run menial errands. You might," he suggested playfully, "if you so desire, insist that I spend an entire hour apologizing to you."

Her lips tightened. "I get the idea," she said briskly. "And I concede that I might find something useful in winning time from you, sir, but what, pray, would you do with a governess for an hour?"

He said nothing, merely looked at her, confused she should ask such a question. Was she serious?

His silent stare unnerved her. Her lashes fanned down against her cheeks, crimson coloring them.

Reaching out to take her hand, Charles thought better of it. He took up the dice cup instead, rolling the ivory cubes into his palm. "I am sure there are many things you might teach me, Miss Stanhope," he said softly.

She looked up quickly, the dark centers of her eyes huge. "You vex me, sir, with such suggestiveness."

He closed his eyes a moment, rolling the dice between his palms. "You grieve me, Miss Stanhope, with your immediate assumption that my motivation is base in nature. Surely you must agree that two strangers would quite naturally have much to learn from one another?"

Her posture was very stiff, the gaze she bent on him a wary one. "Must I?"

He leaned forward, his hand outstretched to hand her one of the dice. "Is there nothing you would learn of me? Or has Grace answered your every question on that score?"

She flinched and looked away. He had hit the mark dead-on. His hand hung between them unnoticed.

"Will you take the first throw, or shall we toss for it?"

She locked her gaze on his hand a moment, uncertainly. "What would you know of me, my lord?"

He lowered his hand onto the backgammon table. What did he long to know of her that he could ask outright? "Among other things, I would discover why your garden has no roses," he said at last.

God, but he wished she might keep looking at him so keenly forever. Her eyes pierced him with unmasked doubt. He longed to watch that doubt change to trust.

She held out her hand, palm up. "To be fair," she said, "we should toss for the first throw."

He handed her a die, holding the other in his own hand, that they might determine the high roller for first cast. "Do we play for time then?"

She shrugged as if it were no great matter to her and tossed the die. "As you wish."

It was in their third and final game that Lord Ramsay began to double the stakes. The first two games had gone swiftly and simply, without conversation, the dice cup's rattle and the clicking progress of their men the only sound. They seemed to be players roughly on a par with one another. Each of them had won a game, effectively canceling one another out, in Prudence's estimation. In this game, from the start, Ramsay took the advantage. Throw after throw, his numbers were high, hers low. Prudence had just decided she had best play a blocking game against that advantage when Ramsay plucked the heavy silver doubling die from the center bar of the table and placed its two side up on the frame that surrounded the board.

"I double," he said calmly.

"You would double time?" She was sincerely baffled by his desire to win time from her. "Surely yours is better spent elsewhere?"

A smile tugged at the corners of his mouth. His brow arched. "Do you forfeit the game?"

She lifted her chin sharply. "I am not beaten yet. Proceed."

Her luck turned. Two high double throws and she had caught up to him.

The spirit of their competition made her a trifle reckless. "I double *you*." She turned the heavy cube to the four. "Do *you* mean to forfeit?"

He made no attempt to suppress a grin. "Forfeit four hours of my precious time? Never!"

On the following play he taunted her, doubling the stakes yet again.

Prudence eyed the silver cube with some concern. Eight hours! What was she doing? What would she do with eight hours of this man's time if she did win? And she had to win, for what might he demand of her for eight hours did she not? Leaving the doubling cube where it sat, she focused her efforts, and the throw of every die, on advancing her men with alacrity.

Her haste made her careless. In a single play two unguarded men were taken from the board. The dice turned against her. For two throws she could not enter the game. By the time she got the first man into play again, she was hopelessly behind. Ramsay won an overwhelming victory. Not only had she not borne a single man off the board, the dice had denied her last man entry into the game.

"Backgammon," she whispered, stricken. "I have never been so soundly beaten."

Ramsay leaned back in his chair, staring at her speculatively. "A good thing we did not play for money, Miss Stanhope. I should not like to have paupered you."

She made an effort to appear unconcerned. "No more than I should have hated to be paupered, sir. As it stands, you are saddled with my company for eight hours, should you so desire it."

He shook his head, his eyes never straying from hers. She thought he meant to relieve her of her obligation, to deny any desire to so detain her, until he opened his mouth to say, "I will not accept eight hours, Miss Stanhope, when in truth you owe me twenty-four."

"Twenty-four?" she breathed in disbelief. "How can it be twenty-four?" But even as she asked, she realized.

"Backgammon triples the score," she whispered in exact unison with his identical response.

He studied her with amusement. He had reason to be amused. Dear God, what folly had she gotten herself into this time?

He leaned forward, both brows raised, his gaze traveling from her eyes to her mouth and back again. "What *shall* we do with twenty-four hours, Miss Stanhope?"

Chapter Nine

*U*ntil we meet again, Miss Stanhope."
Prudence escaped up the steps to Mrs. Harris's boarding-house, Charles Ramsay's parting words ringing in her ears. Twenty-four hours she owed the man. He could afford to smugly assume they would meet again. But what might a man who blithely walked about in a turban think to do in those twenty-four hours? Her pulse quickened with the thought. Closing the door quietly behind herself, she mounted the stairs to the rooms she shared with Mrs. Moore and shut this second door between herself and Lord Ramsay. Knees shaking, she leaned against its wooden solidity.

What would they do with twenty-four hours?

There was a spot along her waist that warmed to the mem-ory of Ramsay's guiding hand helping her down the steps from the carriage. Within the confines of her new gloves, her hand retained the heat from the kiss Ramsay had pressed to her knuckles.

This rash young man who had touched her bare skin in places that had never been touched, who had convinced her that there was within her imagination a garden of repose in which she might find herself—this man had won twenty-four hours of her life. What might he ask of her given so many hours, and all at his bidding? Pru's pulse ran ragged at the thought. Would Ramsay try to touch her? To kiss her? The very idea made her heart pound. Sighing, she reached back to undo the ties on her dress. With a shake of her hips the dress slid to the floor. Out of her evening slippers, then out of the puddled dress she stepped.

She did not want to admit it, even to herself, but all evening she had longed for Rash Ramsay's touch. Strange, how her mind chose to dwell on the idea when Ramsay, of all the men she had been introduced to, had refrained from touching her in any way inappropriately since his inauspicious beginning. It was Ponsonby who had rudely grabbed at her thigh this evening. It was the Prince and two of his cronies who had each made a point of holding her hand too long on introduction. There had been another guest—she could not recall his name—who had drunkenly thrown himself at her as the Ramsay party was leaving the Pavillion. Both Rash and Rue Ramsay had interceded on her behalf with commendable haste.

There was only one moment that sprang to mind when Prudence thought of Ramsay and the effect of his touch. That moment came when he had reached around the back of her chair to poke at Ponsonby with his fork. The cool whisper of his silken sleeve against her skin had—she could not deny it—pleased her. Closing her eyes, she had inhaled the odor of Rash Ramsay's sandalwood cologne with guilty delight. She had not drawn away from him even in the moment she opened her eyes again, though he leaned so close she could count each cinnamon lash above his gray-green eyes.

He had caught her staring at him. One brow had risen speculatively. She had blushed and dropped her gaze. His right hand gripped the edge of the table, while the left reached behind her chair. Those strong, sun-darkened, work-roughened fingers, loosely splayed on white damask, had touched and probed and prodded their way across the map of her body. What would she have done, had it been his hand and not Ponsonby's reaching out to caress her beneath the tablecloth? The wickedness of her thoughts had disturbed her. Such thoughts got one into trouble.

Prudence opened her eyes and bent to release the tapes on her stockings. There was a square of white on the floor in the darkness by the pale puddle of her dress. A note had been slipped under her door. She carried it to the window. There was light enough from the moon to read. Words floated up from the page, like a whisper in the dark.

Pru—

Not content with your letters, I have come to Brighton to see with my own eyes how you get on with Dr. Pratt's treatments. I have been fortunate enough to be able to procure rooms just above yours.

Timothy

Prudence staggered from the window. The paper shook in her hand.

Tim was here? Even now, just above her? He had set out for London, and business, the same day she and Mrs. Moore had left Gillingham for Brighton.

The idea that he followed her, and all its implications, robbed her strength. Crossing to the bed, Pru sank face first into the feather mattress. It enfolded her like a lover's arms. Choking, she rolled over to regard the ceiling with trepidation. He was here to see her! The news was at once wonderful and terrible. She longed to see Timothy. She had imagined what it might be like to have him here, at a time and place where the two of them might be alone, but the difference between dreaming and reality was all too powerful. It brought back in a rush the memory she had suppressed for weeks now in an attempt to deny her own bad judgement.

He had caught her in the hallway late one night, clad in nothing but a thin cotton wrapper and a diaphanous lawn nightshift that had been Edith's before pregnancy had rearranged her measurements. Prudence had taken no real care to be discreet as she passed from her room to the sickroom, where the children lay recovering from fever. It was the middle of the night, and herself the only one awake to hear a fretful child, she had supposed.

Suppositions could be dangerous, she had learned.

"Prudence, my pretty Prudence, come dance with me, my love." His voice had slurred as he caught at her hand and drew her into a brandy-scented embrace.

"I am not your love, cousin," she had protested, all out of

breath, her heart beating faster than usual as he whirled her in his arms, away from the nursery—away from her room and closer to his.

"But you are my love, dear Pru." He had enough sense to whisper, despite the brandy. "You love me. I know you do. I have seen it in your eyes." He had leaned close and peered into her eyes, his own bloodshot and bleared. "There!" He nodded. "It is still there."

His awareness had startled her. She *was* in love with Timothy Margrave, but had thought she kept her illicit feelings private. She and her cousin's husband had exchanged a look now and again, but never more than that—just looks.

He was ready for more, that was clear. He had taken advantage of her surprise, of her lack of resistance, as he brought their giddy dance to an end in front of the door to his room. Boldly he had kissed her mouth, his tasting warmly of the drinks he had been quaffing at the Castle pub, where he spent the evenings more often than not since the death of his unborn son.

"You didn't think I knew, did you?" he had whispered gruffly in her ear.

She had shaken her head, trying to resist, wanting to resist as his hands moved seductively over her back and lower, to stroke the curve of her buttocks. "No, no, you mustn't," she had protested, backing into the wall.

"I know you care for me," he had persisted. "I have been watching you as you cared for Jane and Julia throughout their illness, as you cared for Edith in her miscarriage. I have seen the sympathy in your eyes, my dear Prudence, as your cousin has turned her back on me as though I am in some way responsible for our misery. Do not turn your back on me, too, pretty Prudence." His hand had risen to stroke the curve of her cheek. "Do not deny me the love you carry in your eyes like a torch." He had gently pressed her to the wall then, stroking her hair, peering intently into the eyes he spoke of, his balance unsteady, his words—his touch—tearing her apart inside.

It was true. She cared for him. She had been drawn to Tim from the first moment her cousin Edith had introduced her handsome husband. He was an angel. One could not help but love him. Who would not agree that he and Edith made the perfect couple? They were a perfect matching of temperament and spirit. Pru had loved the promise of union and happiness that existed in her cousin's household. She had even envied it. Her dreams had begun to revolve around the idea of finding herself a husband and helpmate just like Tim.

She loved the way he spoke to his daughters, Jane and Julia. He had sat by their bedsides throughout the worst days of their confinement, reading them storybooks or singing them songs while Prudence changed the vinegar compresses meant to reduce their fever and coaxed them to swallow the foul draughts the doctor had prescribed. She loved his tender manner when the fever that had been passed on to his pregnant wife, Edith, took from him what he had desired most, a son. She loved the gentleness with which he had sat rocking his poor, grieving wife in his arms as she wept deep into the night. She loved the way his fair, silky hair fell down over his forehead when he pored over ledgers or accounts late into the night and the way his clear blue eyes sparkled when he was amused.

There had been little to amuse him of late.

She had become completely caught up in what his misery must be, though he hid it from everyone else behind a facade of even-tempered good cheer. She knew the truth. She had walked past his study the night after his son had been miscarried to hear the ragged, wretched sound of a man's muffled sobbing. She had witnessed in that sound the pain he so carefully hid from everyone else as he tried to carry his family through the wasteland of their sickness and suffering. She had loved and admired everything he was and stood for.

He had leaned against her, there in the hall, his body a seductive weight, pressing her against the wall, a weight she could not push away from her, no matter how wrong she knew such contact to be. Weary after weeks of tending to the fretting children and her morose, despondent cousin, Edith, Prudence had longed for warmth and appreciation. That such warmth might come from Tim had never occurred to her. He was the forbidden, unattainable god she worshipped from afar.

That he settled his head upon her shoulder and his lips, humid and heavy, upon her neck had overwhelmed her. She had allowed him to draw her close in a wonderful and terrible embrace.

Her acquiescence to that embrace had not been enough. He had asked more of her with the guiding pressure of his hands at the small of her back and a needful groan that had issued forth from his throat as he clasped her to him and with hungry lips nuzzled her throat. She had tried to resist. She had tried to push him away. A breathy no had trailed weakly from her lips, but she had neither the strength, nor, ultimately, the desire to adequately fend him off. His lips, his tongue, warm on her neck, had tested her resolve. Her knees had gone weak. When his lips sought hers, her mouth had responded.

That he kissed her was wrong. That she met those kisses with her own desire was wrong, and yet she had wanted him, had needed his affection and his strength, too much to refuse him.

As if he sensed her yielding, he had clasped her chest to his so that her nipples ached with the unaccustomed pressure. His hipbones, too, he drove hard against hers, as he pressed her even more tightly to the flat hard plane of the wall. She had felt trapped, as harried as a rabbit in the jaws of a hound, as he had kissed her again and again, his lips insistent, the heat of his passion, of the danger they risked, consuming.

Tighter and tighter he had held her, ever tighter his weight had pinned her to the wall. His hips had begun to move in a grinding, circular pattern. The hardness of his erection set fire to her through the layers of their clothing in a manner completely foreign to her. Foreign, too, was the throbbing sensitivity of her breasts, the damp heat between her legs, the grasping, almost desperate manner of Tim's advances on her person.

She, who had so recently helped her cousin with the bloody evacuation of the pitiful, stillborn baby and the distress of milk-laden breasts with no baby to suckle them, was filled with the conviction that the sensations she suffered were the hand of God, or the devil, upon her body reminding her of the sin she committed.

Timothy had tried to intrude his hands in the folds of her wrapper.

"No!" She had struck at his hands, gasping, sick with the deceit of her actions against her kinswoman. Poor soul, Edith was unable even for a moment to forget the pain of her loss. She rested only when laudanum had sufficiently dulled her senses. Prudence could not betray the woman who had taken a poor relative into her household and fed and clothed her with no more expectation than companionship and occasional light duties in helping to run a household with two small children.

"No!" She had thrust Timothy away from her with a feeling of revulsion as strong as the passion that still fired her veins. How could they sink so low? How could they allow wicked desire to rule them?

"We cannot . . . cannot," she had whispered fiercely as Timothy reeled back unsteadily. "You are drunk, sir, and I . . . I am a fool." Her voice had cracked in admitting as much. She had whirled away from the brink of disaster and fled to her room.

She had been unable to sleep that night, unable to eat the following day, and completely unable to meet the trusting gaze of her cousin, or the unguarded desire in Timothy's eyes in the week that followed. The illness she had so long been fighting in her cousin's family pounced upon her in this low-ered state. Mrs. Moore, a local widow, had been called in to tend to her as she had tossed and turned in her narrow bed and suffered feverish nightmares of hot hands reaching out to touch her.

A scratching at the door startled Prudence out of the past. She sat up, the bed creaking beneath her.

"Prudence?" Timothy's husky voice reached out to her from the far side of the door. "Are you awake?"

Hand at her throat, Prudence froze. She dared not speak. She dared not open the door. To do so, would be to open the door to desire, to ruin, to destruction. How could Tim, who claimed to care for her, ask so much of her?

"Pru?" He scratched again. Softly came his beloved voice. "Will you not open the door to me?"

Tears welled in Pru's eyes. She covered her mouth with her hand, afraid a sob might escape.

A sigh came from the other side of the door. "Sleep well. I shall see you in the morning."

He went away. She heard the floorboards creak in his wake, and above her, the shutting of a door. Only then did she take her hand from her mouth, bury her face in the pillow, and sob.

The next morning, exhausted by tears and a restless sense of impending disaster, Prudence roused with the dawn. Splashing her face with tepid water from the pitcher on her commode and dabbing at her wetted face with a square of linen, she crossed to the window and looked out across the little green that ran the length of New Steine. She had to see if Ramsay was there again. Lifting the window, she stepped over the sill onto the narrow balcony. She had a boxed-in kitty-corner view of the ocean from the balcony, but it was a view nonetheless.

At the head of the beach stood a man in flowing white robes. She had spotted him, strangely enough, before they had met at the bathhouse. She had watched him in fascination on her first morning in Brighton. She had watched him every morning since, with no less fascination. His morning ritual would have interested her regardless of who he was.

The breeze was warm this morning, and muggy.

Despite the heat, Prudence pulled on her wrapper and cinched it tightly at the waist before leaning out over the balcony railing to get a better look.

Ramsay stood looking toward the ocean as the sun chased away the morning mist. The breeze belled out the India muslin of his robe and the wide legs of matching pyjama trousers like the sails of a ship. Lit by the rising sun, she could see the dark outline of the man's legs, arms, and torso through the fine fabric. The sight was arresting.

She continued to watch as he sat down in the Indian fashion, legs crossed, his hands resting on his knees, palms up. Very still he sat, so still he became an almost indiscernible part of the scenery. Prudence, watching, became very still herself.

The sounds of Brighton waking touched upon her ears with a preternatural clarity. A dog barked. Shod hooves clopped on macadam as the first of the vendors took to the street. The clang of a ship's bell carried from far out on the water. A single gull keened an answer. The caress of the morning breeze through hair that hung unpinned like a waving curtain down her back felt like the brush of angels' wings against her skin. The tangy fresh smell of salty air blended with the heavenly odor of freshly brewed coffee and baking bread rising from downstairs.

Perfectly still the figure on the beach sat. Almost as still, Prudence stood watching him, reveling in the beginning of the day. So still was the surface of the morning that Prudence felt as if a stone had been thrown into it when Mrs. Moore walked briskly into her room.

"Pru?"

"On the balcony," Pru responded.

Mrs. Moore flung aside the waving curtain. The doves that had been cooing and fluttering above the window winged upward in a clattering rush.

As though the birds released him from a spell, the figure on the beach rose and shook the sand from his robes.

"Whatever do you do out there, child?" Mrs. Moore demanded. "Do you mean to make yourself ill? Come in at once, before you are seen. You must tell me all about your evening at the Pavilion."

The figure on the beach turned. Every day the ritual had ended the same way. The figure turned and walked west along the Marine Pavilion. This morning the ritual changed. This morning Ramsay turned and looked up at Prudence! He did not lift a hand in salute, merely stood there, unmoving, staring at her.

Prudence stood a moment, despite the unsuitability of her flimsy attire. What was this stillness they shared every morning? Could it be the attitude of repose he had once suggested she seek? Would their mornings change now that he knew she watched him? Would they cease altogether? She hoped not. She had come to enjoy this strange, bonding stillness he unwittingly shared with her.

"Prudence, shall I go down and order our breakfast?" Mrs. Moore's voice, busy with motherly concerns, brought her back to her senses.

She went in.

It was agreed that Mrs. Moore should go downstairs ahead of Prudence. She would, she declared, order a marvelous breakfast and have it waiting, if only Prudence promised to disclose every detail about the night before at the Pavilion. Prudence agreed, anxious for a moment alone to ponder the significance of Lord Ramsay's stare and her own desire to return it.

She paused before the mirror a moment, her mind fixed on the image of Charles Ramsay in Indian wedding clothes the night before, on Charles Ramsay in prayer robes this morning. What a mystery the man was. He was an exotic taste of the distant places and people she longed to know. What, she wondered, did he see when he looked at her? The thought made her uncomfortable. There was nothing out of the ordinary, nothing exotic, mysterious, or intriguing, in the face that looked back at her from the mirror. Feeling faintly ridiculous for supposing Ramsay might be as intrigued by her as she was by him, she made haste to wash, dress her hair, and button her way into her all too ordinary hand-me-downs.

She opened the door to the hallway, her head still full of Ramsay, and ran smack into Timothy.

"Prudence!" he exclaimed, clinging to her arms to steady her, though his touch inspired quite the opposite effect, leaving her giddy. The sad hollows in his cheeks disappeared for an instant in the warm sunshine of his smile. Shadows passed like clouds over the twin bits of heaven to be seen in his eyes. His joy in seeing her was too bright—too sharp. His hands were in no hurry to leave her arm. When they did, it was by a circuitous route, so that he might lift both her hands to his lips for a kiss.

"You are looking well. It's good to see you."

His compliment, because of its very earnestness, seemed too glowing. He passed a hand through the long, silky locks of honey gold hair at the crown of his head, as was his habit. His gaze passed hungrily over every inch of her. His every word or gesture unsettled her. He had the look about him of an angel on an all too earthly mission. Prudence blushed. Timothy's beauty had always struck her. That his affection evidenced itself so clearly in sky blue eyes, the milky perfection of a straight-toothed smile, and in twin dimples carved symmetrically in the evenness of his features made her heart lurch uncomfortably. Prudence feared greatly he could drown her in the treacherous beauty of his smile.

The fortification around her heart that she had allowed to drop away in the past few days, so that she might relax, sprang firmly back into place.

"Timothy," she said stiffly, "what brings you to Brighton?"

"You do. I had to see how you were getting on." His gaze traveled over the planes of her face as though he had forgotten them in some way and would never forget them again. She shivered. "Business brought me to London, and so close to Brighton that I could not resist dropping in to see how you get on with Dr. Blair's treatment. I could not have you thinking we had forgotten you, now could I?"

His smile was too tender, too loving. It would not do for Mrs. Moore to witness such a smile. Again he brushed back the soft, blond forelock from the high forehead that gave him an endearingly angelic appeal.

Prudence was both touched and troubled. "You are most kind," she said softly. "Perhaps you should partake of the waters yourself, as you are here. I've no doubt they would do you good."

He made a face and held out his arm to her. "I would much rather partake of breakfast. Will you join me?"

"But of course. Mrs. Moore will have a table waiting."

Mention of Mrs. Moore seemed to dim the sparkle in his eyes.

"Of course," he said. Taking her hand, he raised it to his lips for another heated kiss, before tucking it into the crook of his arm. "I am so very glad to see you looking well." His hand patted hers with his every word, as if for emphasis.

Together, they went down to breakfast.

Mrs. Moore was overjoyed to see the master. Tim wisely started the meal with an explanation, for Mrs. Moore's benefit, of his reasons for stopping with them, none of which had to do with his dire need to see Prudence. He went on to charm them both with an account of the latest doings in London.

"How is Edith?" Prudence asked as soon as their food had been placed before them. "Any word? We have yet to receive any mail from Gillingham."

Timothy was as easy to read as a book. Though he guarded his words, his expression had a way of telling all. Sadness pulled at his mouth and clouded his eyes. He chewed for an instant on the corner of a triangle of toast before saying with a shrug, "There has been no change."

"And the girls?" Mrs. Moore briskly set about filling their cups with tea. "Are they completely recovered?"

The sadness fled Timothy's expression. He smiled broadly, unknowingly charming several ladies at a nearby table, so sunny was his expression. Prudence was herself unable to resist returning such a smile. "The girls are up and about, terrorizing the upstairs maids and into all sorts of mischief with their governess gone." The blindingly beautiful smile was turned full upon Prudence. "They have both instructed me to lavish you with their hugs and kisses should I chance to see you." His eyes warmed at the idea.

Prudence blushed.

A cloud of guilt darkened the brilliance of Tim's eyes. He turned to ask Mrs. Moore what she found to do with herself while Prudence was occupied with the baths.

Prudence's heart twisted. Poor little Jane. Dear sweet Julia. How she hated to hurt them, and hurt them she would if she held fast to her resolution to find a new position. They were too young to understand the danger of their father's lavished kisses—too young to understand she hurt them less in leaving them, than in staying. For hurt and disgrace them she inevitably would if she returned to Gillingham and the daily draw of Timothy Margrave's beautiful smiles.

"What shall we do with ourselves while I am here, when you are not compelled to take your medicine?" Timothy was ready to smile at her again, ready to tease her with the twinkle in his eyes. He leaned in over the table, his boot stretching out to touch upon hers beneath the table. To Prudence there was implicit in his every word, every glance, every move, his intention to seduce her, now that they were distanced from the watchful eyes of his wife and children, servants and neighbors.

There was only one who stood in his way here in Brighton —Mrs. Moore.

"There's always the chance you will receive an invitation to dine with the Prince," the woman said coyly.

Prudence would have liked to thrust the remark back down Mrs. Moore's throat. She had not intended for Tim to hear of last night's escapade.

She need not have worried. He evidenced no interest in the suggestive remark.

"Small chance," he said. "I am not now, nor do I ever plan to be, part of the Prince's rather risqué set."

In a rush, before Mrs. Moore could do further damage, Prudence raised the most mundane topic she could imagine.

"After breakfast we must make a point of stopping in at Donaldson's Circulating Library in Old Steine Street."

"Must we?" Tim asked lightly, though his boot beneath the table lent weight to the question.

Prudence edged her foot away from his. "Indeed. We must see that your name is entered in the Master of Ceremonies registry."

"Do you think I shall find the time to participate in the local entertainments, Pru? A week seems so short a period." His foot bumped hers again. "I thought we would no more than have a good chat and a hand or two of cards and I would be off again."

Prudence had trouble meeting the questions that lurked in the heaven of Tim's tender gaze. "There is always a card game running at Donaldson's," she said. "In addition, there are billiard tables and sometimes an orchestra, as well as a multitude of good books and the latest editions of the London papers."

"Well then," Timothy agreed, dazzling Mrs. Moore with his smile, "Donaldson's it is. Tell me, Mrs. Moore, what card games do they favor here?"

Chapter Ten

L oo was the game of choice at Donaldson's. The stakes were very low. Those who longed for deeper play ambled across the street to Raggett's Subscription House, but if music, quiet conversation, and penny stakes pleased, Donaldson's Circulating Library was the haunt of choice. More like a club than a reading room, a wooden rotunda at one end was generally occupied by a chamber orchestra, and the back room held the billiard table. A small subscription fee provided members access to all.

Timothy paid for the fees as well as for a handful of chips for each of them.

"It's nothing," he said, laughing when Prudence objected. "Can't have you two wasting away of boredom while I am here."

"We have never been in danger of that," Mrs. Moore murmured sarcastically.

Tim gave no indication he heard her. "We have all had enough of sickrooms and mourning, have we not?" The look he shared with Prudence added weight to his words. "Life is all too brief not to enjoy it while we may."

Prudence turned away, but he would not let her ignore him. "How is the shampooing treatment Dr. Blair prescribed? Is it the cure-all he promised?"

Mrs. Moore let slip a little bark of laughter.

Prudence blushed, reminded of the treatment she had received at the hands of Lord Ramsay. "It is too soon to tell," she said. "Perhaps a shampooing would do you good as well."

Tim pushed his golden mane away from his forehead, lines of sorrow for a moment etching harsh around his eyes. "No physicking for me while I am here, Pru. I mean to escape for the entire week all contact with doctors and their treatments."

He was remembering the loss of the baby, a day full of doctors who could do nothing to cure what ailed his stillborn son.

"You mean to stay the entire week, sir?" Mrs. Moore was too interested in securing them places at the loo table to give the idea her full attention.

Tim looked not at Mrs. Moore, but at Prudence, his expression lit once more with the promise of what a week together might bring, his sadness for the moment forgotten, safely tucked away in the depths of Dorset.

Prudence cared not for cards. They reminded her of her folly.

Tim, on the other hand, enjoyed cards as much as Mrs. Moore. He had turned to cards throughout the extent of his recent bad luck. He had played for hours with Edith in the early days of her pregnancy when she was too ill to do anything else in the evenings. As her pregnancy had progressed, her tolerance for extended card games had dwindled. She was too tired, too moody to play without shows of temper. She had forgone the nightly interchange with her husband, had gone off to her bedchamber to sleep, while Tim played solitaire for hour upon hour into the night. With the loss of the baby, he had tried to return the pattern of their lives to some sort of normalcy, instigating the card games of old with his grief-benumbed wife. Edith had been unable to focus, unable even to agree to sharing a bed with her husband. The nightly solitaire games had seemed more solitary than ever to Prudence. One evening, she had foolishly agreed to a hand or two of casino with Tim.

Perhaps that had been her mistake. Camaraderie was born out of card play, or backgammon for that matter, both battles of luck and wits that drew two people together in an unaccustomed manner. Over a backgammon board Prudence had lost twenty-four hours of her time, but it was over cards that Prudence had lost all sense of the proper perspective with regard to her cousin's husband.

Two chairs came open at a table for seven players. Mrs.

Moore leapt upon one. Timothy held out the other for Prudence.

Mrs. Moore watched the two of them expectantly. Prudence knew the older woman liked to play almost as much as she liked to sit in silent judgement of the actions of others.

She shook her head, handing Tim the playing chips he had given her. "You and Mrs. Moore play. I have the headache and would be far happier quietly reading a newspaper. Perhaps, if the headache disappears, I will come and join you."

Her hand briefly met Tim's in the exchange of the chips. His angelic blue eyes locked tenderly on hers for a speaking moment. Disappointment hovered about the mouth that had introduced her to her own passionate nature.

"All right," he said. "I hope the headache goes away."

Prudence did not really suffer from the headache. It was her heart that was hurting, not her head. She could not bear to sit across the table from the source of that heartache for another hour, as she had over breakfast, with the sun pouring over Timothy's shoulder catching his hair in a halo of gold while his eyes, twin pools of clear blue azure, promised to quench her every desire. She could not resist another tender word or glance. Timothy had only to look at her to muddle her thinking. She would forget her purpose, looking into his eyes. She would forget what was right or wrong or proper or decent if he blessed her with another of his blinding smiles. She could not keep her gaze from centering on his lips when he smiled. She knew too well the heated promise of them, their tender allure.

The affection she felt for Timothy Margrave weighed heavy and aching in her chest. It was, in a way, as if his affection for her reached out as much as his arms would like to, as if that stifled affection squeezed the very breath out of her. What she wanted, what she longed for when Timothy was near, went against all that Prudence held dear.

She cared for Timothy. She knew he cared for her, and yet she feared his intentions. She feared even more, her own overwhelming desire. She could not turn off the feelings, but she could distance herself from them, and from Tim. Plucking up one of the many papers made available to those who frequented Donaldson's, she buried herself in the pages of the *Sussex Advertiser* and vowed she would not surface again until she had found a position in the "Wants." It was time to get on with her life.

A quarter of an hour later, no closer to her goal than when she started, Prudence had viewed all of the available papers save one, the *London Times*. That one paper hung almost before her nose, clenched in the hands of another of the circulating library patrons. He had been in possession of the *Times* for the entirety of the time Prudence had been leafing through the rest of the world's news.

Prudence squinted at the pages suspended before her. She could see the "Wants" almost clearly enough to read them where they were. A long row of capital *W*'s ran the length of the back page. She leaned forward in her chair. There, just a little closer. The first line of each of the advertisements was headed boldly with the word "Wants," and then in smaller type followed a description. She nervously eyed the hands that held the paper before leaning still closer to scan the black-boxed entries. Footmen, grooms, and stable boys, cooks, maids, schoolmasters, shoemakers, butchers, and bakers were needed. There were dogs lost and dogs found, horses, harness, and vehicles for sale. There were "Wants" for boarders and boat passengers, for the loan of monies, and the buying and selling of properties. The entire page was covered in the tiny type of hopes, of promises, of possibilities. Surely among so many there was someone who wanted, who needed a body with her unique qualifications.

Prudence was drawn to the suspended page as a thirsty man is drawn to water. She had no idea how intent, nor how rude was her perusal until the page dropped out from in front of her nose, and she was faced by the gentleman who had been reading the other side of the page.

"Did you want something?" he asked.

It was Lord Ramsay—not in a robe and turban this time, but dressed very much as one might expect an Englishman to dress, barring the colorful paisley sash at his waist. Prudence found him new and fascinating all over again.

He was staring at her, in the same knowing way he had stared at her that very morning—as he had stared at her on the street in front of the bathhouse, as he stared at her every time they came together—one eyebrow raised, as if in amusement, his mouth set in an uncompromising line. His unsettling gaze held no questions, only answers to questions she had yet to ask.

"Miss Stanhope, I would like to think it is me you find so engrossing, that you have come with no other purpose in mind than to tell me you would begin payment of our twenty-four hours' time together; however, as I am sure it is *this* you would rather spend your time with, be my guest." He neatly folded the paper as he spoke and held it out to her.

She was too embarrassed to take it.

"I do beg your pardon." She ducked her chin, blood heating her cheeks.

"We seem to have formed the odd habit of constantly apologizing to one another," he said softly, dropping the paper to his knee. It bridged the narrow gap between them, grazing against her knee as well.

Prudence jumped. She looked up self-consciously, so overblown had her reaction been to the touch. Was that a twinkle in his strange, gray-green eyes?

He tapped the newspaper and leaned closer. "What is it you want, Miss Stanhope?"

Prudence was startled. She had been wondering what Ramsay expected of the twenty-four hours he had won from her. His simple question placed undue emphasis on *her* deepest desires, not his. What *did* she want?

She flicked a glance in her cousin's direction. Her twenty-four hour dilemma with Rash Ramsay seemed inconsequential compared with the dilemma Timothy Margrave posed in arriving here. She had left Gillingham convinced she must separate herself from Tim and all he stood for. She knew that in wanting him, she wanted the unattainable. She would not, could not, find what she sought beneath her cousin's roof, in Timothy's arms.

Rash Ramsay waited an answer. As he waited, he stared at her, as had become his habit. She could tell him none of this.

She thought of the garden in her mind that this man had revealed to her. She wanted to free it from the vine that choked its growth. She wanted the garden to flourish, as the tropicals in her glass house flourished.

What did she want? It suddenly became clear to her that the tropicals were the part of her that wanted to travel, to visit foreign lands, to explore the unknown. "I want . . ." she began to blurt out her desire, but stopped as her gaze settled on the newspaper resting on his knee. "*Wants*"—the word leapt off of the page in a long row of *W*'s. Perhaps he wanted to know only what it was she sought in the newspaper.

"I want a new position," she said simply. "You may recall my mentioning before, I am desirous of a new position as a lady's traveling companion or as a governess to another household."

"Is that all you desire?" He studied her face as the question hung between them. "Is your current position so intolerable?" He passed the paper from his knee to hers. "If so, I would not prove an obstacle to your search. Please peruse to your heart's content. I wish you luck in finding exactly what you are looking for."

Again the emphasis he placed on simple words made them seem vaster in scope than the mere finding of a position. Uneasy, Prudence took the paper, that she might focus her perusal on the advertisements, rather than on Ramsay's searching gaze. He just as eagerly took advantage of the opportunity to continue staring at her. She could feel the weight of his gaze pass over her. Looking up, she realized he was not the only one staring. Her cousin had lost interest in his cards. His gaze met hers across the room.

"You are staring." She reproved Ramsay uneasily, hoping he would stop looking at her so intently and go away before Tim saw the need to join them.

Ramsay's response startled her.

"Yes. I am not quite sure what it is about you that seems so familiar to me, but I have the feeling every time I look at you, most especially when our eyes meet, that we know one another remarkably well . . . for strangers. Have you the same sensation?"

Prudence set aside the paper. Her search had been fruitless, but this conversation was as intriguing as every other she had shared with Charles Ramsay. "I admit there is something about you I find familiar. We have never had occasion to meet before the day we"—she forced her voice to remain even—"encountered one another at Mahomed's bathhouse, have we?"

He smiled mischievously. "Perhaps not in this life, but another."

She blinked in dismay that he openly suggested such heresy. "You speak of reincarnation?"

"Ah!" His eyebrows rose and fell. "I must keep in mind that there is very little one can teach a governess." He tried to make light of his remarks with the arch elevation of his errant brow, but it was remarkable how quickly they delved into meaty topics whenever they had a moment together. There were people she had known all her life with whom she had never broached thought-provoking philosophies. Quite probably she never would, but with Charles Ramsay there were none of the conventional limits or boundaries to their conversations. There was something absolutely exhilarating about such freedom of expression.

"Do you believe in reincarnation, then? And is it a meditation in which you engage every morning?"

"Yes and yes." Something changed in his eyes as he looked at her, as if a door to a deeper part of himself opened. "I make a practice of meditating every day."

"You sat so very still. Is that the attitude of repose you once mentioned to me?"

Before he could respond, before she could ask him how one went about the mysterious art of meditation, they were interrupted.

Tim had abandoned his cards.

"Whatever is the topic of this charming tête-à-tête? You two do seem to have your heads bent together in an admirably cozy fashion."

Tim sounded nonchalant, but Prudence knew every nuance of his voice. There was nothing nonchalant in his interest. She knew him, she thought, too well.

"Cousin!" Prudence opened her mouth to explain, and as quickly snapped it shut again. She could not tell Tim the truth. Reincarnation and meditation did not figure into his accounting of the world. He would be shocked by their unorthodox topics.

Ramsay came to her rescue. He seemed to be doing that rather often of late. "Would you be interested in an outing to the tidal pools along the westward shoreline between Portslade and Saltdean? I am putting together a party for tomorrow and thought Miss Stanhope might care to join us." His tone was gracious in the extreme, but Prudence could not dismiss the feeling that he studied her cousin with far more interest than such a question merited.

Timothy looked from Ramsay to Prudence and back again, confusion dimming the brilliance of his eyes. "I do not think Pru has the energy for outings. She suffers terribly from the headache, you know."

Ramsay nodded. "Your cousin"—he seemed to be absorbing the implications of their connection—"has told me they trouble her on occasion. It occurred to me that a carefree day in the sunshine might be just the thing to clear her head."

Tim frowned. "I do not think you can have thought at all carefully, sir. I am convinced that too much sun and wind would be just the thing to provoke the headache." He turned to Prudence, as though he expected her to agree.

It annoyed Prudence that these two arranged her life without consulting her. She was only a little mollified when Ramsay turned to ask, "Miss Stanhope? Am I misinformed? Did you not tell us yesterday that you meant to collect shells for your charges?"

Prudence looked uneasily from her cousin's face to Lord Ramsay's. Another moment and she would succumb to the appeal in Timothy's eyes. She must not succumb. Timothy had no right to try and determine her future, not even for an afternoon. *What do you want?* The question Ramsay had earlier posed to her rang in her ears. What did she want? She wanted to see the tidal pools. She wanted to pay off the debt of time she owed Charles Ramsay. She wanted to free herself from the spell of Tim's endearing presence for a few hours.

"I would be pleased to be included in your plans," she said to Ramsay.

"And you, sir? Do you care to join us?" Ramsay graciously extended the invitation to Tim a second time. Prudence was pleased to hear no hint of triumph in his voice.

Timothy shook his head, the look he turned on her that of a disappointed angel. "No, I thank you. I have a limited time to spend in Brighton and better ways to spend it."

Ramsay ended the conversation. "We shall call for you at dawn tomorrow, then, Miss Stanhope."

"Yes." She expected him to take her hand in farewell, perhaps to kiss it. Her fingers tingled in anticipation of such contact.

He bowed instead and touched two fingers to his forehead in an oddly exotic gesture, almost as if in blessing.

"Until we meet again," he said.

Chapter Eleven

Timothy waited until they began the walk back to Mrs. Harris's boardinghouse, before he questioned Pru's judgement. He waited, too, until Mrs. Moore begged leave to step inside one of the shops they were passing to look at wool. She required more for her knitting. For a moment in the deserted street he was alone with her.

Prudence knew what was coming. She was, in a way, relieved when at last he broached the topic on both their minds.

"I am confused, Pru, and more than a little wounded that you choose to spend time with others when I have come so far to see you. Who was that rude fellow?"

"I am sorry, Tim." She could see a distorted reflection of his face in one of the shop windows before them. She was sorry to see his reflection frown. Sorrow swelled in her chest, threatening to overwhelm her. She was sorry for so many things in connection with this man. "I should have introduced you to one another. I do not know how I can have been so remiss in my manners."

"You have yet to tell me who he is." Tim's jaw had a hard look.

She turned away from his reflection, moving slowly along the window, as though the millinary goods inside fascinated her. "His name is Ramsay, Charles Ramsay. I met him, his brother Rupert, and Rue's wife, Grace, here in Brighton."

"Ramsay?" He followed her, his hands clasped behind his back. "He is not one of those much-talked-of Ramsay brothers who have just lost their inheritance to Miles Fletcher, is he?"

She had reached the end of the window. She could not continue to edge away from him. Neither could she lie to him. "I'm afraid he is. Will you not come with us to the tidal pools? I had it in mind to find some sort of sea treasure for Jane and for Julia—shells, starfish, sponges, and the like."

She looked back at him. He shoved his hair away from the dear, troubled features Prudence longed to caress free of all care. Dear God, would she ever love another man as much as Tim? He smiled at her as if he found something touching in her plan. "They will enjoy that enormously." He considered a moment, his jaw working, before surprising her with an insistent "You must go! But, surely, there is someone better suited to the task of escort on such an outing than a Ramsay? Surely you realize you risk all reputation in associating with such a man?"

She pressed her lips together and fought the words that wanted to spill from her mouth.

"He could ruin you," he pressed.

"And you would not?"

He would not recognize the parallel. "How can you say such a thing? Do you mean to grievously wound me, Pru?" His eyes were dark with too much sorrow. Prudence longed to comfort him, but could not. Would not.

She wished she might take back her words. "No." She fought the tears that threatened to undo her voice. "But neither would I grievously wound my cousin Edith or your children. I wish only the best for all of you."

He closed his eyes a moment, jaw working, and leaned against the dark mathematical tile that decorated the building's exterior. When he opened the blue of his eyes to her again, she could see he was pained by her reminder of his loved ones. "You know then why I had to come, why I had to see you?"

She clasped her hands together before her and stared as if intrigued by the display of lace in the window. She could not look at him. If she looked, she might go to him and beg him to take her in his arms. "I do."

"And do you feel nothing for me?" His voice was very low. Sadness, loneliness, and desire reached out to her even in his reflection in the windowpane. She bit down on her lower lip and resisted the impulse to turn to him.

"Feel nothing?" Her voice broke. "You know that is not the case. I feel too much. It is tearing me apart inside."

"Oh, my dear Pru . . ." She could hear the wonder in his voice. He pushed himself away from the wall and moved toward her.

She dared to glance at him.

It was a mistake to have done so. The intensity of his feelings shone from his eyes like a sword with which he meant to cut away her resistance.

She backed up a step, her hands before her like a shield. "Please, Tim. You should go home—home to your wife and children. You should stay away from me."

He would not hear her plea. He took a step closer. "Ah, but my dearest Pru, is it not yet clear to you? I cannot stay away. If I could, I would not be here with you in Brighton today."

She was saved from further advances by Mrs. Moore, who came rushing out of the shop, a bulky packet in her hands. Breathlessly, she apologized, "I am sorry to keep you waiting. You do not forget you have an appointment at the bathhouse, do you, Pru? Shall we go straight there? Will you be coming with us, Master Margrave? It is a curious place, Mohamed's. One meets the most interesting people there."

Timothy declined, for which Prudence was genuinely thankful. There was something far too seductive about the bare skin and steaming temperatures of the baths for her to feel comfortable sharing the experience with Tim. As it was, the herb-scented steaming followed by a shampooing not at all unlike the one she had received at the hands of Rash Ramsay, reminded her all too vividly of the feelings she wanted to deny in connection with that other gentleman—with any gentleman.

Those feelings had made her overwrought. The eggshell crunch was back in Pru's neck, and her chest felt constricted. As the shampooer worked to loosen her neck and shoulders, thoughts of Lord Ramsay crowded into Pru's mind. The sham-

pooing he had given her was, as he had said, very much like
the one she had since received. That he had proven trustworthy in that respect pleased her. He had bypassed more than one
opportunity to touch her far more intimately than the shampooing allowed. Most men would not have resisted such an
opportunity.

The garden he had conjured forth from her imagination
reappeared. It was, perhaps, the rhythmic clicking of Mrs.
Moore's knitting needles that brought it back so clearly.

Prudence entered the garden again. Nothing was changed.
The vine she now thought of as a representation of Timothy
still threatened to overtake the place. The marble fountain in
the middle of the garden did not flow. In her mind's eye she
examined the fountain with interest. What part of her life did
this pale, still cherub represent? Tears springing to her eyes,
she realized the marble effigy looked like the pale, perfect,
stillborn babe she had helped her cousin to deliver. It made
sense that this fountain did not flow. It made sense, too, that it
stood at the center of her tangled garden. The death of Edith's
babe stood at the center of her current circumstances. Had the
baby lived, her cousin would not be sunk in despair, and Tim
would not have turned to her in his grief. She would never
have revealed her feelings for him.

Prudence turned her back on the silent fountain to examine
the overgrown beds in the garden. Twisting tendrils of vine
smothered everything. Moved by the meaning of the fountain,
by the tenacity of the vine, she began to clear the plants it
smothered. She could see the tops of the carrots now and rows
of stunted cabbage. What pleased her most was the unexpected uncovering in the fertile soil of her imagination a
thorny sprig that could be nothing less than the beginnings of a
rosebush, a bush with but a single, tight green bud to promise
a future flowering. Prudence had cleared the vines from the
rosebush when she was jolted from the garden of her imagining by the songlike voice of the shampooer.

"Time for your bath, miss."

With a groan from her chair Mrs. Moore stood up and
tucked her knitting into her bag. "The bath is too wet for my

wool, dear. If you need me, I shall be on the seaside balcony in the shade."

The bath Prudence sank into as the final step of her shampooing was large enough to hold half a dozen patrons, but for the moment she shared the blessed cool with only one other female, a rather large female, to be sure, but only the one.

There was something about the woman that struck Prudence as familiar. She could not immediately place the drenched creature who lifted an eyelid to gaze at her, but just as much as the surface of the pool was disturbed by her stepping into it, so, too, was her mind disturbed by a sudden rush of memories—Charles Ramsay and his brother on the steps outside the bathhouse—a dangling hand, proof that a body lay beneath the mound of sheeting borne by six straining men—a heart-rending cry from a carriage in the street.

Memory triggered realization. Her somnolent bath mate was the woman from the carriage. Sensing she was being observed, both the woman's eyes opened abruptly.

Prudence could not pretend she had not been staring. "How do you do?" she asked softly.

"Not well," the woman replied tartly. "I would not be here else, would I? How do *you* do?"

Prudence thought a moment before she replied. How did she do? It was not often she was asked the question, rarer still that she honestly considered her reply. "I feel as if I have been run over by a coach and four," she said earnestly.

The woman laughed weakly. "Your first time here?"

"First week," Pru said. "I am Prudence Stanhope." She held forth a dripping hand.

The woman regarded her hand a moment in surprise before clasping it wetly for the briefest of moments, saying, "Rose Thurgood."

Rose, Prudence thought. Was this the rose she had just uncovered in her garden? The woman mumbled something incoherent about this having been the worst week in her entire life.

Prudence regarded the poor woman with sincere sympathy.

"I understand, more than you may realize. I was here for the first time on the day your sister died."

Rose Thurgood's face sagged. "Were you? Did you perhaps speak to her?" Her expression lifted with hope.

"No, I am sorry. I did not. But I can well understand that you do not feel well today."

"Can you?" Mrs. Thurgood sighed heavily and sank a little lower in the water. "Have you lost someone as dear to you as my sister is . . . was to me?"

Prudence nodded. "I have no sisters, no siblings at all, but my parents were killed in the overturning of a carriage six years ago. I was devastated."

Mrs. Thurgood closed her eyes and rubbed at her forehead, dribbling water down her nose. "Both of them at once? How dreadful."

"Yes. I do not know how I would have survived had I not been taken in by my cousin, a dear lady who suffers her own tragedy now in the loss of a child."

"Dear, dear," Rose said sadly. "Life can be a wrenching business at times. I am quite flattened by Ester's unexpected demise. We had planned to travel together . . . to collect some pretty. . . ." Tears choked off her words.

Prudence strove to ease her pain and the embarrassment of losing all control in front of a stranger by inquiring with real interest, "Where did you mean to go?"

Rose Thurgood sniffed unhappily. "China. Perhaps a side trip through Tibet." She burst into tears again. "Now I shall be forced to remain here, alone, in the midst of brick dust and paint fumes while my house is being finished."

Prudence reached out to pat the woman's hand. "How awful for you," she crooned. "Your sister did not want that."

Mrs. Thurgood splashed water on her swollen eyes. "No, she did not," she agreed. "It was Ester's suggestion we take ourselves off together in the first place. She is ever so daring . . . was." Again she fought to control tears. "She suggested we travel to China. It is in chinoiserie I intend to decorate the house, you see. Ester said we could go and select, firsthand, the lacquered furniture I wanted, along with all manner of pottery and china."

"Then you must go," Prudence said with conviction.

Rose Thurgood eyed her in dismay. "Go? I couldn't. What would people think of me if there was not a proper period of mourning?"

"They might think you honor your sister's memory more by carrying bravely on with the trip the two of you had planned together."

Interest lit Rose Thurgood's expression briefly. It was as swiftly extinguished. She shook her head. "I could not go alone," she said. "Not to a place so completely foreign to me. I haven't the strength."

"Perhaps another relative, or a friend . . . ?"

Rose shook her head. "None of them likes to travel as much as Ester did."

"You could hire someone."

Mrs. Thurgood frowned. "A perfect stranger? I am not at all comfortable with that idea. No, there's nothing for it. Brick dust it must be."

Prudence hid her disappointment. "Well, should you change your mind, please call on me. I would not turn down the chance to explore the Continent. I love to travel, and while I could not in any way begin to fill your sister's shoes, I am conversant in several languages that . . ."

Mrs. Thurgood began to weep in earnest. Prudence felt dreadful. She should have kept her mouth shut. How could she think of pushing her own agenda upon the woman when she was so recently bereaved?

"I am sorry." She patted the woman's shaking shoulder. "How silly of me to suggest such a thing at a time like this. Please forgive me."

The woman continued to sob wetly into the bath.

"There, there," Prudence crooned. "You must do whatever feels right. If you think it best to stay and oversee the construction of your house, you should do just that. I would, in fact, recommend to you a very kind and trustworthy gentleman who has just returned from India and the Orient with all manner of lovely china and textiles. I daresay he has contacts who will ship you the lacquered furniture you mentioned."

Rose Thurgood's interest returned. She grabbed at a towel and dried the tears from her eyes. "How very kind you are, my dear. Who is this gentleman?"

Chapter Twelve

Charles Ramsay could not stop thinking of Prudence Stanhope as he bore his brother's weight with care across the slippery shale that led them into the surge of the tide. Rupert, breathing hard, gave another hop, leaning into Charles's shoulder. Most men would have considered the one-legged walk to the water too much effort for the pleasure of a swim, but Charles and Rupert made daily practice of performing this ungainly ritual. Today their efforts promised to be unusually satisfying. The air was increasingly close and muggy. The sun seemed all the hotter for it. The brothers, clad in nothing more than full-cut Turkish pantaloons, the left leg of Rupert's tied in a knot at the knee, the free end flapping in the breeze, made slow progress to the water's edge.

"I feel almost whole again in the water," Rue had explained to Charles. "The water lends me legs. And as a result of these daily exertions, what's left of me grows stronger."

Rue's daily trek to the beach was a source of inspiration to Charles, a symbol of his own resolve to fight the odds of his financial defeat, to stagger on, though the very legs had been cut out from beneath him. A man could not ask for a more admirable, a more cheerfully courageous brother. As much as Rue leaned on him physically, Charles leaned in turn upon his one-legged brother emotionally. It was to Rupert Charles had originally turned to sound out his ideas with regard to travel in the Far East. It was to Rupert Charles had written of his progress. Now, in the daily three-legged, arm-in-arm jaunts to splash about in waters that were reputed to have great healing properties, both of the brothers found opportunity to reveal their misgivings, their fears, their hopes for a happy future despite the strange turn of events that bound the Ramsays, who had lost a fortune, inextricably to the Fletchers, who had won it away from them. It was during one of these daily trips that Rupert told Charles, "I had no idea it was Miles Fletcher to whom your inheritance had passed when Grace and I ran away to Gretna. I do not know that I could have married her, had I known."

"Silly gudgeon. Of course you could have. Never have I seen a pair more in love. I find myself longing for just such a happy union whenever I am alone with the two of you."

"I am immensely pleased you should say so. Grace lived in fear that you and she might never be friends when you returned from overseas. Aurora must suffer similar fears."

"It will be difficult for me to like Miles Fletcher," Charles admitted. "But I have made up my mind that I must welcome him, if not as a brother, at least as a relation I will tolerate, for my sister's sake. Karmic forces must have been at work to so firmly enmesh our families."

"Karma? Is that anything like kismet?"

"Very like."

"Then why confuse me with another silly term?" Rupert took another hop, slamming into his shoulder, just as Charles stepped down on a stone that turned beneath his foot. The two staggered as one.

Rue's breath caught in his throat as Charles fought gravity and rebalanced their weight. "If you fall and take me down with you, Chaz, embarrassing me in front of an entire beach-front of watching females, among them my lovely wife, I shall kick you."

"Idle threat," Charles said, pausing at the water's edge to more securely grasp his brother. "You land on your ass if you do. Besides, Grace must have seen you make an utter fool of yourself already, at least once. You are in love with her."

"What has that to do with anything?"

"Lovers always make complete fools of themselves."

Rupert laughed and made another graceless hop. "When will you begin to be foolish?"

"Me? I suppose I shall be as foolish as the next man when I allow myself to fall in love."

"Allow yourself? There's no allowing involved so far as I can tell. It just happens when one least expects it."

"I haven't the means to fall in love," Charles said with a grimace as he stepped into the chill water. Rue had no choice other than to splash after him.

"Is it?" "*You* haven't the means? Christ, that's cold."

Charles was not sure whether Rue referred to his attitude or the temperature of the water.

"Enough to shrivel me manhood."

"Ah, it's the water you mean. I thought you impugned my approach to love."

Rupert laughed. "As to that, you stand holding up a one-legged man without a penny to his name, at least not until his book begins to sell, and have the gall to tell him *you* haven't the means to fall in love?"

"That's right. You have a leg to stand on, Rue. Financially, I have none." Charles moved deeper into the chill waves. They would be warmer when they had completely doused themselves.

"Doing it a bit brown, aren't you? I thought the Prince had committed to a number of the expensive items you have shown him."

"The Prince has committed to a cartload of stuff, but I have yet to see so much as sixpence."

"No!"

"Yes." Charles tried to make light of his dire straits. "Do you know that in all my years of buying things, it never once occurred to me how inconvenient it is for a tradesman to collect payment on past due bills until I began billing customers myself."

Rue laughed uneasily. "But the Prince has not been your only customer."

"True. I have enjoyed any number of illustrious promises as a result of the Prince's favor, however none of the beau monde see fit to promptly paying their bills."

"I suppose that was to be expected. How much of a hole are you in?"

"I'm not in over my head yet. Not to worry, Rue. I have merely adopted the habit of delaying payments myself. Unless, of course, you happen to have noticed an irresistible heiress like Grace dangling after me, I've no other choice."

Rue would not let the matter lie. "No heiresses, but there has been a governess about."

Charles sighed. "Do you recommend I succumb to the charms of a young woman as bereft of fortune as I am myself?"

Rue laughed heartily. "I highly recommend falling in love with the woman you are most drawn to, no matter what her circumstances. Fortunes can be made or lost in an instant. You should know that better than anyone. But love, precious and fragile flower that it is, must be plucked where and when it blooms."

Charles squeezed his brother's shoulder. "You begin to sound more and more the poet, little brother. You have changed while I have been gone."

"As have you," Rue admitted. "But not so much, I hope, that you will refuse to tell me just what it was happened between you and Miss Stanhope the day you met at the baths." He paused significantly. "You were gone for the longest while. Did you, in all truth, give the girl a shampooing?"

The water, thigh-deep now, pulled gently at their legs, first one way and then the other. Rupert's questions pulled at Charles in much the same manner.

"I think you deserve a ducking for asking."

"Shall I take that as a yes?" Rue laughed and flung himself away from Charles's support, splashing mightily with a sweep of his arm. In the water he was agile enough to evade pursuit.

"You would not take advantage of a crippled man," he protested when Charles splashed back.

"Oh wouldn't I?"

Determined to prove him mistaken, Charles flung dripping hair away from his eyes and dove into the water after him.

* * *

Prudence paused on the bathhouse steps. It was almost as humid on the streets today as it was in the steam baths. King's Road was strangely quiet, empty but for a single carriage pulled up to wait for its owner, a familiar black barouche, it had once brought Rose Thurgood to claim the body of her sister. It came today to claim only Rose.

Prudence was glad the street was still today, glad no sheet-covered body followed them out the door, but it would have been nice to encounter Lord Ramsay again. She felt quite keenly his absence, so strongly had she felt his presence here before.

Mrs. Moore stopped at her heels. "I know what you are thinking."

Prudence hoped with all her heart Mrs. Moore was mistaken. "Do you?"

"But, of course. I, too, cannot help but think of the last time we were here." She looked over her shoulder, nodding toward the door through which they had come. "That poor woman dying here, so that six men must carry her out. How strange that you should encounter her sister today. What was her name? Rose? Poor dear. She seemed a nice enough person."

"Very nice," Prudence agreed, an unexpected sadness overwhelming her. It was odd, really, even fanciful, but she had half expected to encounter Ramsay here, if only for a moment. He had said little to her this morning at Donaldson's with regard to the twenty-four hours she owed him. She had expected him to swiftly follow up on that. Surely, if the man was as interested in her as she had convinced herself he must be, he would make a point of claiming his prize.

That she encountered Rose Thurgood instead only served to accentuate Ramsay's absence. The woman, too, reminded Prudence of the brevity of life, of the dreams she still clung to, perhaps foolishly, of traveling to distant shores. Most devastating of all, she had reminded Prudence of the loss of her parents. There was a deep abiding loneliness attendant to such memories, a loneliness that was echoed in the knowledge Prudence carried of the misery she would suffer soon in separating herself from Edith, Jane, Julia, and Tim.

Tim waited for her even now. He waited to take her in his arms, little knowing that in so doing he pushed her away from happiness even as he sought to bestow it. The thought was as cloying as the weather.

"Shall we return by way of the Marine Parade?" Prudence suggested, in no hurry to face him.

Mrs. Moore eyed the sky. She plucked up the watch that dangled from a chain about her neck. "I do not think that is at all wise, Pru. Mr. Margrave is waiting. Perhaps we should go straight back. I fear we will be overheated walking the longer route in this warm weather."

Prudence drank in a breath of the sun-warmed salty air. There was something calming, something infinite and timeless about the muggy breeze that plucked at her bonnet, the sun that warmed her cheek, the muted lapping of water on the beach. This was, she thought, a place of repose. There was no reason to hurry oneself in Brighton. Here she had responsibility to no one but herself. She meant to regain her strength, to reestablish the direction of her future, to rediscover her lost state of repose. None of these goals was met in hurrying back to face Timothy.

"Perhaps *you* should go straight back," she said agreeably. "If only to tell my cousin that I have taken the longer route along the beach. I have every intention of enjoying the sunshine. There are clouds gathering. We may not be so fortunate in tomorrow's weather."

Mrs. Moore was not at all pleased with her suggestion. "I cannot leave you alone to walk back with so many uniforms about," she huffed.

Prudence laughed. Brighton did have more than its fair share of the military. "Come along then." She linked her arm through Mrs. Moore's. "Timothy will just have to wait."

Mrs. Moore seemed bent on a brisk pace despite the heat.

Equally determined that their progress should be leisurely, Prudence disengaged her arm to search her reticule for the pretty painted fan she always carried. "The Channel is looking particularly beautiful today," she said, wafting the fan breezily.

Mrs. Moore was not interested in the scenery. "Do you mean to tell Mr. Margrave?" she demanded.

"About?" There was so much that had happened of late that Prudence did not care to tell Timothy.

"About that awful Ramsay fellow and what he did to you at the baths."

"Of course not. What purpose can it serve? Timothy already holds Lord Ramsay in contempt. I would not have him calling the fellow out for pistols at dawn or some such nonsense when no real harm has been done."

"He ought to know. He can protect you from the rogue."

How could a rogue protect her from a rogue?

"I've no need of protection. Not from Ramsay anyway. He has behaved the perfect gentleman of late."

"Has he now?" Mrs. Moore shrugged her shoulders defensively. "I would not know, seeing as how I have yet to hear a word about what went on at the Pavilion, which I notice you did not mention to your cousin either."

So that was it.

"Oh! Do you know it completely slipped my mind, so unexpected was the appearance of my cousin. The Pavilion was absolutely remarkable! I wish you could have been there to see. Shall I tell you about it now?"

"If you've a mind." Mrs. Moore failed completely in her attempt to sound disinterested.

Prudence launched into a description of all the aspects of the prior evening that were sure to entertain Mrs. Moore. She began with a detailed account of how the Pavilion was decorated, dropping occasional remarks about who else had been invited to dine.

Mrs. Moore begged to know what the guests had worn and what dishes had been served for dinner. Prudence described almost everything. She neglected to mention Ramsay's remarks with regard to dragons and lotus blossoms, his rescue of her leg from Ponsonby, and his winnings over a backgammon board.

"Miss Stanhope!" A female voice cut into her narrative.

From the shade of Walker's Circulating Library, Grace

Ramsay waved to Pru. As Donaldson's main competitor, Walker's attraction lay in its proximity to the Marine Parade and its fabulous view of the ocean. Grace took full advantage of that view. An easel was set in front of her, and in her hands she clasped a long, brass spyglass.

"Who is that?" Mrs. Moore demanded.

"Grace Ramsay," Prudence said, turning toward Walker's.

Mrs. Moore uttered a little noise of impatience. "Your cousin disapproves of the Ramsays. I heard him say as much over breakfast."

"Yes," Prudence replied evenly, "I do not, however, agree with my cousin's opinion in all things." She wondered if Mrs. Moore even began to understand her reasoning when she said firmly, "I must choose my path just as he must choose his."

Again came the little noise of impatience. "If you mean to stay here conversing with the woman, perhaps I had best go on, to inform Mr. Margrave as to your whereabouts."

Prudence knew Mrs. Moore was miffed that their conversation had been interrupted. She knew, too, that Mrs. Moore was uncomfortable with the idea that Prudence challenged her cousin's authority in any way. As Prudence had no intention of explaining how dangerous his limited authority might prove, she made no move to stay the woman. "Perhaps you should," she agreed. "We must each do what we think best."

She and Mrs. Moore parted company.

Grace waved again. Pru trudged up the incline of the beach to join her. It was unusually hot today. Already she began to perspire. Languidly, she plied her fan.

Grace looked genuinely pleased to see her. "You are looking well this afternoon, Miss Stanhope, if a trifle flushed. Have you just come from your ablutions?"

Prudence nodded.

Grace swung her spyglass in the direction of the expanse of water behind Prudence. "I have come to watch my husband and his brother partake of theirs at this unfashionably advanced hour. In this heat I am tempted to join them. My paint refuses to dry, so humid is the air. Care for a peep? I am proud to say that Rue is almost the equal of his brother in salt water, due to its buoyancy."

She held the spyglass out for Prudence, who set aside her fan to hold it to her eye.

"Do you see them?" Grace asked.

Prudence adjusted her gaze to peer through the eyepiece. The glittering brightness of sun-touched waves momentarily blinded her. She saw nothing, though the Channel looked cool and inviting.

"There," Grace pointed. "You cannot miss Charles's dark coloring. He is burned as brown as the sailor he has been pretending to be."

Prudence raised her eye above the spyglass a moment to pinpoint the distant figures and refocused the glass. There Ramsay was, suddenly so sharply focused before her she felt as if she might reach out to touch him.

Prudence almost dropped the glass. The man who dived and rolled and splashed like a happy otter in the sea was intimidating in his glistening, wet, near-naked state, even at a distance. Prudence had studied the human form, male and female, in any number of books and paintings. Here, in Brighton, at the beach, no matter how unusual it might be to see a bared body elsewhere, exposed chests, torsos, and limbs were the norm. What little bit of clothing was worn, clung wetly, disguising little. None bared themselves so well, in her estimation, as Rash Ramsay. His shoulders were broad, his chest wide and sculptural, his waist flat, his hips narrow, his legs beautifully muscular. Ramsay was better clothed in nothing than most men were in the most perfectly tailored garments. God and good health had graced him with excellent bones, perfect musculature, and firm, sun-browned flesh that draped over what lay beneath it like heavy satin.

Beside him splashed his brother, Rupert, the contrast of his pale imperfection heightening Charles Ramsay's flawless physique. Prudence held her breath to watch, unwilling to lose for a moment, due to the trembling of her inhalations, the vision that swam before her.

A wave of heat blossomed in her chest, rising to burn in her already heated neck and cheeks. This was the man who had run his hands over so much of her own bare skin. This was the man to whom she owed twenty-four hours. She dragged her eyes away from him.

"What . . ." The simple word fell ragged from her lips. Clearing her throat, she managed to say in a more normal tone, "What did you mean when you said he has been pretending to be a sailor?"

Grace had taken up her brush and was daubing paint at her canvas. "In order to more easily afford his passage back to England from India, Charles signed onto a freighter. He tells me he immersed himself in the part, that he took to wearing the native colors and clothing of the Indians on board. He also learned to swim like a dolphin, swear in four languages, and to play backgammon like a master."

Prudence closed her eyes in chagrin. Small wonder that she now owed the man twenty-four hours of her time, though he made no move to claim them. Men were not to be trusted. She raised the glass to stare at Ramsay again. Why, she wondered, had he made no attempt to redeem his winnings?

Grace was unaware of her straying attention. "He claims it was quite the adventure," she went on, "but I cannot help thinking there is more to this story than he will reveal to me. There are, if you look very carefully, faint scars across his back—as if he has been beaten."

Prudence squinted thoughtfully through the glass. She could not deny her interest in Rash Ramsay. He was uncharted territory—a foreign country she wished to explore, though it frightened her to consider the journey.

As if he felt her gaze, Ramsay turned, scanned the shore, and stopped when he spotted them. It was ridiculous to believe he could see Pru as clearly as she saw him with the aid of the spyglass, but so intently did he look in her direction that for the breadth of an instant she believed the laws of physics had been broken. He raised his hand to salute her with a wave, drops of water raining, the sun catching on the water that gilded his deeply bronzed body like carelessly hung diamonds. The water looked very inviting.

Prudence lowered the glass, panicked. She did not trust this man. She was not sure she even liked him, and yet she found him too intriguing to ignore. She was, truth be told, consumed by wanton desire at the sight of him. The idea of throwing herself fully clothed into the water, of pressing her wet body to his in the same wicked manner Tim had once pressed himself to her, crossed her mind. To suffer licentious longings for two men was surely completely depraved, was it not? Had she been possessed of an uncontrollable passion? Why was she now beset by carnal desires when in all her life she had never had such thoughts enter her head? She felt as if liquid fire ran through her veins, as intoxicating as wine, a threat to her control. That frightened her.

Prudence lowered the glass and picked up her fan again, to cool the sheen of perspiration on her neck, her face, between her breasts. She felt confined by her clothes, indeed by her entire situation.

Ramsay was leaving the water, his brother leaning into his arm. They meant to join her and Grace. Prudence was tempted to drop the glass and run. Ramsay was intimidating enough from a distance. He would be overwhelming up close. She had been unable to keep her eyes off what she could see of him through the spyglass. Where was she to look when he stood right in front of her in near-naked and drenched condition?

Prudence was not prepared to find out. To this man she owed twenty-four hours of her time. She must keep her wits about her. She must rein in her unruly passions.

"Handsome devil, isn't he?" Grace said with a naughty grin.

"Rupert?" Prudence deliberately misread her. She must extricate herself from conversation with Grace before the brothers Ramsay tottered together to join them.

Grace laughed. "Well, of course I think Rupert is gorgeous, but as I am sure you would not do me the disservice of vying for my husband, I was referring in this instance to Charles."

"Oh, I . . ."

Grace laughed again and waved a paintbrush at her, flinging wet color onto the stones at her feet. "He likes you, you know."

Prudence blushed, confused as to which Ramsay she referred. She plied her fan with vigor.

"My husband is not easily impressed . . ."

Ah, it was Rupert who liked her then.

Grace was not finished. "But Charles . . . well, Charles has the uncanny habit of befriending everyone, even when friendship would seem an impossible expectation. Do you know I was terrified we should never become friends, so awkward were the circumstances when first we met?"

"You refer to your brother having come into the Ramsay inheritance?"

Grace cleared her throat uneasily. "Yes, dreadfully awkward that. I was sure I would be rejected out of hand by all of the Ramsay brothers, but especially by Charles. He has, to my amazement, been the most congenial of the lot. I asked him about it once. He said the strangest thing."

"What?" Prudence could not deny her curiosity.

"He said, 'In every encounter we learn more about ourselves. The Fletchers have taught me a great deal.' Now, I had no idea what to make of that, until he went on, saying, 'All things happen for good reason. Even if it required my entire fortune I would gladly relinquish it again, that Rupert might find happiness, having already suffered more than his fair share of grief.'"

The sentiment moved her so much she dabbed at her eyes with a handkerchief. "I only wish that he may find a similar happiness with the one he loves."

"He is in love then?" The heat of Pru's passion deserted her.

"I think so." Grace's voice steadied. She no longer resorted to her handkerchief. "He shows all the proper signs."

"Oh." Prudence was surprised by her own disappointment, by the hollowness Grace's words seemed to find within her. She noted again the slow, steady progress of the Ramsays. What was it Rash Ramsay felt for her? She knew he liked to test his wits against hers and his skill at backgammon. But did he care for or about her? Whom did he love, this man who had touched her body as no man had ever touched her, this fellow who spoke of gardens and repose? Was he drawn to someone else as much as she was in this instant drawn to him?

God, he was beautiful. Not angelically so, as Tim was, Ramsay's beauty was of the more earthly variety. He tossed back his head, laughing at something his brother Rupert said, his teeth flashing white in the dark tan of his face, his coppery hair glittering in the sun as it dropped diamonds of water down the stout column of his neck and onto a chest as muscular as any sailor's.

Grace cocked her head to one side, her brush busy on the canvas. "Charles tells me you mean to go with us tomorrow to the tidal pools."

"I am concerned that the weather may turn against us." Pru peered skyward at the gathering clouds, and then out to sea again to check on the progress of the Ramsays. It would take time for the two to reach them.

Grace was undeterred. "Well, if the weather does sour, we must simply put off our plan until the next clear day. Agreed?"

"Of course. If the tides are with us."

"Charles also tells me you have family in town. Cousins?"

"A cousin—by marriage. Timothy Margrave is my benefactor. His children are the ones I teach."

"How kind of him to visit. He has come some distance, has he not?"

Grace was examining her intently. To be stared at while questioned about Timothy disturbed Prudence.

Grace sensed her discomfort. "Now do not move too much, and please forgive me if I seem to stare quite madly at you. I have just worked you into my painting."

Prudence was embarrassed to have been caught off guard in such a manner. She reached up to brush a loose strand of hair from her cheek.

"No. Don't touch," Grace barked. "You need not concern yourself with your appearance. You are perfect just as you are. Just relax and tell me more about your cousin. Where is it he has property?"

Prudence tried to hold still. The effort reminded her of the day at the bathhouse when she had tried to sit still, waiting for her shampooer. Her eyes strayed once more to Ramsay. "Gillingham," she said. "In Dorset."

"My, your cousin must be fond of you indeed, to come so far."

"Tim had business in London. I am merely a side trip."

"No more than that? Your cousin . . . what is her name?"

"Edith."

"Has she not recently suffered ill health?"

"A miscarriage."

Grace clucked her tongue and frowned. "How sad."

"Yes. Poor Edith is inconsolable."

"Her husband must be anxious to return to her."

Prudence shifted uncomfortably. The day was too warm for Grace's questions. "They both suffer horribly," she said. "It was their first boy."

"Umm. A disappointment indeed. As females, you and I are only too aware of how much stock is placed in at least one child possessing a penis."

"Grace!" Prudence was shocked.

Grace shrugged. "The line of inheritance depends upon adding to the family jewels. You know that as well as I."

Pru laughed. "You are right, of course." She wondered if she sounded as bitter as she felt. "My own parents' wealth, due to their lack of sons, was passed on to my uncle, who has three boys to assure the continuance of the Stanhope line."

"Your uncle did not take you in?" It was Grace's turn to be shocked.

"Yes." Prudence bit her lip. "No. I stayed a week after the funeral, but could not remain. It pained Uncle Theodore to have me about, reminding him he owed his entire fortune and the improved prospects for all his offspring to the death of the elder brother he had adored."

"I see."

Prudence felt she had said too much. She was not accustomed to pouring her troubles into anyone's ears. She slipped another wary look in Rash Ramsay's direction. Best be on her way.

"Will you be so good as to tell Lord Ramsay he may expect a visit from a Mrs. Rose Thurgood, a fine and decent lady, who is interested in decorating her new house in the Oriental style?"

Grace put down her brush. "Why not tell him yourself? He and Rue are almost upon us."

Prudence had no desire to admit her reluctance to encounter Rash Ramsay in his current, wet condition. "My cousin expects me," she said, her eyes straying nervously.

Grace left the easel and took her hand. "I will tell him. May I tell him, too, that we shall see you in the Steine this evening?"

Prudence was pleased that Grace cared enough to suggest such a thing, but she made no absolute promises. She had yet to see what Timothy had in mind. "I suppose we may."

"Prudence!" A man's voice hailed her.

She thought it must be Ramsay, but in whirling to regard his progress, she saw that his attention was drawn not to her, but to a spot on the road above her. Her gaze followed his. Timothy stood looking down at her from the stairway that led to the beach.

She waved to him. She could not tell if he scowled so fiercely at her, or at the brightness of the sun. He waved back. With a few hasty words to wish Grace good day, she went to join him.

"Is that Miss Stanhope's cousin?" Grace asked Charles when he and Rue, both of them breathing hard from their exertions, made their way to her easel.

Charles frowned at the retreating figures. "Yes. Is he the reason she ran away without so much as a word of greeting?"

"Her last words were for you, Charles." Grace looked far too pleased with the fact.

"Were they now?" Rue's tone was suggestive.

Charles helped Rupert to a chair and threw a towel at him. "Wipe that smirk off your face, little brother." He made a point of sliding his arms into a shirt and buttoning the cuffs before asking Grace. "What were these words, pray tell, Gracie." It would not do to appear too interested.

"She said you were to expect a Rose."

"A rose?" Ramsay's thoughts flashed back to Miss Stanhope's roseless garden. "Is this a riddle?"

"Oh dear, what was the name?" Grace's paintbrush stopped while she considered the matter.

Beneath the concealing tail of his shirt Charles dropped the trousers that clung wetly to his legs and stepped into a dry pair. "Name?"

"The Rose's name."

"The rose has a name?" Charles looked over Grace's shoulder as he buttoned the trousers. There, on the canvas, was Miss Stanhope's lovely profile. The painted Prudence, against a backdrop of ocean and sky, had turned her head to gaze at two men who waded companionably, side by side, at the edge of the water. A strand of hair trailed seductively across her painted cheek. The men were too distant in the painting to possess much in the way of faces. Both had reddish brown hair.

"Rupert and I?"

"Yes. Do you like it?"

"I do. You've given Rue back his leg."

"She always gives me my leg when she paints me," Rue said cheerfully.

"Of course I do," Grace said as if it were the most natural thing in the world. "I can repaint history if I choose, and generally I do."

Charles could not take his eyes off Miss Stanhope's profile. There was a hint of longing in the painted eyes. Had she really stood here staring at them this way, or was this merely more repainted history?

"It's a very good likeness of Miss Stanhope," he said.

"Good!" Grace crowed. "The woman's name is . . ." She painted the air with her brush, her tone uncertain. "Something good."

Charles looked at Rupert, confused. Rue shrugged.

Grace smiled. "Thurgood! That's it. Rose Thurgood."

Chapter Thirteen

At the heart of Brighton lay the Steine, a flat, treeless, grassy triangle skirted by the Grand and Marine Parades. Once used for drying fishing nets and storing boats in bad weather, the Prince and the Duke of Marlborough had built their homes almost on top of the space. It was thereafter drained, and small, wooden fences were erected to keep the fishermen and their nets away. Fashionable businesses had sprung up along its perimeter. When the weather was amenable, as it was on this day, most of Brighton gathered in the Steine of an evening, for the promenade. Anybody who was anybody gathered to take the air and exchange the latest gossip and pleasantries. The Steine, above all else, gave Brighton a sense of community, even deluged as it was by wave after wave of ailing strangers.

As the shadows lengthened and the light of the sinking sun turned golden, Prudence, Tim, and Mrs. Moore made their way to the Steine from one direction; Charles, Grace, and Rupert from another. Across the Steine, they spotted one another. Bonnets nodded, hats were tipped, fans fluttered.

"I would prefer we did not make a point of conversing with the Ramsays," Tim said in the most reasonable of tones. "It is too hot to pretend to be civil."

Prudence replied, just as reasonably, "I will not make a point of avoiding them."

On the far side of the Steine, Rupert murmured in his brother's ear, "I daresay you'll not get much more than a nod out of Miss Stanhope this evening, unless kismet deigns otherwise. Her cousin clings to her arm."

"Like a vine," Charles agreed.

"This vine has a possessive way with our Prudence." Grace observed.

Charles nodded. "I cannot help thinking an excess of vine may be the reason Miss Stanhope seeks a new position."

Grace chuckled. "You are an observant fellow, Charles. I like that in a man. You and my brother, Miles, would get along splendidly."

"Do you think so?" He stiffened at the suggestion. "If there is anyone in the world right now with whom I doubt I would get along splendidly, it has to be Miles."

Grace squeezed his arm. "I know that circumstances are not conducive to a friendship between the two of you, but I am determined you *shall* meet. The rest will be up to you. I have every hope that you will become quite comfortable in one another's company."

His brows arched skeptically.

"Yes," she insisted. "It makes great sense that you should establish some sort of connection, if only to make your dear sisters happy."

"For that very reason, I shall make a point to be civil, Grace, should your brother and I ever cross paths."

"I expect much more than mere civility, my lord, and as to your paths crossing, I have assured they shall. Has Aurora not yet written about the upcoming races?"

"Am I to surmise that you have invited my sister and her husband to join us so that I am forced to meet your brother?"

She chuckled richly. "But of course."

Charles looked keenly at Rupert, eyebrows raised.

Rue laughed. "This is Grace's doing, not mine. I have just been wondering if this carefully engineered arrangement might be considered a form of kismet?"

"A very contrived form," Charles admitted.

"Kismet? What is kismet?" Grace wanted to know.

Kismet, in that very instant, arrived upon the scene, in the form of Rose Thurgood's carriage. The horses were drawn to a halt in the Grand Parade. From the window a plump hand waved.

* * *

Prudence recognized Rose's barouche immediately.

"Come," she said to Tim, drawing him toward the vehicle. "There is someone I should like you to meet."

Rose's black bonnet filled the carriage window. A wan smile beneath its netted brim evidenced her pleasure that they chose to approach.

"I will not get out, Prudence," she said, busily fanning herself. "Not while the weather is so beastly. I suffer the heat more than most, dressed as I am in deepest mourning. I thought that might be Lord Ramsay you walked beside, and so anxious am I to meet him, I dared to stop."

Tim frowned at mention of Ramsay. Prudence hastened to introduce the two.

"So, you are the kind cousin who took in Miss Stanhope in her hour of gravest need." Rose held out a black gloved hand.

Timothy's frown disappeared. He made proper salute to the extended digits.

"A pleasure indeed, sir, to meet someone whose sensibilities are so very proper—so very appropriate—in another's time of grief."

Judging by his expression, Tim felt undeserving of the praise.

Rose went on. "Is it Dorset you come from? My sister and I were once acquainted with a family in Dorset by the name of Stowe. Millicent and Egbert Stowe. Did you know them? They had a daughter who would be close to your age."

"Edith!" Timothy and Prudence said in mutual surprise.

"She is my cousin," Prudence said.

"She is my wife," said Tim.

A tear came to Rose's eye. "What a small world we live in. Why the last time I saw little Edith she was no more than ten years old. That she is all grown up makes me feel quite old. How is the dear girl?"

As Timothy tactfully explained his wife's depression, Rose resorted to her handkerchief more than once. "Oh dear," she said. "How sad." So genuine was her concern in prodding him to reveal detail that Tim opened up to her as if he had known her all his life.

So much did these two seem willing to share with one another in their mutual grief that Prudence dropped back from the conversation, filled with a sense that they had been meant to meet today to take solace in one another's complete understanding of their suffering.

The Ramsay party, in the meantime, made their slow way around the Steine. Prudence did not hesitate to break away from the carriage in order that she might speak to them. She wanted to introduce Lord Ramsay to Rose.

"Do we interrupt?" Grace asked softly, though they stood too distant from the carriage to be overheard.

Prudence looked over her shoulder. Small wonder Grace asked. The emotional intensity of the conversation Timothy and Rose were engaged in was painted on their features.

"I would not interrupt just this minute, but that is Mrs. Rose Thurgood . . ."

Charles Ramsay examined the carriage with interest. "Ah! The Rose I was to expect."

"Yes. She is decorating her new home in the Oriental mode. I thought you might be able to help her."

"Business, again," Rupert said with a yawn. "This would seem an excellent opportunity to seek out the comfort of a bench, my dear, preferably one in the shade."

Grace agreed. "Will we see you at the Assembly this evening?" she asked Prudence.

"I am not sure." Prudence had no idea if her cousin meant to take her to the Assembly.

"We mean to drop by briefly and thought we might encounter you there. Do not forget we mean to be up with the dawn in order to visit the tide pools."

"I do not forget," Prudence said warmly. She was looking forward to the proposed excursion.

That she had been left alone with Rash Ramsay never crossed her mind until she turned to find him watching her, as he was always in the habit of watching her, with a narrowness of focus and the calm, knowing look that never failed to unnerve her.

Nervously, she fanned herself. Ramsay seemed not to feel the heat at all. Perhaps tanned flesh did not perspire in the same manner as did skin unused to the sun's touch. Prudence took the little gold watch that had been her mother's from her pocket. Determining the time, she put it away again.

"Have you another engagement?" Ramsay asked her.

"No, but I owe you a debt, sir. A twenty-four-hour debt if you will recall."

"I do not forget," he said emphatically. "But you need not worry over our time together, Miss Stanhope. We two are destined to spend time together."

"But I do worry, sir. I do not welch on debts. I mean to see that you get every minute you have won from me."

"Despite your cousin's objections?"

She could not look him in the eye.

"Or have *you* so little interest in my company?"

Her chin rose. "To the contrary, I find you very interesting."

"And yet you ran away this afternoon."

She blushed. "I thought you might prefer privacy given the sparseness of your attire."

"To the contrary, Miss Stanhope," he echoed her own words. "I thought you might like to honor part of your debt to me in taking a dip with us."

She blushed furiously, shocked by his suggestion. "Sea bathing is not included in my treatment."

"Are a doctor's orders the only way to get you in the water? A dip is most refreshing when the weather is as warm and sultry as it is today."

The idea of cool water against heated skin had undeniable appeal.

"I have heard that dipping should be done only in the coolest parts of the day, to avoid colds."

"Nonsense. Do you think I would in any way risk my brother's health? Do I, for that matter, look at all ill to you?"

She could not tell him she had never seen a healthier specimen, nor that the idea of a dip in his company elevated her temperature almost beyond bearing. Fluttering her fan a little faster, she took the safer route of changing the subject. "I should be in fear of drowning."

"You need not fear. I would not let you drown."

No, he would not let her drown in the ocean, she thought, but in looking into his eyes she felt herself in danger of drowning in his rash suggestiveness.

"You are called Rash Ramsay."

"Yes."

"Are you so called because of your propensity to make wholly inappropriate suggestions, sir?"

He looked first at her and then focused on the far horizon to be seen beyond the buildings at the end of the Steine, where the glitter of the ocean met the sky. His eyes, reflecting the sky, seemed clouded with doubt.

"In a way, you have the right of it. I had no idea I was referred to as Rash Ramsay until I returned from India to find all I had once possessed was lost. That I had left the family finances in the hands of the most reckless of brothers was justly considered a rash act."

"Why did you?"

"Why did I what?"

"Leave the finances in your brother's hands. Surely you must have known his gambling habits?"

He sighed, squared his shoulders, and looked at her again. All uncertainty vanished from his demeanor. "I knew. Perhaps it was naive, but I thought I did Jack a favor in entrusting him with responsibility. I believed responsibility would be the making of him—that it would settle him. I was wrong."

Silence hung between them. Prudence had no idea what to say in the wake of such an admission. He did not appear to expect a response of her.

"Leaving Jack in charge was not my only perceived rashness." His frankness was unexpected.

"No?"

"No." He bit his lip. "I have, you see, crossed over a boundary of which I was not fully aware, in attempting to make my own money rather than allowing tenants to make it for me. I think you, of all people, will understand when I say that the social order has been disturbed. There are any number of people I once considered friends who will have nothing to do with me now."

Prudence nodded. She understood. She had herself stepped over the boundary he spoke of in becoming governess to her cousin's children.

"I wanted . . ." He looked at her intently, as though it were important to him she understood. "I wanted to be courageous—at least as courageous as Rupert had been in losing his leg for king and country. I wanted to plumb my own depths, to test my own boundaries, to take a journey within as great as the one I embarked on without. I saw great potential—still do—in the exchange of goods and ideas between East and West. Some of the items I have brought back with me are amazing: porcelains, textiles, spices, jade, ivory, and lacquerware. The trading system, or lack of same, is remarkably challenging."

"Tell me more."

"There is so much to tell, I would not know how to begin."

He seemed content to leave it at that, with nothing more said of the wonders that made his voice vibrate with emotion had she not encouraged him to continue. "Begin at the beginning."

He searched her expression doubtfully. "Are you sure I do not bore you? Most of the people I spill these tales to say they want to hear, but before I have much more than begun, their eyes glaze over."

She regarded him in amazement. He was marvelous. His sense of purpose moved her far more than anything she had encountered before. "I am not *most* people," she said.

He was regarding her again with his uncannily knowing eyes, as if he read every thought that crossed her mind. "No, you are not *most* people. Far from it, Miss Stanhope. You are quite incomparable. In all my travels I have never met anyone in the least like you."

High praise, and heady, from one so well-traveled. She was troubled by a stab of doubt that his compliment was genuine.

And yet, so much feeling did he place in wording it, that Prudence felt he said far more to her than that she was unique. She felt he meant to convey to her that he found something he had been searching for in her, just as she found something she longed for in him.

Before he could recount to her anything more, they were interrupted. Timothy had detached himself, at last, from Mrs. Thurgood.

In turning from the carriage, Pru saw Tim's face clearly. His every expression registered. Rather like the wilted condition of his shirt points in the heat, there was a worn, sad, almost beaten look about him, the look of someone who had just poured out his troubles to another, wearing himself down even as he found relief. His gaze settled on her, eyes brightening, and then on Ramsay, his neck and jaw stiffening, his beautiful blue eyes narrowing with patent dislike. When Pru stepped past him to inquire of Rose if she still felt up to meeting Charles Ramsay, the chilling look of distaste turned to follow her for a brief, disturbing moment.

The power of that telling array of negative emotion, passing so freely over the face of one whom she had come to love beyond reason, struck her very hard.

"Are you all right, my dear?" Rose Thurgood peered at her with concern from the depths of the carriage.

Prudence laughed ruefully in an attempt to disguise her true feelings. "I should be asking you."

"A lovely man." Rose nodded her head toward Tim. The lovely man stood stiffly gazing at the ocean, pointedly ignoring Charles Ramsay, who stared at Prudence. "A pity about Edith."

"A great pity," Prudence agreed, her heart heavy. That Edith's husband should be here, rather than at his wife's side at this very moment, and all on her account, struck her afresh. With a sigh she said softly, "If you feel up to it, there is another lovely man to whom I would introduce you."

Chapter Fourteen

Timothy was subdued in the walk back to Mrs. Harris's boardinghouse. There was a moody bleakness to his demeanor that matched the gray clouds that promised rain. Timothy had always seemed golden to Prudence—touched by the sun. The darkness that hung over him now prevented her from raising the subject of the biweekly Assembly Grace had mentioned. Tim was clearly in no mood for music and dancing, crowds and conversation.

She was not herself in the mood for such gaiety. Her head was aching, too full of important things unsaid between her and her cousin, between herself and Lord Ramsay. There was no room for idle chatter. Her heart ached as much as, if not more than, her head. She felt empty, completely hollowed out by a sense of longing she could not name. Her back and shoulders ached. She stretched her neck, first one way and then the other, trying to release the tension. The relief the shampooer had brought to her only that morning seemed a distant thing.

Ramsay filled her thoughts. His words, the bald admission of hopes and dreams—powerful dreams, courageous dreams, dreams she could not dismiss filled her pounding head. "I wanted to plumb my own depths" he had said to her "to test my own boundaries—to take a journey within as great as the one I have embarked on without." He seemed, she thought, always to be moving forward. An admirable endeavor, moving forward into the unknown when it was far easier to wallow, motionless, in the known, no matter how miserable and hopeless that known might be. She wrapped her arms about her shoulders, wishing he walked beside her up the hill. She would spend the evening wallowing in the known, chatting or playing cards with Tim. She listened to the eggshell crunch at the base of her neck and wished Charles Ramsay were there to soothe her ache.

Her wishes were pointless, of course. She left Ramsay behind her.

Prudence paused at the end of the street to look back down the hill and watch the dying embers of the day extinguished, to catch a glimpse, perhaps, of what might have been. Brighton glowed in the fading light. The Channel flickered silver and bronze. Darkness had begun to swallow up the edges of things.

Timothy stopped a stride in front of her. When he turned, the light of the setting sun gilded his complexion. His hair, flicked back out of his eyes with an all too familiar gesture, shone like spun gold. His lashes, his eyebrows, his very complexion seemed touched by the hand of Midas. This beautiful, golden angel of a man came to Brighton for no other reason than to be with her. The power of the idea stopped her very breath—it roused the same passions that she had been fighting into submission all day.

"A penny for your thoughts," he said lightly, sliding his hand from his pocket to throw a coin into the air, where it caught the light, glittering almost as brightly as he did.

She caught the coin. It was not a penny, but a silver sixpence, the coin most of the brides in England tucked into their shoes for luck on their wedding day. No sixpence for her shoe with this man as groom. The payment of their union was scandal and shame.

He retraced his steps to stand before her. She regretted that she stood between him and the sun. Her body blocked the light that made him beautiful. Of all things she might be to him, she did not want to throw a shadow on his brilliance.

He took up the hand with which she held the sixpence. "What are you thinking, Pru? You have the oddest expression."

His hand on this sultry evening was too warm enwrapping hers. She could not deny the affection, the attraction, the love that lived in her heart for this man and yet, she found no pleasure in his need to touch her. She dropped the coin into his palm. He released her, that it might not slide through his fingers. Brow furrowed, he sent the sixpence spinning into the air, caught it, and tossed it high again.

"Will you not confide in me, Pru?"

Uneasy with his question, Prudence set the two of them in motion, by stepping onto the grass of the narrow green that stretched the length of New Steine. Part of the green basked in the light of the failing sun. Shadows from the hotels and houses on the west side of the street would soon blot out that light.

"I am thinking of endings," she said, the words sticking in her throat. There, she had said it. She could be courageous. She could test boundaries. She turned her head to gauge his reaction.

Tim missed catching the sixpence. Its glittering brilliance was swallowed by the grass. He stopped, but made no move to find it. He looked not at the grass, but into her eyes. "Endings?"

"Yes." She wanted him to understand. She looked steadily into the heaven of his eyes, willing him to understand her purpose, to accept the idea of endings. "Here we stand, bathed in the *ending* of a sunny day, blessed with the recent *ending* of illness and pain, troubled by the *ending* of our hopeless hopes and unattainable dreams . . ."

He held up his hand to block the too bright light or to block her words. She could not be certain.

As ruthless as the sun, she went on. "We come, dear cousin, to the *ending* of my time in your household."

He reached out to squeeze her hand, as if he could stop the flow of her words with a touch. "No!"

Sadness and a sense of enormous loss threatened to overwhelm her. She felt dizzy, the price of breaking out of a downward spiral, such a loss of equilibrium. Her voice dropped to a whisper. "I cannot stay. Surely you see that."

The hand at his brow was shaking. It fell down to cover his eyes, that he might not see anything, not even her beseeching expression. "I cannot lose you, Pru. Not now. The idea is too bleak to be borne. Surely you must see that. I have lost too much of late. I need you more than ever I have needed anyone."

Prudence felt hot—uncomfortably hot—her dress too heavy, too confining. A languid breeze was stirring, but it was not enough to cool her. She felt sticky with sweat. Her hair clung to the nape of her neck. The sight of the Channel, stretching cool and green as far as the eye could see, made her long to break away from the heat of his words, the heat of his gaze, the heavy, clinging heat of his need. She wanted to wash herself clean and cool again.

The shadows were lengthening. His words tested her resolve. Tears blurred her eyes. She turned from him, determined to be strong, determined to be persuasive, determined to keep moving toward the unknown, no matter how painful such movement proved.

"For the sake of all that I hold most dear: my cousin, my nieces, for the sake of all that is good and right and true within you, Tim, I must find another place to call home."

He knew it was true. She could see the knowledge in the beads of sweat that gathered along his upper lip. He shook his head, denying the truth. Raking golden strands of hair out of his eyes with a hand that trembled, he turned to glare at the setting sun. "I will not speak of this, not now, when I came with no other intention than to forget all that pains me." Abruptly, he strode toward the boardinghouse, as if the matter were settled between them.

Up the steps he bolted before her and through the door.

She followed at a more leisurely pace, her footsteps leaden.

Neither Timothy nor Mrs. Moore were to be seen when she stepped inside. Mrs. Harris and two of the other boarders were bustling down the stairs however, dressed to go out, and looking very fine.

"We are off to the Assembly. You do know it is held every Tuesday and Thursday at the Castle Inn?" Mrs. Harris asked gayly. "Should we look for your little party to join us later, or are you feeling too pulled for so much noise and company,

Miss Stanhope? You are looking a trifle off color this evening."

There was nothing more lowering, Prudence thought, than to be told one looked poorly. "I have yet to ask my cousin if he has any desire to go," she said. "But we will make a point of looking for you if we decide to come."

"Off we go then," Mrs. Harris said cheerfully.

The door closed behind them. As if they took with them all the energy she possessed, Prudence started up the stairs in weary disappointment. She stopped when Timothy called her name.

"Pru?" His voice came, soft and hesitant, from behind the door to the breakfast room. He meant no one to hear but her.

Curious, and hopeful that she might finish the conversation they had begun, Pru pushed open the door. Tim reached for her as she entered, his grasp urgent and sudden. She gasped. With his heel he kicked the door shut behind them as he drew her possessively into the warm circle of his arms. He leaned his head against hers, his breath fanning humidly against her hair. Prudence stood rigidly in the circle of his arms, tears brimming but not shed, her heart beating fast. It was a wonderful thing to be cradled in another's arms, but she must not give in to the wonder of it.

"How can you speak to me of endings when I came to Brighton for no other reason than to be with you? For no other reason, Prudence. Please do not push me away. Do not remind me of the responsibilities that must tear us apart in the end. Just be with me, please, be with me."

She made no effort to push him away. She did, in the end, return the aching pressure of his clasp, her fingers alive to the texture of the fabric of his coat, her ears keen to the rasp of his breath as it fanned her hair. He was, she thought, too warm. His breath in her hair was uncomfortable. The idea of abandoning such heat forever however, was chilling. This, too, was part of their ending.

She listened to the creak of footsteps crossing the flooring above their heads. Mrs. Moore would be wondering what had become of them. In the corner of the room a case clock ticked.

Through the open window came the lonely sound of the distant washing of waves upon the shore. Prudence longed to submerge herself.

Tim clasped her tighter. He turned his head slightly so that his lips were pressed to her temple. "I want you, Pru."

The shadows deepened. The sun slipped below the buildings on the far side of the street. The tick of the clock and the ragged sound of their breathing seemed to grow louder in the silence. The breakfast room, its lace tablecloths, glittering silver, and shining crockery readied for the following morning, seemed to be a room in waiting, a room that held its breath.

The warmth of the lips at her temple shifted. Tim gently nuzzled her ear. Prudence knew this lingering embrace was wrong. She knew she should protest. She should raise her hands and push him away. But the promise of Timothy's lips upon her ear filled her with an almost uncontrollable desire to forget her best intentions. Her body swayed into his.

"Oh yes, Prudence." He sighed into her hair.

She squeezed her eyes shut. The sound of her name on his lips was sweet. Despite this brief spark of happiness, one of the dammed-up tears trickled through her lashes. She turned her head, breaking away from temptation, away from the promise of filling the yawning hole of loneliness that had troubled her since the day her parents had been killed.

Anticipating her intent, Timothy tightened his hold.

Prudence opened her eyes, panicked. How could she plan to behave in one way and act in quite another? Was there no courage within her left to call upon? Had she lost the strength to move? Tim's hands traveled seductively along her spine. His lips traveled in a tantalizing path from her ear to her neck. Blinking back tears, she forced her eyes to remain open. God help her, she must not allow this to go on.

The word she needed formed at the back of her throat. *No.* She needed to say it. *No.* She had to say it. *No.* Now, before he closed her mouth on all her *Nos* with a kiss.

On the wall was the shadow of a vine, its source a brass planter full of lush green ivy. The shadow refocused her thoughts.

"This is wrong," she said in a voice that grew stronger as she pulled from his clasp.

"Can love be wrong?" His voice shook. He stopped her movement toward the door with a touch.

"It is undoubtedly wrong if it destroys all else we love. Go home, Timothy," Prudence begged. Her voice wavered, so intensely did she feel the truth. "Go home to Edith. The time you spend with me rightfully belongs to her."

Prudence stood at the open window in her room, examining her kitty-corner view of the Channel as it faded into nothingness in the dusk. She could no longer see the water clearly, but she could still hear it, washing in, washing out, calling her.

"Your cousin speaks of leaving us if the weather is clear tomorrow," Mrs. Moore said in a voice lowered by awe as she tiptoed up behind her. "I thought he intended to stay the week."

The end, Prudence thought. "He must be missing Edith and the girls," she said.

"No doubt." Pru could see Mrs. Moore's reflection nodding sagely in the periphery of her vision. "Do you mean to join us downstairs for cards? Master Margrave did say he would like to play a hand or two before he leaves us."

Pru sighed heavily. "No, thank you, Mrs. Moore. I have no patience for cards in this heat."

"I shall just go down and tell Master Margrave."

Prudence nodded. "Please do." Before Mrs. Moore had cleared the doorway, she said softly. "There is no reason why you should not indulge him with a game or two, Mrs. Moore."

Mrs. Moore gone, Prudence stepped onto the balcony to watch the last traces of light fade from the sky. Endings were difficult. To keep saying no to one to whom she had long imagined saying yes was a challenge. To test the unknown was frightening. *Dear God*, she prayed on the first star that appeared in the darkening sky, *let there be an end to my desire for my cousin's husband.*

Chapter Fifteen

Hot, tired, and more than a little discouraged, Charles went to meditate—to find his peace again after mingling with so many people from whom he needed something at the Assembly. To need, to reach out to others with that need, was draining. He went to the beach where he made a habit of meditating, to fill himself up again. The moon, the ocean, the breeze that began to lift away the oppressive heat of the day—all of nature would fill him. He arranged his thoughts as carefully as he arranged his posture this evening. He needed a miracle. In order to survive the week, he needed nothing less than that, and yet he needed to release his own neediness, like a pigeon on the wing, for the meditation to bring him peace. He closed his eyes, emptied his mind, and listened as the tide whispered to him of the largeness of life.

A miracle came to him. Not clothed in the form he might have expected, but she was a miracle nonetheless.

The noise of furtive footsteps sliding on shale and the little whispered exclamations of feminine surprise as an ankle turned or toes bruised on stones unseen in the dark returned him from his meditative wanderings to the beach head.

Across the shale, moonlight silvering the upswept cloud of her hair and the pale shimmer of her cotton wrapper, went a woman whose form and figure he would recognize anywhere, no matter how disguised.

To the water's edge Prudence Stanhope crept, her head turning this way and that, as if to make certain she was alone. He thought she must see him. He was sure she must. He even opened his mouth, words forming at the back of his throat to let her know she was not alone at all, when to his dismay she slipped the sash on her wrapper and, spreading wide her arms, let the freshening breeze catch its fabric, so that it billowed out behind her like pale wings. She arched her arms back, her breasts and torso forward, relishing the breeze. As if it were a lover come to undress her, the breeze slipped the garment from her shoulders. With a laugh and a last look around to be sure she was not observed, she dropped the wrapper to the ground.

Like some naiad of the deep, come to wade upon the shore-line, clad only in a fine lawn night shift that revealed her every curve, she stepped shamelessly into the water, hem lifted high. The cold drew a gasp, but she did not hesitate. Higher and higher the hem of her shift rose to avoid being soaked as she wobbled out among the rocks, her arms flailing occasionally to maintain balance. When she had waded in up to her knees, she stopped, with a contented sigh. Winding the raised hem of the shift in her hand, she knotted it at thigh level and bent to cup a splash of water for her neck, another for her face, a third she dribbled into the hollow between her breasts.

With a laugh, perhaps at her own audacity, she lifted her arms above her head as if to capture the moon. Charles was re-minded, as his eyes worshipped her and his loins fired with desire, of Ovid's *Metamorphosis*. A king, stumbling upon the goddess Diana, in the midst of bathing with her nymphs, was punished for his lustful stares by being changed into a stag that was hunted down and killed by the king's own dogs.

Charles understood the king completely. He could not move. He could not stop watching. He could not spit in the eye of fate and turn his back on Prudence Stanhope.

She was the one who turned, and in turning lost her footing. With a little shriek she splashed, very ungoddesslike, into the water.

Charles lurched out of the lotus position, ready to leap into the water after her, ready to save her.

She did not require saving.

"Oh bother!" he heard her say breathlessly as she stood up again, her night shift soaked, her hair drenched and bedrag-gled, half come down from its pins. Raising the waterlogged hem to squeeze it dry, she began to laugh. A little guffaw at first, the laugh grew and expanded upon itself, until with another, breathless "Bother it all" she abandoned her efforts to be dry and sank into the knee-deep water again, still laughing.

Charles thought he had never heard a sound so gleeful. He watched her, happy in her happiness, until she decided to abandon her ablutions. Out of respect for her he closed his eyes. No more than a peek or two did he steal as she stepped out of her drenched night shift, wrung it out as much as she could, used it to blot her body, and then muffled herself away in the cotton wrapper she had left lying on the shale. He did follow her when she left the beach, as furtive going up as she had been coming down. Not for lascivious reasons did he shadow her return to Mrs. Harris's boardinghouse. He went to guard her from other shadows in the night. He need not have worried. The moon looked out for her. She returned, laughing softly on occasion at her own daring, unnoticed but for him.

Prudence lay in bed, staring at the candlelight that played games of light and shadow across the ceiling. She felt refreshed, revived, and in a way transformed by her audacious moonlight swim. What an adventure it had been! And the adventure was not yet over. Her heart still raced. She still felt laughter bubbling up within her chest. Her night shift was draped, dripping, over the windowsill. Without it, she had slipped between the crisp linens, her flesh cooled by the recent dousing and sensitive to its nakedness. How odd it was to crawl into bed without one's clothes on! How sensual! It was almost as audacious as stripping off one's clothes outdoors with no one but the moon to see.

She closed her eyes and took a deep breath. She could not lie naked without thinking of her first shampooing, of Charles Ramsay's gloved hands on her feet, hands, back, and shoulders. And with thoughts of Ramsay came the image of her garden. The vine had invaded the vegetables. It reached again for the tender green shoots and newly unfurled leaves.

There was a change in the fountain. It pulsed with life, water splashing from the marble figure in its center. No longer a cherub, the figure of a bathing Venus had usurped its position. Despite its entanglement, the rose was growing. The rosebud had begun to plumpen. It began to rain in the garden, a heavy drumming rain that soaked Prudence to the skin in her imagination, a rain that encouraged both the rose and the vine to new growth.

The rain, as it turned out, was not just in Prudence's imaginary garden. It was real. It came drumming down on Brighton in the middle of the night in unending sheets of gray. Without ever realizing she had slipped from her state of repose into a deep slumber, Prudence overslept. When she roused at last, she sat up abruptly in bed troubled by the uneasy feeling she was late for an important appointment.

"Oh no," she groaned. "The tidal pools!"

Had she slept right through the choice of going, or not going? She did not want to know; she did not want to get up out of the safe haven of her bed. She pulled the sheet over her head.

But lying with a sheet over one's head listening to the rain did not accomplish anything. Prudence knew her problems would not simply disappear if she remained where she was. Movement was required. Thrusting her feet from their cozy confines she raced to the window, thrusting her arms through her wrapper as she went.

Rain pelted the balcony. Her night shift was wetter than ever. She wrung it out again, leaning over the sill to do so, and then closed the window. There would have been no point in rising early today. Her choice of going or not going to the tidal pools had not been missed, merely delayed. With a sigh she leaned her cheek to the cool surface of the windowpane and shook out her wadded night shift. There would be no excursions to the tidal pools today. There would be, instead, many hours to while away in the company of her cousin. He would not set out for home in this miserable wet. The day promised to be as trying as the weather.

She stared out across the green to the rain-lashed area of the beach where Rash Ramsay had yesterday sat so still, lost in meditation, where last night she had stolen under cover of darkness to cool herself in the Channel. The beach was deserted today, bleak and lonely—not at all enticing.

Mrs. Moore breezed into the room, her arms full of white roses. "Your excursion is canceled, my dear," she chortled, "but it is almost worth gray skies if one is to be lavished with roses. Only smell them, Pru. They are quite heavenly."

Prudence leaned obligingly into the bouquet. Could these be from Tim? "Lovely!" she agreed. "Who . . . ?"

"I've no idea. They arrived by messenger, along with this." She held out a wax-sealed square of heavy vellum.

Prudence broke the seal while Mrs. Moore arranged the roses in a vase. The note was from Grace. She read aloud from it.

Our plans to go to the tidal pools are regrettably delayed—rescheduled for the first morning the sun shows itself. As for today, we mean to play parlor games to while away the hours. Please join us. Bring along Mrs. Moore and your cousin if they care to come.

It was signed with a flourish, the name Ramsay being followed by a postscript which Prudence kept to herself.

Charles is responsible for the roses. He said your garden was in need of them. I quite sensibly pointed out to him that roses that have been cut are quite useless in a garden. He said you would understand. Do you?

Prudence examined the roses with fresh interest. Charles Ramsay chose to send to her plump white buds kissed with pink, each poised on the brink of unfurling their petals. What a beautiful and extravagant gesture. She leaned down to drink in the sweet perfume of the bouquet.

"Miss Ramsay's invitation sounds like a bit of fun, Pru," Mrs. Moore said, "but my guess is Mr. Margrave will not want to have anything to do with the idea."

"Quite right," Prudence agreed. They both knew it was not parlor games her cousin would object to so much as it was Ramsays he deplored. With a sigh she sat down and composed a message to Grace, declining her kind offer. Finished, she paused to pluck a rosebud from the bouquet. Clipping it short, she arranged it artfully in the silver and glass bud brooch that had been her mother's. She might not be able to join the Ramsays today, but she meant to carry a reminder of their kindness with her. She pinned the brooch to her breast pocket and went downstairs to breakfast.

Tim was distant, cool, his brow as overcast as the skies. He did not open his mouth to say a word to Prudence until Mrs. Moore, uneasy with the silence, went to great lengths to explain the invitation and the flowers that had come.

"You wish to play games with the Ramsays?" Tim studied Pru coldly through the steam that wafted over the rim of his coffee cup.

"No," Prudence said simply. Pushing away her half-eaten egg she pulled out her note to Grace. "I wonder if you will arrange to have this message delivered to the Ramsays."

He glanced over the note. "You decline!"

"Yes. I mean to spend the morning catching up on my reading at Donaldson's." She meant to search the "Wants" again, but she refrained from explaining her purpose.

By the time the gig had been readied and brought around to them, Tim had unbent enough to chat quite amiably with Prudence on several matters of complete insignificance. When they had all three squeezed quite uncomfortably into the gig, furled umbrellas dripping on their shoes, Prudence pressed thigh to thigh beside him, he warmed to her completely.

"I had hoped to take you to the chalybeate spring for the waters sometime while I am here. Perhaps, if the rain lets up, this afternoon would suit you?"

"You are kind to offer," Prudence said, though questions troubled her appreciation of the kindness with which she credited him. She bent to sniff the rosebud at her breast. The sweet perfume of the flower masked the unpleasantness of her doubts.

The rose was not the only sweetness in the day. Prudence found three promising ads to respond to in the "Wants," and contrary to expectation, the rain let up for about an hour. The question of the chalybeate spring having been raised again, she found herself alone in the gig with Timothy, Mrs. Moore opting out of a damp, crowded ride to a muddy spring.

"I've no reason to drink the waters, you see," the older woman had reasoned. "My health is not to be complained of, and I would not be sending contrary messages to my system, you may well understand."

Mrs. Moore was perhaps the wisest of their lot. Tim said little. The sky threatened rain, and everything she touched was wet, despite the cessation of the downpour. The seat of the gig was wet, the leather top that covered their heads dripped wetly on her skirt, and she had drenched her left boot in a puddle in stepping from the curb into the gig.

The dreary, dripping tone of the day seemed personified when Timothy pulled the gig into the dogleg turn in North Street that carried one into Upper North Street, where the rain-washed flint tower of St. Nicholas's Church dominated the landscape. The road was crowded with vehicles gathered for a funeral, their purpose evident in the abundance of sodden black crepe and drooping plumes.

Timothy slowed the horse. Ahead, a woman carrying an infant and dressed all in black, crossed the road. Three small children, looking like nothing so much as dour-faced ravens clad as they were in dark, shin-length cloaks, followed her. Slipping on the wet, uneven cobblestones, the smallest child sprawled face first in the middle of the road. With an oath Timothy yanked the horse to a wall-eyed stop. The animal cavorted sideways, wet flanks bunching. A yowl erupted from the youngster in the street.

Shrieking, the woman ran back into the road for the child, her face contorted with fear. "Have you killed my boy?"

"No." Tim's mouth had a grim look. "No harm done. Have *you*, madame, any idea how to look after your children?"

The woman dismissed his remark with a tongue wagging, delivered in an accent so thick as to be nearly incomprehensible. With a toss of her head she picked up the boy, examined his sodden knee britches, and wiped his muddy palms with a shake and a scold.

"A woman like that does not deserve to have children," Tim muttered gruffly, slapping the lines across the horse's rain-damp rump. The animal lurched nervously into motion.

Prudence was surprised he judged the woman so harshly, but anything she might have said in response was interrupted by the somber peal of bells from the church tower. Released by the sound, a river of black-clad mourners flowed from the church. Unfortunate as funerals were under any circumstances, this one seemed doubly so to Prudence. She was acquainted with the deceased. Rose Thurgood figured prominently among the mourners who stepped from the church, wringing their hands and weeping. Given the enormous size of the coffin under which double the usual number of pallbearers staggered, there was no doubt for whom the bells tolled.

"I know whose funeral this is!" Prudence said in a hushed voice, more to herself than to Timothy. Catching Rose Thurgood's teary gaze, Prudence lifted her hand in mute acknowledgement and blinked back the threat of unwarranted emotion from her own eyes.

"This is Ester Childe's funeral," she said unevenly, dangerously close to tears.

"Child? Whose child?" Timothy's eyes swam with his own ill-concealed grief.

Prudence blinked sympathetically. The last funeral they had attended together had been that of a child, this man's stillborn son. Small wonder he thought she said child and not Childe.

Her hand went out to his. "No one's child. The woman's name was Childe."

"Oh." Tim's face had a blankness that disturbed her. He slapped the reins, the more quickly to carry them away from the funeral and its attendant pall of memories.

* * *

St. Anne's Well, when they reached it, was not very impressive. There was a rain-soaked green and a muddy track that led to the little building that covered the well, which was, itself, nothing more than a basin to catch the iron-rich waters. It had been erected, a plaque mounted at its base told them, by the famous Dr. Richard Russell. Ironic, really, Russell had spent most of his lifetime promoting Brighton's seawater's restorative properties rather than the value of natural mineral springs like this one.

The water was as unimpressive as the basin it trickled into. It welled forth in a faintly reddish brown stream that had, over time, stained everything it touched.

Prudence was reminded quite rudely of another basin, the basin in which she had bathed the blood from Edith's stillborn son.

Tim peered into the well, his face drawn. "Dear God," he whispered. "You cannot drink that. It looks vile."

"It looks like . . ." Pru cleared her throat ". . . rust." Bravely, she dipped the cup they had brought with them into the stream of water, taking care not to stir the sediment that darkened the bottom of the basin. Her voice was stronger, as was her resolve when she said, "It is the very iron deposits discoloring it that make this a strengthening drought. It will not kill me."

Tim wordlessly turned his back on her and walked out of the confines of the building.

Pru frowned. *It will not kill me.* Poor word choice, considering the funeral they had just passed and the emotions it had triggered. Closing her eyes, she sipped at the water. The flavor was strong, flat, and faintly metallic. With a grimace she tipped up the cup and swallowed another mouthful like the medicine it was.

She followed Tim outside. He was pacing away from her, back down the muddy track to the rented carriage, his shoulders slumped in a manner most uncharacteristic.

Prudence watched with concern. Had he been more moved by the funeral than she had imagined? She came up behind him as he checked the carriage wheels to see if they had become mired. She touched his arm. "Tim, are you all right?"

His arm jerked from her touch as if he were burned. Face averted, he held up his hand, fending her off with a weak wave. "You forget yourself," he said gruffly. "I am not the one who comes here for the waters, Pru."

"I think you are far more in need of them than you know, Timothy Margrave," she scolded in the gentlest of voices.

Timothy turned, his face wet with tears. "Dear Pru," he whispered. "Always concerned for other's pain when you suffer your own without complaint." His voice was unsteady.

"Is it the funeral upset you?" she asked gently.

He shook his head. "No!" The word came out with the force of an oath. "No!"

"What then?" Her hand wavered uncertainly above his sleeve.

Her touch released a rapid flood of explanation. "The boy! It was the boy. I might have killed him, falling down like that in front of the horse."

A sob wracked him. It was a rough, ragged, violent sob. He turned his back, shoulders shaking under the onslaught of too many tears, too long repressed.

"I know," she said, patting his back. "I know. I know."

He turned into her arms. His head sank heavily on her shoulder. A burning warmth soaked her shoulder where his head rested, tearing into the very heart of her. She stroked his hair. She stroked his back. She murmured soft, soothing, meaningless words, knowing he wept not for the boy who tripped on wet cobblestones and skinned his knee, but for the son he would never see across any streets, for the son whose knees he could not dust off and kiss better again. She held him until he gave a deep sigh and lifted his head.

She thought he would wipe away his tears then and blow his nose. She never dreamed he would kiss her.

Hot, salty, needy—the kiss was as violent, raw, and passionate as the recent spate of tears. It drew strength from her. She could not refuse Tim such a kiss, but neither could she take joy in it. This was not a kiss for love; it was a kiss for sorrow. When Tim withdrew his lips and her knees threatened to buckle beneath her, she turned her head into his shoulder for a moment, then pulled away and turned her back on him. She could not bear another such kiss. He would drain the very life from her with many such kisses.

Chapter Sixteen

It began to rain again. As if it were the hand of God, giving them a nudge, the rain drove them away from St. Anne's Well, away from the possibility of more kisses, more touching, more heartache. It drove them back to the boardinghouse, where, soaked to the skin, Prudence dashed upstairs to change into dry clothes, while Timothy drove the gig back to Donaldson's to fetch Mrs. Moore.

Alone in her room with the smell of roses all around her, Prudence felt safe. There was nothing that comforted her so much on this rainy day as the soft color, the delicate perfume, the gentle message of Charles Ramsay's gift of roses. From buds they had begun to open their petals to her as though shyly unveiling their faces for a closer look. Whenever she looked at them, the moments she had shared with their sender played and replayed in her mind. She could not deny, when she glanced at the roses, that her feelings for Lord Ramsay had blossomed as much as these roses did.

She was in great need this afternoon of someone with whom she could share her dilemma. It was Ramsay who leapt first to mind, not Grace, who would share her every confidence with her husband and who had a way of delving for information she might not be prepared to reveal. Not Rose Thurgood, though she would make an excellent confidante. Rose suffered too great a sorrow of her own for Prudence to think of troubling her with more. Rash Ramsay struggled with his own financial crisis, of course, but in the midst of his struggle he thought to send her roses that he could not afford. It was not so strange then that she sat at her desk, composing letters of inquiry in response to the "Wants" she had seen, fortifying herself now and then, when her pen ran dry, with the sweet perfume from the roses on the table beside her.

The rain continued into the second day.

Charles rose from the prayer rug on which he had been sitting cross-legged, listening to the sound of rain on the roof. His mind was too overwhelmed by the concerns of Mammon to meditate. Jarett, the boy he had hired to assist him, ran in response to the bell at the door. It opened on Rose Thurgood—potential savior or final death knell to his business? Which, remained to be seen.

Dripping umbrellas with feet beneath crowded into the narrow space Charles had rented in Kemp Street in the North Lanes. Others had crowded in, some to browse and stare and walk away empty-handed, some to purchase and then ignore his bills with equal enthusiasm. Ramsay was in desperate need of money. Without it he would not be able to meet his rent. He already owed Jarett two week's pay. He had prayed for a miracle. He had meditated, waiting for an answer. He had touted his wares wherever he showed his face.

Rose Thurgood collapsed her umbrella, shedding rain in all directions and handed it to Jarett. Dainty for one so large, she maneuvered her way with aplomb down the narrow aisle Charles had carved between numbered boxes and crates piled in neat towers on either side. She held a lorgnette to her eyes on occasion to peer curiously at a piece of sculpture here, a pile of jewel-hued rugs there.

In the shadow of Mrs. Thurgood came another female, her face hidden by the brim of her bonnet as she peeled away her pelisse and handed it, along with another damp parasol, to Jarett. If Mrs. Thurgood purchased nothing today, Charles would have to let Jarett go, but today the boy would be the one to fetch and carry and turn back the carpets in their stacks should Rose Thurgood care to search for something among the floor coverings.

The woman with the bonnet looked up, her gloved fingers pulling at the bow that bound a dripping hat to her head.

Miracle of miracles—his moonlit maiden!

"Miss Stanhope!"

The intensity of Charles's pleasure in seeing Prudence Stanhope surprised him, as did the sudden roses in her cheeks. Her face was a beacon lit with pleasure and joy, real joy, in seeing him. Her presence now, so unexpected, was a gift—a gift of hope—on a day when he was desperately in need of hope. She came into the darkness of the narrow space that held his treasures, his future, his hopes, and dreams. Where there had been none, there was now light.

"My lord," she said with a breathlessness that matched his own. "Thank you for the roses." Her hand went to the clasp at her breast, wherein one of his roses nestled.

"A gladsome flower, the rose," he quoted Wordsworth. "She lifts her head for endless spring." His own heart was lifted by the feeling of spring Prudence Stanhope brought with her, but his words were directed rather pointedly at Rose Thurgood. "I welcome this rose you bring to me," he said with a formal bow. "I am so very pleased to see you both again."

"Good day to you, too, young man," Rose said with mock severity, her plump cheeks rosied by a blush. It occurred to him that she was a woman unused to receiving compliments.

Charles turned his attention at last to Prudence. "How do you do, Miss Stanhope?"

As happy as he was to see her, he could not help noticing the wanness of Pru's complexion once her initial blush had faded. There were dark circles under her eyes. Sadness pulled at her eyes and mouth. Could it be this young woman's health was compromised more than he knew? Did she find no cure here in Brighton for what ailed her? There were mysteries still to be solved with relation to Prudence Stanhope.

Prudence could not meet his eyes when she answered softly, "I am fine. Thank you for asking."

It occurred to Charles that there were many things in life far more fearful than the mere loss of one's worldly goods. He asked with increasing concern, "Shall I fetch you a chair? You look . . ." he grappled for the best word "fatigued."

"A chair would be lovely," she admitted.

Jarett, ever observant, brought each of the ladies a chair.

Charles could not be satisfied. "Is there any other way in which I can make you comfortable?"

"Perhaps you can if you have a cure for the headache." Prudence Stanhope tried to speak brightly, but he could see pain in her eyes.

"Your head aches, dear?" Mrs. Thurgood cooed sympathetically. "I had no idea. Why did you not say something? Had I known I would never have dragged you out in this nasty weather."

"I've nothing medicinal at hand," Charles admitted with regret, "but I know a bit of Far Eastern magic that relieves headaches." He spoke softly, unwilling to further aggravate her pain.

Prudence eyed him dubiously.

"Far Eastern magic? How diverting, my lord." Rose Thurgood was fascinated. "Give it a try, my dear. You've nothing to lose but the pain in your head."

"What is involved in this magic?" Prudence was unconvinced.

He held out his right hand as he went down on one knee, smiling to reassure her. "Will you give me your hand?"

In the instant the words passed his lips he realized how very like a proposal this was, to kneel before a young woman and ask for her hand. A flash of recognition touched her features. The corner of her lips quirked upward, as her lashes dropped down to veil her gaze.

She placed a gloved hand in his. "Is this a proposal, sir?"

He laughed. "Absolutely."

Her gaze met his in surprise.

"A proposal to cure your head," he amended.

"You mean to cure my head through my hand?" She sounded doubtful.

He nodded. "As a matter of fact I do, but I would ask you to remove your glove, if you please. As damp as yours is, it may serve to restrict circulation."

Miss Stanhope cast an uncertain look in Mrs. Thurgood's direction.

Rose raised her brows, but it was clear from her expression

that curiosity completely overrode any censure with which she might have objected to the liberty he suggested.

Prudence removed a glove.

"Both of them," Charles instructed.

She slipped the second glove from her fingers and gave it into Jarett's care. He cheerfully offered to hang them in a warm spot to dry. Mrs. Thurgood was offered the opportunity to warm her gloves as well, but she declined, urging Charles, "Get on with the magic, dear boy."

Charles held out his hand. Miss Stanhope entrusted him with hers. Their eyes met over joined hands. Charles was sure, from the look they exchanged, that Miss Stanhope felt the impact of flesh against flesh as potently as he. Her hand belonged in his.

"This may be uncomfortable," he warned, encircling her wrist with the fingers of his left hand. He could feel the accelerated beat of her pulse in his palm. With the thumb and forefinger of his right hand he began to pinch at the padded V of connecting flesh between her thumb and forefinger. "Tell me when I hit the spot that hurts."

"Ow," she said uncertainly.

He pinched the spot harder.

"Ow! Ow!" She glared at him. "That hurts. Stop!"

He stopped, his fingers resting just above the tender spot on either side of her hand. There was nothing malicious in his gaze. He did, in fact, look at her with touching tenderness and undisguised sympathy.

"How can hurting my hand help my head?" she demanded crossly.

He shrugged. "I was told that the release of blocked and built-up pressures at certain points in the body alleviate pain. I don't know why a point in your hand can affect your head, I just know it generally works. Shall I stop, or can you stand the pain a moment longer?"

"Steady on," encouraged Mrs. Thurgood. "The best medicine generally involves either dreadful taste or a bit of pain."

Prudence exhaled heavily. "All right. I am too curious to cry craven now, but depend upon it, sir, if I end this exercise with both head and hand hurting, I shall take great pleasure in boxing your ears."

He nodded. "Consider them yours for the boxing. Are you prepared?"

She nodded.

He took a firmer grip on her wrist. Her pulse was faster than before.

"Try to relax," he recommended. "All pain eases a little if we do but relax a bit."

She nodded. Her hand went limp in his.

"Excellent!" he said with approval. He pinched hard at the spot that had made her cry out before, his thumb moving in a gentle, circular motion. "Tell me when it stops hurting," he directed.

"Stops hurting?" she snapped. "You have only to stop hurting it for it to . . . to stop . . ." She halted in mid-sentence, her mouth open, a curious expression wrinkling her brow.

"It doesn't hurt anymore," she said incredulously.

"Good." He released her hand. "Shall we try the other one?"

"So you can pinch it as well?" she chided him, even as she gave him her other hand.

He smiled. "Not for long." He repeated the circular motion with his thumb and forefinger.

A few seconds later, she nodded. "That has stopped hurting as well."

"And the headache?"

"Yes, how is your head, my dear?" Mrs. Thurgood sat regarding the entire proceedings with rapt attention.

Prudence considered the question thoroughly, turning her head first one way and then the other, a look of surprise dawning. "My headache is gone," she said with disbelief. "Completely gone." She tilted her head from side to side, as if to test her words. "However did you do that?" She regarded Charles with more than a trace of awe.

"Are you sure?" Rose asked in wonder.

"Yes. It really is a bit of magic."

Rose chortled in delight. "I do believe you could charm cobras, sir. If your goods are anywhere near as miraculous as your headache cure, I shall count myself very fortunate to walk away with a portion of them."

Miracles, Charles was later convinced, fell to *his* lot that day. Not only did Mrs. Thurgood indulge liberally in the items he showed her, but, miracle upon miracles, she handed him a promissory note before they parted, made out to her bank. "I shall pay the other half on delivery, my lord. You may bring my treasures to me some time after Wednesday next. The plastering is supposed to be finished by then."

As for Miss Stanhope, he managed to find a moment alone with her while Mrs. Thurgood deliberated over the colors of a rug.

"How's the head?" he asked her.

"Fine. Amazing, really." She smiled sweetly, as if in the movement of her lips she might convey to him how much she appreciated her cure.

"I have been thinking about the hours you owe me."

Her smile fled. "Yes?"

"Yes. I have an idea how we might spend a few of them."

"How?"

"There is another Assembly tonight. We did miss you at the last one. I should like to dance with you if you do not think it will provoke another headache."

She frowned.

"You do not care for the idea?"

"My cousin . . ." She hesitated.

"He does not care for the idea?"

She lifted her chin and looked him forthrightly in the eye. "My cousin does not approve of my keeping your company."

He sighed. "Not surprising, given my family's highly publicized misconduct. But Miss Stanhope, your cousin's opinion of me does not trouble me so much as yours. Do you approve of my company?"

Her lashes swept down to hide the answer in her eyes. "I do, sir," she said with a nervous laugh, her manner uncertain, as if such an admission might be misconstrued. "It would be a lie to tell you otherwise." She frowned, as if uncertain she should speak, and then blurted, "My cousin likes to think it is his responsibility to determine where, when, and with whom I come and go. I am, myself, determined to choose my own path. But I will not flagrantly flout propriety in arriving without escort at an Assembly."

"What of our excursion to the tidal pools? Do you mean to join us? Or shall I make your excuses to Grace?"

She considered the question far longer than he had anticipated. "It has been my intention from the start to view the tidal pools. See them I will."

Prudence felt she had been touched by magic. There had been a magic of form, color, and texture in Ramsay's assembled treasures: in glowing brasswork, in iridescent jade, creamy ivory, shimmering fabrics, and richly piled rugs. Every treasure that was brought out for their observation and appreciation had helped her to see a little deeper, she thought, into the mind of the man called Rash Ramsay. Nothing had moved her more, however, than the magical touch of his hands in stopping her headache.

Pausing at the bottom of the stairs that led up to her room, she pinched experimentally at the spot that had given her so much pain earlier that day. Her hand was still faintly tender, but her head remained curiously pain free. What a wonder that Ramsay could touch a spot and banish pain. Why was not everyone possessed of such knowledge?

She stopped rubbing the spot on her hand with a sharp intake of breath. Her gloves! She had forgotten them! To leave a personal article of clothing in a gentleman's possession smacked of flirtation. Her lapse of memory might be misconstrued. Lovers made a habit of keeping token gloves, proof positive that they had held one another's hands.

"Where in blazes have you been all morning?" Timothy's anger broke on the crown of her head as though it had been hurled from the top of the stairs. With guilty haste Prudence tucked her naked hands in the folds of her skirt.

"Good morning, cousin. I have enjoyed a pleasant morning,

despite the rain. Have you?" There was a hint of reprimand in her tone, the same sort of reprimand she would have used on either of the girls had they met her with such rudeness.

"My morning was spent worrying over your sudden disappearance."

She did not allow him to ruffle her mood. She was, she reminded herself, still touched by magic. "Did you think to check with Mrs. Harris? She saw me out the door herself and into Rose Thurgood's carriage."

"Mrs. Harris has herself been out this morning. Shopping—or some such nonsense."

"Oh! Had she been here, she might have told you that shopping was my errand as well."

"You went shopping? In this weather?"

"Yes. Rose has a new home to decorate. She wanted my opinion on some Oriental carpets, brasses, and porcelain."

"And did she buy anything? Or is she the type of female who stands dithering over every item she examines for an absolute age and then walks out empty-handed, unable to make up her mind?" Tim was in a pet.

Prudence refused to let him drag her along in his foul temper.

"She found any number of marvelous things. It was, all in all, a magical morning. What shall we do now to enjoy a magical afternoon?" She smiled, willing his temper to sweeten, and in fact her unruffled composure mollified him.

"Shall we spend part of the day at Donaldson's?" he suggested gruffly. He had begun to descend the stairs. She began to climb them. "If we get bored we can walk to the Royal Circus Ampitheatre where the local children learn to ride. There is a confectionery there."

Such a creature of habit he was. Funny, she had never noticed it before, but in Gillingham one had little choice but to become a creature of habit.

"Lovely idea," she agreed. "There is to be a violin concerto at Donaldson's this afternoon. Shall I fetch Mrs. Moore while you arrange our transport? Perhaps we could try the Greek eatery Mrs. Thurgood pointed out to me today. She says their fish dishes are marvelous."

They had come together on the steps. She stopped and waited for him to decline the adventure of trying a food he was unfamiliar with.

"Greek?" He pursed his lips. "You know me. I would much rather stop in at one of the inns for a bite of lemon sole or poached whiting."

She nodded. She had known the nature of this man without any real awareness of what it was she knew. They were not suited to one another at all. Could it be she loved the idea of him more than the reality?

"Shall we plan to take part in the Assembly tonight? Rose wondered if she might see us there." Again she tested the limits of his horizon.

As if he sensed the importance of her question, Tim studied her face. Was there anything he might see in her features that revealed her changed perception of him? Was there anything in her eyes, in her mouth, in the set of her chin that might reveal her desire to see Ramsay again that evening? The idea of dancing in the arms of a man who considered the entire world his to explore, a man who made magic with his hands, had undeniable appeal.

"The Assembly? That's an idea," Tim said noncommittally.

Chapter Seventeen

They did not go to the Assembly. It should not have surprised Pru, but it did. Her cousin's excuse over dinner left her with no argument.

"I fear you will find yourself quite ill in the morning if you engage in too much noise and frivolity tonight in a smoke-filled room amongst strangers, especially on such a dreadfully damp evening." His face was a picture of concern, but his booted foot touching hers beneath the table reminded her of other concerns between them.

It would seem everyone else had gone to the Assemblies. They had the sitting room virtually to themselves. Prudence felt stifled by their very solitude. The windows were closed on the sound and wet of the rain. A fire had been lit, filling the room with muggy warmth. The distant hushing of water, the pop of burning wood, the ticking of a clock upon the mantle lulled them, hushing their conversation and slowing their movements over the cards. Mrs. Moore's head began to nod.

Beneath the table Tim crossed his legs, his boot brushing against Pru's skirt. She flinched and pulled away. In time with the ticking of the clock, Tim's boot swung against her skirt again. Prudence moved the position of her legs, so that her cousin no longer collided with the fabric of her dress. He readjusted as well. Pru wondered irritably how Mrs. Moore could possibly drowse with the clock ticking so insistently, counting off minutes that slipped away forever.

The clock and the rhythmic contact with Tim's boot echoed a dull throbbing in Pru's head. Her headache had returned. The throbbing grew more painful when Tim's boot stopped swinging and with marked intent found the edge of her shoe.

Another subtle shift in his stance and his leg leaned purposefully into hers.

Prudence played out her cards and tried to ignore the alluring angel at her elbow, the angel with blue eyes that sought hers with a look of such open desire over the fan of his cards that it set her heart to racing the clock. *Endings, endings, endings* the clock reminded her. She must put an end to the dalliance beneath the table, to the admission of desire in the meeting of their gazes. She must put an end to her longing and move on.

And yet, the only movement was beneath the table. Tim's hand was warm and heavy on the fabric that covered her knee, moving upward with unmistakable intent to her thigh. Prudence thought of Ponsonby. She thought of Charles Ramsay.

"No!" She gathered her courage and grabbed at his hand.

Mrs. Moore roused from her snoozing with a snort. "My turn?" she mumbled. Even as she said it, she faded away again, her head bobbing back to its resting place on the wing of the Queen Anne chair in which she made herself comfortable.

Tim's hand had paused in its explorations of Pru's thigh. It began to move again.

"No," Prudence whispered. Her body rebelled against the reasoning of her mind by enjoying the meanderings of this hand. "No!" She shoved him away and jumped up from her chair, frightened not so much by Timothy's hand as she was frightened by her desire to let his hand go where it would.

"Mrs. Moore," she said, emotion thick in her throat. She shook the woman awake. "Mrs. Moore. We must to bed early if we are to be up at the crack of dawn for our trip to the tide pools."

Mrs. Moore roused, bleary eyed and confused, looking as rumpled and groggy as Prudence felt inside. "To bed? But of course." As if to prove she had not really been asleep, she barreled out of her chair and crossed the room with some semblance of her usual brisk energy.

"Prudence?" Timothy stayed her at the door. "A moment, please."

Her foot already on the stairs, Mrs. Moore, paused and looked back, a blinking owl trying to keep its eyelids properly open.

With a wave Prudence motioned her onward.

Tim forced a smile. It held no joy, only sadness and disappointment at her proposed desertion. "You know I do not approve of this excursion."

"Yes."

"Yet you persist in going?"

"Yes." Her voice almost left her. That she possessed the courage to flout his will surprised her. That she did it more than once this evening was astonishing.

His jaw tightened, all traces of his smile gone. "Had I the right to forbid your going, I would. You do not—cannot—know the treachery that lurks in the hearts of men, Pru."

"I think I do," she said softly.

His hand rose to rake the golden strands of hair away from a troubled forehead. "I have been asking around with regard to Ramsays—"

That got her attention. "Yes?"

"They are all that I feared and worse."

"How so?"

"They are notorious, my dear. There are no end of rumors. Five brothers and a sister, all of them known by dreadful nicknames. One of them a drunkard, another is said to be dying of the pox. The sister is a wild, neck or nothing rider they call the Amazon. They are all poor as church mice due to the reckless gambling of the one known as Rakehell—"

"You forget," she interrupted quietly. "I am just as poor."

"Through no fault of your own." He said it as if that made all the difference in the world.

"Is it the fault of Charles or Rupert Ramsay that they are cursed with dreadful brothers?"

"It *is* unconscionable that Charles Ramsay, as eldest, left the family finances in the hands of a wastrel."

"He would agree with you today. He thought, at the time, it might be the saving of his brother's character to so entrust him."

"He pours out his heart to you?" His mouth twisted, and his eyes had a wounded look. "I fear for your good name, Prudence. The Ramsays can do nothing but tarnish it."

Prudence held her tongue. She would not tell Tim again that she felt far more in danger of ruining her good name in his company than in any other. Her silence spoke louder than words.

Tim scowled and jumped up to pace the room.

"I am touched by your concern." She carefully maintained her distance from him.

"Yet you ignore my advice." He flung the words like darts. "Can it be you have allowed Rash Ramsay to seduce you, too?"

Prudence felt as if he had struck her. "Seduce me? A man I have known no more than a few days! How can you imagine such a thing?"

His eyes flashed angrily. "I am told you chased him down the street in broad daylight."

It had been foolish in her to believe she could keep that secret. It had been foolish in her to believe he would not attack the very weakness he had fostered in her.

He was not finished. "How is it that this stranger has been encouraged to escort you to dinner at the Pavilion?"

She was obliged to defend herself. "At the Prince's suggestion, I accepted Lord Ramsay's escort."

"The Prince? A man who makes no effort to be discreet in his indiscretions? On his advice, you thought it wise to entrust your person to one who is known to everyone as Rash Ramsay?"

"I did not then know him by that name."

"Ignorance is poor excuse for folly, Pru. Twice now I have asked you not to go to the tidal pools. If you persist in accepting Ramsay's escort—"

"What?" she demanded. "Would you cast me out over an imagined fall from grace when you are yourself responsible for the only tumble I have been in danger of succumbing to?"

He exhaled heavily and passed a hand through his hair. "I give you my word; I mean to return to Edith as soon as weather permits, just as you have suggested, Prudence, but I must warn you that if you consort with the Ramsays you will no longer be welcomed in my home."

She gasped, unprepared for so brutal a stance from him.

His jaw worked, his mouth set in a hard line. "Jane and Julia . . . I will not have them touched by gossip, the sort of gossip that must accompany your association with the Ramsays."

Choking back her disbelief in his hypocrisy, Prudence fled his company.

Prudence took herself off to her room, not to sleep, but to write letters. Timothy threatened to cut her off. One moment he was clutching at her thigh, the next he threatened to ban her from his home forever. What was she to do? She had no situation readily available to her. She had no one to turn to, certainly no one in the family. She armed herself with a pen and wrote letters.

To her cousin Edith she explained how much she appreciated the hospitality of her home. At length she proclaimed her desire no longer to be a burden to the Margrave family. Life is a journey, she wrote. Our paths move in opposite directions. She ended by urging her cousin to make every attempt to regain her health. She heartily recommended Mahomed's Baths as a source of comfort. Into this missive she tucked a shorter page just for Jane and Julia. She sealed the letter with a heartfelt sigh.

In response to the "Wants" she had collected that afternoon, more letters. Then, quill resharpened, she dipped into the standish and wrote to everyone she knew or was related to, explaining her desire for a new position. It took hours and all her concentration. Her fingers ached from clutching the quill by the time she was done. She pushed away doubt and fear. She refused to resign herself to the hard truth that all her scribbling might come to naught. For the moment letters meant hope. She was determined to be hopeful.

Almost in tandem with the sealing of her letters, there came another ending. The rain stopped. An absence of noise drew her to the window, that and a desire for a breath of cool, fresh air. The beauty of the night sky drew her onto the wet balcony, her fine, white lawn wrapper floating around her like one of the filmy clouds that dimmed the moon. For the first time since the rain had started, stars peeked through rents in the passing veil of clouds. Prudence found hope in their presence, hope for sun on the morrow.

She was not the only one to recognize the significance of stars. A carriage pulled into the street as she gazed heavenward. She paid it no mind. The driver was hunched in his box. The occupants were hidden away inside. They could not see her, above them on a dark balcony, gazing at the night sky. The carriage stopped at the door beneath her. A female voice professed she would only be a minute. The voice was that of Grace Ramsay. Prudence knew it well.

The bell pull rang and rang again.

The door opened below.

Prudence, ready to race downstairs to see what brought Grace here, was stopped in her tracks by the sound of another voice she recognized. Charles Ramsay had stepped out of the carriage to admire the night sky. His brother Rue hung out the window of the coach chatting with him.

"What a beautiful night," she heard Rupert say.

"Is it?" Charles gazed at the clearing sky, his spirits oddly downcast. He should be in a good mood. He had, after all, seen Miss Stanhope that morning. She had brought him Rose Thurgood, who had ordered far more from his collection than he had dared anticipate. One of the Prince's compatriots had seen fit to pay his bill today as well. The tide was turning in his favor. The rain had stopped. Why then was he miserable? Why could he not find it within himself to agree that this was a beautiful night?

"Insipid affair—the Assembly," he grumbled.

"Especially as Miss Stanhope did not attend." Rupert put his finger squarely on the sore spot.

"Yes. I must admit I was looking forward to seeing her. I wanted . . ." Charles's gaze rose to the balcony where he had once caught Prudence Stanhope watching him. He wanted to see her again, to talk to her. He had been possessed of the most pressing desire to dance with her this evening, to have legitimate excuse to touch her again, not as he had touched her hands this morning, in a healing capacity, but as a man touches a woman. He had her gloves in his pocket—small white gloves, soft kidskin permeated with her jasmine scent, cut in the exact shape of her hands. She had left them behind, a small part of herself that he had carried about with him all day.

"You wanted to thank her for introducing you to Rose Thurgood, I know. You have said as much at least ten times already." Rupert brought his mind back to the thought he had stopped in midsentence.

Was that movement on the balcony? Surely, it was too much to hope that he might catch Prudence standing there a second time? The balcony was dark. It was difficult to discern anything that might be there other than a flash of white, a bit of curtain blowing through the open window he thought. It fluttered in the breeze.

"Are you become foolish at last, Chaz, on account of your pretty governess?"

Charles paced away from the door of the carriage and glanced again at the balcony. The white splotch of curtain had the look of a ghost about it.

"What was it happened between the two of you that day at the baths?" Rue would not abandon his line of questioning. "As I recall, last time I dared to ask, you did your best to drown me."

"Foolish of me," Charles admitted sarcastically, "not to have finished the job, so that you would no longer plague me with such questions."

"Foolish?"

"Very foolish. I have been foolish from the moment I first laid hands on her," he admitted softly.

"Aha! So you *did* give her a shampooing! I thought as much. Otherwise she would not have been so furious with you afterward. And yet, methinks she looks upon you with a kindly eye of late. Can it be Miss Stanhope has become as foolish from this bathhouse encounter as you, Chaz?"

Charles sighed. The flicker of white drew his gaze again. "I think Miss Stanhope's cousin would like to stop her from associating with Ramsays, and if you persist in plaguing me with these unseemly questions, I shall be forced to agree with him."

Rupert laughed. "Are we Ramsays such a bad lot then, Chaz?"

"We are a miserable assortment of penniless misfits and scoundrels, Rue." The last words came out sounding a trifle strangled. The moon had slipped from behind the dimming veil of clouds for a heartbeat. In its silvery light Charles saw that the ghost on the balcony was not blowing curtains at all. Prudence stood above them, the flimsy lawn wrapper she clutched about her shoulders floating in the wind, like seaweed in the surf.

The door to the boardinghouse opened, blinding him to the sight of her with a flood of light. Grace came slowly down the steps.

"Well," Rue said. "Did you speak to her?"

"No." Grace sighed heavily, waiting for the door to close off the light—and listening ears—behind her before she went on. "It was her cousin I spoke to. Handsome fellow, but a bit of a cold fish. He said Pru was not feeling well, that she went to bed early. I told him we had missed them at the Assembly. He said, 'What a pity.' I went on to explain we meant to come by at half past six in the morning if the weather held and if she was still interested in joining our excursion to the tide pools. He said he did not think she would feel up to it."

"Was he rude to you?" Rupert asked. "He does not care for Ramsays, or so Charles has just been telling me."

"He was not rude, but neither was he particularly polite," Grace said as Charles helped her into the coach. "Do you know I was possessed of the disturbing impression the entire time I was detailing our plans, that he had no intention, whatsoever, of passing on the information."

Charles stepped up into the coach after her. "Not to worry," he said firmly. "I have no doubt Miss Stanhope will be ready and waiting for us at half past six if she sincerely wishes to accompany us."

"How can you be so sure?" Grace fretted. "I tell you, I am absolutely convinced this Margrave fellow means to tell her nothing of my visit."

Charles stared up at the balcony as he settled himself in the carriage. Still as a statue, Miss Stanhope stood watching and listening.

"Trust me," he said, calmly tipping his hat to the pale figure. "I have good reason to believe Miss Stanhope will join us if that is her intention."

Chapter Eighteen

Prudence leaned into the rocks that surrounded the still pool of salty water she had chosen to examine out of several possibilities. Where her shadow touched the water tiny fish darted away from the potential danger in the abrupt darkness that fell across their underwater world. She understood the sensibilities of the frightened fish. Her own world, her immediate future, was threatened by the fearful shadow of the unknown.

And yet, in this moment, if she focused all her thoughts and feelings on the present, she was happy. The morning air, washed rainy fresh, was brisk without any bite. The breeze played with her hair. The sky, with only a skimming of high white clouds and the flicker of birds on the wing, promised a fair day.

Before her lay entire worlds to explore. Each placid tide pool was its own underwater kingdom, each as foreign and as intriguing to examine as the Prince Regent's Marine Pavilion. Here were worlds in miniature of wet stone, waving seaweed, delicate sponge, and darting sea life. Sea squirts clustered together like bunches of yellowish grapes, while breadcrumb sponges, dead man's fingers, and spider crabs fulfilled the strange promise of their names. Among the branches of the bladder wrack chameleon prawns drifted like pale ghosts. Barnacles encrusted the rocks, their feathery legs combing the water for food. She was looking for shells, of which there were plenty, but few suited her purpose. There were tiny, cone-shaped limpets that clung to the rocks around her like miniature volcanoes, and periwinkles in a variety of colors, though she did not want to kill the snails inside if she could find some of the larger whelk, cockle, or mussel shells already vacated by their owners.

The shells were for Jane and Julia. Odd to think she might never see the girls again—odd and troubling.

Charles Ramsay's reflection joined hers on the placid surface of the tide pool. He reached out to touch her shoulder, this man who had come very close to admitting he loved her to his brother the night before. Had he meant it? Did he really love her, or was he capable only of ruining her reputation and breaking her heart, as her cousin would have her believe? Was it true, as she had so long assumed, that no man could be trusted? Ramsay's hand hovered as uncertainly as her opinion before making contact with her shoulder.

She turned her head toward him, her cheek unexpectedly brushing the warmth of his fingers. She would not believe Charles Ramsay's intent was to ruin her. Her eyes closed involuntarily, the better to savor the sensation of his touch, before with a sharp intake of breath she pulled away from the surface of the tidal pool and stood up beside him.

"Yes?"

He held out his hand to her, to assist in her progress across the rocks. "Come," he said. "Grace has found the most amusing fellow."

An amusing fellow. She brushed off her skirts and took his hand. Some might describe Rash Ramsay as such. He had amused their entire party on the drive from Brighton with stories of his travels. He had spoken of snake charmers, belly dancers, opium dens, and dragon dances, holding Prudence rapt with his every word.

He was a snake charmer of sorts himself. Rose had been right to say the man could charm a cobra. Could one trust a snake charmer? Could she trust the words that had hinted of his love for her the night before? Or did Charles Ramsay pull a ruse on her again as clever as he had in making her believe him a bathhouse attendant? He had seen. He had known she was standing on the balcony. He might have said anything and expected her to believe him sincere.

"Come see, come see." Grace waved to her from another of

the tidal pools cupped in the rocks along the beach. "You must see this marvelous creature."

The marvel was bizarre and flesh-colored. Fleshy appendages at the front end of its caterpillarlike body resembled the horns of a cow. Long, brown feathery appendages along its back gave it the look of a pincushion.

"My, isn't he the dandy!" Prudence breathed with suitable awe. "A sea slug of sartorial splendor."

"Is that what it is? A slug?" Grace frowned. "How disappointing. I thought he looked rather like an underwater badger."

"He does." Prudence laughed. "And there is no reason you may not continue to identify him as such. He is a marvelous fellow, no matter how unprepossessing his name."

"Well, I'm off to see what engrosses Rupert so," Grace said cheerfully. "He is determined to find a crab with blue legs." She moved on to the next of the underwater kingdoms.

Prudence looked up. Charles Ramsay stood regarding her as if she had said something quite remarkable.

"What's in a name?" he asked softly.

A name? Was it the Ramsay name he referred to? No, he was quoting Shakespeare, a line from *Romeo and Juliet*.

"That which we call a rose, by any other name would smell as sweet."

"Do you refer to Rose Thurgood? Or do you mean to play Juliet?" Prudence teased him.

"I will play Romeo to *your* Juliet." Charles offered graciously, "but not until I have thanked you for Rose Thurgood."

"She is a lovely lady, is she not?" Prudence tried not to blush at the idea of the two of them assuming the roles of Romeo and Juliet, as he had suggested.

Charles was not done with bringing her to the blush. "A lovely lady and an even lovelier customer. I was pleased you chose to come with her yesterday, despite the discomfiture of the headache and the disapproval of your cousin."

She found it difficult to look at him, choosing instead to look deeper into the tidal pool.

"You left these behind." He pulled from his pocket the gloves she could ill afford to lose. His fingers played a moment with the soft, kid leather fingers before he held them out to her.

"Thank you," she said, taking them—surprised he had not found excuses to hold onto them longer. "And thank you again for chasing away my headache yesterday."

He nodded. "Tell me" he said, shifting his position, "how does your head today?"

"Fine." She glanced up. He had chosen his position with forethought. It allowed him both to stare into the tidal pool and to stare directly into her eyes whenever she chanced to look up. A trifle disconcerting.

Both of his brows were raised at the moment, as if to question the veracity of her claim. "You started out saying fine yesterday."

She blushed. "I am truly fine today. Trust me. I would readily tell you otherwise, that you might work your magic on my hands again."

He smiled. "And your cousin?"

Unprepared for the question, she frowned, swallowed, plastered a smile on her lips, and made light of his query. "As far as I know, he suffers not from the headache either."

He laughed. "You do not think me satisfied with that for an answer, do you?"

"My, what a nice specimen of a dahlia sea anemone." She pointed into the pool, hoping he might yet be distracted.

He rose, skirting the end of the pool to position himself beside her against the rocks. He was a trifle overwhelming, so close did he lean into her shoulder in order to see the anemone, which he examined with gratifying appreciation and concentration before turning his head to say, almost directly in her ear, "You were saying?"

"Saying?" she repeated.

"Yes, about your cousin? Yesterday you were forthcoming enough to confide in me that he cares not for Ramsays. Does he know you are here?"

"Yes," she said softly. By now he must.

"He told you of Grace's visit last night then?"

"No."

"Uhm." He studied her profile a moment as if waiting for more. "Will you suffer for honoring us with your company?"

She licked her lips uneasily. "Possibly."

"Will you trust me with specifics?"

Trust? Prudence frowned. She had trusted Tim. Men were not to be trusted. That was the root of the problem. She wanted more than anything to confide that distrust in someone, but she could not speak ill of men to a man. Neither would she malign her cousin to Ramsay.

She shook her head. "My fears may prove unfounded."

He seemed unhappy with her answer. "If they do not," he said, "will you promise to come to me for assistance?"

She took a deep breath and bit down on her lip to stop its shaking. She wondered if he knew how relieved she was to say, "Yes, I promise. You are very kind."

"It is not really kindness, Miss Stanhope, that drives me, when your safety and happiness are concerned."

"No? What then?"

"Come now, Miss Stanhope, surely you do not mean to deny overhearing last night the declaration of my feelings for you?"

"You admitted only to foolishness last night, my lord," she whispered, almost breathless with surprise that he chose to refer to the matter.

"Dare I hope that you may become equally foolish, Miss Stanhope?"

"Foolish?" She lost all composure. "I do not know just what it is I feel for you, but I will not call it foolishness."

"Will you look at me, Miss Stanhope?"

She turned her head to look directly into his eyes with the wary tension of someone who had looked too openly into another man's eyes.

Charles met her gaze with no such wariness. His eyes were awash with interest, amusement, and something else, something she could not define. It questioned her wariness. Far more eloquently than he might have verbalized his feelings for her, his expressive eyes let her know that he cared deeply for her, that he did in fact feel desires for her. There was a softness to his expression, an affection and a kindness that made his face radiant.

"Are we friends? Good friends?"

She was surprised by the question. After a moment's thought she nodded. She did consider this man a friend, no matter that he was a Ramsay and despite the doubts she still harbored with regard to his intent.

"Are we friends enough that I might call you Prudence, and you might refer to me as Charles?"

"A rose by any other name?" she suggested archly.

He nodded, eyes shining.

A moment's hesitation, and she nodded a second time.

"You may call me Prudence . . . Charles." His name felt strange on her tongue. She had almost called him Chaz, as Rupert did.

He smiled, delighted. "Thank you, Prudence."

He surprised her by cupping the crown of her head with his hand that he might he kiss her twice on the forehead. The kisses were unexpected. Prudence drew back, confused.

She had expected Charles Ramsay to kiss her one day. She had been expecting kisses from this man almost from the moment they had met. She could not gaze into the open door of his features, could not watch his gaze wander from her eyes to her lips and back again, without expectation of kisses. That he chose to kiss her now, not on the lips, but on the forehead, his actions matching his words of friendship rather than love, touched her heart in a manner most unexpected.

On the basis of the unorthodox manner in which they had first met, on the basis too of Rash Ramsay's reputation, Prudence had lived with the expectation of this man's taking advantage of her. He had been blessed with plenty of opportunity. He had, in fact, won twenty-four hours' time from her, to use or abuse as he wished. Had he, in fact, followed such a pattern, her opinion of men would no more than have been confirmed.

But, with a kiss to her forehead all Pru's preconceived notions seemed questionable. It occurred to her that it was restraint she witnessed here. That Rash Ramsay, of all men, restrained himself in such a manner pointed up to her how highly irresponsible, how rashly licentious, her cousin's kisses were. What irony, that her cousin, who should not be drawn to kiss her, was interested in little else, while Ramsay, whose lips she would like to taste, kissed her chastely on the forehead, more like a kinsman than her kinsman.

She felt herself a little foolish and more than a little wanton to have expected a kiss on the lips from Charles Ramsay.

"Come," he said, rising. "The tide is turning."

And indeed, the tide had turned. It was eating away at the beach that had been exposed to them, licking at the rocks nearby, swallowing up the tidal pools that had held them captivated.

It had taken every ounce of Charles's self-control not to kiss Prudence Stanhope full on the lips. There were any number of reasons why he exercised such restraint. There was, after all, much they needed to know about one another before he bound her to him with a kiss. A kiss, at this point, was tantamount to a proposal. Charles was prepared to admit himself foolish, but he was not foolish enough to commit himself to any woman when he had nothing more to offer her than hopes and dreams and—he reached down to pick up a shell that floated in the foam near his feet—an angel's wing.

He held out to her the fragile white shell that almost filled his palm. "Do you know what this means?"

"An angel's wing!" Her eyes sparkled with delight as she turned the shell in her hands. "An almost perfect specimen."

He smiled. The shell reminded him of Prudence Stanhope standing on a moonlit beach, arms uplifted like wings. "I did not ask what it was, Miss Stanhope, but what it means."

"Means?" Her brow wrinkled. "What do *you* mean?"

"Finding an angel's wing means that an angel from the sea has outgrown hers. She has left them on the beach so that some lucky mortal may be touched by what is left of the magic in them."

"What a lovely notion," she said. "Did someone tell you the tale when you were a child?"

He nodded and reached out to touch the shell, as if in touching it he might touch the past. "My mother told me stories of angels and fairies, trolls and elves."

"And did you believe her?"

"But of course. I trusted her every word implicitly, and she would have me trust in angel's wings. By so doing, my childhood was a time and place of adventure and wonder."

"Your adult life seems to me a time and place of adventure and wonder as well." Prudence held out the angel's wing, to return it to him.

"Keep it if you like." He clasped his arms behind his back, afraid he would touch her if she stood there much longer holding out the shell to him. "For one of your girls," he suggested. "Shall we go up? Grace is waving."

He pointed to the cliff top. Grace stood waving her hat.

"Thank you for the shell." Prudence tucked the angel's wing into her pocket. "The girls will enjoy seeing this. They have yet to visit the seaside."

They headed up the beach.

"Were you raised on fairy tales?" He returned to the topic they had touched upon.

"I wasn't." She bent to pick up another curiosity from the shoreline. "Another bivalve," she said, "though not a very good specimen." She cast the bit of shell down again. "My mother, though not as keen as I have been for reading about foreign lands, was always ready to use nature as a classroom to teach me things."

"Things like bivalves?"

"Yes. She firmly believed that any female with good sense should educate herself by reading extensively, or by attending lectures on subject matter that appealed to her."

"A bluestocking?"

"I suppose she was, though I never heard anyone dare to say as much to her face. She was too much the lady. Her thirst for knowledge was passed on to me. I know three languages, the globes, mathematics, some science, and a dabbling of most of the known world's politics and religions. Were I born a male instead of female, there are any number of careers I might have pursued. As I was a girl, I make an excellent governess. I should like to make an even better traveling companion."

"Thence the want ads."

"Yes. I have always longed to see the world."

"I know it might seem very selfish in me, but I am very glad you were not born a male."

She blushed.

"Is that why you intend to leave the bosom of your family?"

"Because I am a female?"

She sounded defensive—too defensive given the question.

"No. Travel."

She started to answer, shook her head, and said with a finality that discouraged further questions, "That figures into it. I would not remain forever dependent upon my cousin's good will and generosity. I've no desire to outstay my welcome."

"And yet," he prodded, "your cousin seems as fond of you as any brother."

She concentrated on their climbing pathway. The footing was not, he thought, as treacherous as the subject he dared to broach. "Yes, he has been good to me, but I would be dependent on no man when I can capably stand on my own two feet. I feel too much like this fellow here at times."

She bent to pick up a rough, sand-covered piece of cockleshell on whose back clung a smooth, flesh-colored slipper shell. She prodded the slipper shell. "I have come to depend too greatly on my host." The slipper shell, long since dried out, fell away from the cockle under her prodding.

She pressed her lips together, her gaze focused on the ocean that had begun to drop away behind them. "Have you ever been too close to someone to see them clearly?"

Charles thought immediately of Jack and the fortune he had so blindly entrusted to his brother's care. "Yes. My fortune is lost because of my blindness to my brother's weaknesses."

She nodded. "I have been equally blind with regard to my cousin."

"Do you love him, then?" He had to know.

Her eyes closed on the idea. "Yes," she admitted softly.

Charles studied her face as she purposefully returned her attention to the climbing pathway again. Every bone in her jaw seemed set with resolve.

"Do you think it possible you might learn to love another?" he called after her.

She stopped in her tracks, then turned to face him, her gaze uneasy as she studied his face. "Why do you ask?"

He continued to mount the path until he came even with her. "I ask because . . . because I still believe in the magic of an angel's wing . . . in a way."

She smiled, her hand straying to the pocket where she had put away the shell. "And what way is that?"

He found himself reluctant to explain. He had tried to explain his philosophy to those he loved most and had been met with disbelief, even horror.

"I believe . . . ," he said hesitantly, unable to watch her reaction as he spoke "in the Hindu and Buddhist philosophy that fate brings us together with people and events for good reason—that we may learn and grow." He ran a hand uneasily through his hair, prepared for her laughter or disbelief.

"You speak of kismet then, or karma?" she asked calmly.

He was rendered speechless by her cool, unruffled acceptance. Of course she knew what he referred to. Of course she would understand better than any—this governess who traveled the world by way of books. "Do you understand me then? Do you agree?"

Her brow furrowed. "The idea is intriguing, but I have faced a great deal of hardship of late. I am not convinced we carry debts from one life to the next, nor am I convinced that growth and learning stem from all our troubles."

"No?" He was disappointed. "What hardship have you endured that does not fit into my picture of the cosmos? Can you tell me?"

She closed her eyes, her expression troubled. "What growth or learning comes from the death of an innocent child? What debt so dear nips life in the bud? There can be no good in such pointless tragedy, surely. To the contrary, I have seen additional hardships come from devastating losses."

He sighed heavily. "You may be right. There seems to be neither rhyme nor reason to the death of an innocent. And yet, such an event touches deeply the lives of everyone involved. Have you not been touched?" He reached out to touch her arm. "Has your life not in some way been changed? Have you not wrestled with thoughts or choices that would otherwise have never entered your realm? Have you not a better appreciation of life as a result of this death you speak of? Has life, perchance, been pushed in a new direction?"

She bowed her head, studying his words. A struggle went on between her knitted brows. She threw back her head with a sigh. "I have learned a great deal, far more perhaps than I wanted to. My life, as you say, has been thrust in an entirely unexpected direction."

He was pleased with her response, pleased that she opened herself up enough to admit as much to him. He held his tongue, hoping she might have more to say. She paused. She had taken the angel's wing from her pocket and stood looking at it with unwarranted attention. What she chose to reveal, when she spoke again, caught him completely off guard. "I would not, I realize, be here today had it not been for . . ." She stopped and began again, reminding him, "You asked me, sir, if I might learn to love another."

He went very still. "I did."

"I will admit I did not think it at all possible"—she spoke slowly, haltingly, her gaze uncertain, as it rose from her examination of the shell, to dart a look his way—"until I encountered a man at a bathhouse with as much magic in his touch as may be found in an angel's wing."

Hope, like wine, made Charles giddy. He reached out to touch her face, his finger tracing the line of her jaw. Her eyes widened with surprise. Her lips parted as she inhaled abruptly with a little gasp. Drawn by her lips, he bent to kiss her.

She closed her eyes, anticipating his intent.

And yet, he stopped, his lips no more than a fraction of an inch from her lips, his heart beating fast and hard. "I would not win you with just the magic of a touch, Prudence," he said softly, his lips so close to hers he could feel the heat of her breath like a sensitive caress. "No, not even with a kiss."

She turned from him, her hand flying up to cover her mouth. He caught the hand in his. Resistant, she balled it into a fist.

"I would win you, here"—he carried her fist to her forehead touching it—"here"—he carried her fist to her lips, to the center of her chest, pressing it firmly between her breasts—"and here"—he carried her fist one last time, below her waist. "I would not presume to win you at all until I have dealt with . . . prior commitments. I must have more to offer you than kisses."

She gasped. Wrenching her fist from his hold, she set off up the pathway. He could not be sure she heard the words, but he said them anyway. "You deserve more, Prudence, far more."

Chapter Nineteen

To the top of the cliff they climbed in silence, Prudence mulling over all that had been said and done. Ramsay refused to kiss her! She had wanted him to kiss her. She had freely offered up her lips to him. Why did he reject her?

She deserved more than kisses, he has said, *much more.* What did he mean by that? What *did* she deserve? What was she worth, or worthy of?

Food awaited them on the downs. Cold meat and cheeses, fresh bread, and fruit were spread out on waterproof tarps and blankets in the shade of the carriage, from which the horses had been unhitched that they might graze. Food sated not the emptiness inside her, no more than Rupert and Grace's chatter filled the silence between her and Ramsay.

"You must meet my brother, Miles, Miss Stanhope," Grace insisted. "He is coming for the races. He may be able to recommend a position to you as traveling companion to one of his many acquaintances."

"If anyone is in a way to help you, it will be Miles," Rupert agreed. "He is a capital fellow and very well connected. Aurora will be pleased to make your acquaintance as well. There is nothing she likes better than a lively day at the races."

"Unless it be Miles," Grace corrected him playfully.

He laughed. "Unless it be Miles," he agreed.

Prudence listened to the continuing conversation not so much with an ear for specifics, but with a growing comprehension of how loving were the exchanges between Grace and Rupert.

Their playful banter suggestively hinted at the affections special to newlywed husbands and wives. Prudence wanted just such happiness and compatibility in her own life. Could Charles Ramsay love her as Rupert loved Grace—as Miles would appear to love his Aurora? He had yet to say as much. He admitted only to foolishness. He asked permission to call her by her given name. Yet, he refused to kiss her. Prudence stared at the man whose eyes had always seemed to hold not questions, but answers. Did the answer to her quest for happiness, for stillness, for love and affection, lie waiting in Ramsay's eyes? She thought it might.

"Do you mean to go?" Grace's question hung in the air, awaiting an answer.

Prudence shook the milling thoughts from her head. They were all looking at her. The question was hers to answer.

"Go?" she repeated.

"To the races," Grace said. "Do you mean to go to the races?"

"I had not given it any thought," she admitted.

"Ask your cousin if you may not come with us."

"Yes, please do." Charles Ramsay seconded the notion.

He wanted her around. That was surely sign of affection, was it not?

Prudence nodded. "Thank you for the invitation."

With little more to fuel it, the conversation ran dry along with the wine. Grace announced her intention to spend some time at her easel. Rue took out his notebooks and arranged himself comfortably on the blanket.

"This is," he declared, "the perfect place to get some writing done."

Uneasy with the prospect of another thought-provoking conversation with Charles Ramsay, Prudence went for a walk, alone with her thoughts, along the cliff top. The sky was boundless, the Channel dulcet in the afternoon sunlight. Thoughts wheeled and banked and screeched at her like the occasional gull that winged its way above her head. Did Charles Ramsay love her? Did she love him? Were they destined for one another? Did she believe in destiny? What did she want? Prudence sought answers and a sense of peace in her perambulations. She found neither.

Restless and still seeking answers, she returned to the picnicking spot. Perhaps a chat with Grace would clear her mind. But Grace was busy with her paints. Rupert sat to one side of her easel, comfortably sprawled on one of the waterproof tarps, his pen scratching busily at the page. There was something so satisfactory in their arrangement, something that spoke to Prudence with subtle poignancy of the interests these two shared, the love, that she could not find it within her to interrupt.

Neither could she interrupt Charles Ramsay who alone remained beside the carriage. He sat, as Prudence had seen him sit before, facing the ocean, perfectly still, his eyes closed, his legs folded, the backs of his hands resting comfortably on his knees, so that his palms seemed to cup the sky. He was a compelling and peaceful sight. He looked rather like a candle flaring in the wind, dressed as he was, in white, with his hair, the only moving thing about him, tossing like flame in the breeze.

Prudence turned in her tracks to return to her solitary perambulations.

"Please stay," Charles said softly, without turning. He seemed to address the water spread before him.

Prudence paused.

"May I take advantage of one of the hours you owe me."

The quiet voice drew her nearer.

"Take advantage? How so?" She feared the worst.

"Will you sit and meditate with me, Prudence?"

She hesitated. "Why do you meditate?" She needed the answer before she could agree to his request.

He turned from his examination of the Channel. He did not seem surprised by her question, nor was he hesitant to reply, "In meditation I find answers. In answers I find peace."

"I should like to find answers." Prudence bent to unlace her boots with the feeling she bared more than her stockinged feet in joining this man.

"You were meditating when you found your garden."

His words surprised her.

"That was meditation? That was no more than my imagination."

His brows rose in the amused manner with which she was so familiar. "Really?"

She frowned, puzzled. It had just been her imagination, had it not? "How do you sit so still?"

"The key is to become completely comfortable with the position of one's body, so that it may be forgotten."

"Forgotten?"

"Yes, when one's flesh stops talking, it becomes a simple matter to hear the more subtle voice of one's spirit."

"I don't understand."

"You will." He sounded so certain she began to believe she would.

"How shall I sit? As you do?" She sank onto the blanket opposite him, studying the placement of his hands and feet.

"Sit or lie down—whatever you find most comfortable."

"Lie down?" She could not lie down! She would in no way be able to forget her body if she lay down next to this man. "I choose to sit," she said firmly, trying to arrange herself in the same pretzeled position Charles assumed.

"This is not the easiest posture," she complained as her legs tangled in her skirt. She felt quite ridiculous.

"You need not sit this way," he said calmly, his eyes sparkling with amused expectation. What he waited for, she could not fathom, but that he seemed to think it would come from her, made her a little nervous.

She adopted his pose uneasily. Her hands felt odd, completely useless, resting as they did on her knees.

Ramsay nodded when she was settled. He closed his eyes. "Now, ask your toes how they feel."

Her toes? Was this some elaborate hoax again? He could not be serious, could he? His eyes remained closed. He rocked a little on his haunches, as if to find a more comfortable position.

She closed her eyes. How did her toes feel? She had never paused to wonder how any part of her body was feeling unless something was markedly wrong, like having a cough, or the headache. It was strange now, to think about how her toes felt when it was the rest of her body that clamored for attention simply because she sat opposite Charles Ramsay. His very presence stirred anxious anticipation in her stomach and rib cage. Her heart was beating faster than usual. Her ears were keen to his every movement. Her back felt stiff, and her knees and ankles were uncomfortable. Most unusual, heat seemed to have fired in her private parts. Perhaps it was no more than the decidedly unladylike posture, legs splayed, skirts puddled in her lap. A lady did not sprawl upon the ground after all, like a toddler on the nursery floor with a pile of building blocks.

"If your toes are relaxed and comfortable," he went on, "ask your ankles how they are doing. When you find a body part that is not relaxed and comfortable, adjust your position until it is."

Her toes had been fine, but her ankles were not at all happy. She rearranged her position.

His voice touched every part of her, his tone even and undemanding, recommending she relax her calves, knees, thighs, hips, and posterior. Her posterior! That he openly mentioned the particulars of her every limb was enough to make her eyes pop in surprise on several occasions. Yet, he sat so still, so comfortably, his suggestions made so blandly, without any sense of the provocative, that she closed her eyes again and focused on making comfortable her every body part.

"Your back and neck," he languidly suggested, "should be as limber and as flowing as a willow. Your head may sway a little when you are truly relaxed. You may feel heavy and warm and then weightless, as if your limbs float, or have disappeared entirely."

He was right. She could not feel her feet at all!

"Generally," his voice very soft, very low, "thoughts and images will flow through your mind like scudding clouds at this point, distracting you from a true state of repose. Let the thoughts flow. You may find answers to questions that trouble you. You may visualize dreamlike images that make no sense to you. Let the clouds float by. Do not think, do not dream, do not worry. You have come here to be still."

He fell quiet and still—so still she might have thought he left her, but for the sound the wind made occasionally in flapping the fabric of his shirt. Basking in the warmth of the day, her lungs filling with fresh air, she sat in the lee of the rocks, listening to the sound of her breathing. Air rushed in, air rushed out, echoing the unending breath of the ocean far beneath them. Water rushed in. Water rushed out. The sun warmed the top of her head, and a breeze kissed her cheek.

Unbidden thoughts drifted through her mind—panicky thoughts, worrisome thoughts. Images rushed in, images rushed out. The vine was dying away. The rosebush flourished in the sun. Hands touched her neck and shoulders, hands that pushed and prodded, pinching at the aches, searching out truths. Thoughts washed over her like waves. She was white and fragile, an angel's wing riding the surf. The tide rushed out, the tide rushed in drowning the rocks, spawning generation upon generation of sea life in the tide pools, kingdoms under the sea. Long before she was born, these waves had washed the shore; long after she was gone, they would continue to slide in, slide out. The voice of eternity whispered in the wash of the water. Her troubles and fears were hushed to insignificance by that whisper.

"Sit still a moment," she was in the habit of telling Jane and Julia when they had trouble mastering their lessons. "Sit still and let the universe tell you the answer if it will." More often than not, in that moment of stillness an answer would come, not always the right one, but mistakes were essential for growth, for learning to take place. Mistakes like Timothy. The teacher within had to remember her own lessons. *Sit still and let the universe answer if it will.*

The sun's heat lulled her. The wind was a low-keyed lullaby humming off the cliffs. A bird hung above her, riding the music of wind and water, keening. Prudence heard none of it. For a moment—or was it many moments—she drifted into nothingness, a place without sound or thought or imagery. She sat completely still.

A fly, buzzing too near her ear, brought her back to reality with a jerk. She opened her eyes, disoriented. She had been floating, or was it flying? She had been for an instant a mote of dust in sunlight, a seed pod floating in the wind, a drop of water among many flung against the rocks below. She felt relaxed, replete. Her senses rejoiced in the blue of the sky, the cry of a tern, the sweet smell of the breeze. How long had she been sitting here?

She unfolded her legs quietly, her gaze darting to focus on Charles Ramsay, who sat, eyes closed, his body absolutely still but for the slow rise and fall of his chest and the wild flailing of his glowing hair. He was fire, stirred to new heat in the freshening breeze.

She stared at him, as if seeing him for the first time. Never had she been at liberty to examine him so minutely. He was always looking at her when his eyes were open. She could not return his gaze without concentrating her attention almost exclusively on the expression in his eyes. To see him now, eyes shut, was to see him afresh. His hair, his eyebrows, his lashes were quite wonderful seen in sunshine, which tindered them with its fire and accentuated the deep glowing tan of his skin. His mouth was his most attractive feature. His lower lip was full, one might almost say sensuous. She could not look at his mouth without thinking that he might have kissed her anywhere and had chosen to kiss her forehead.

He opened eyes as green and distant as the ocean. He blinked, focused on her, and smiled. His smile surged over her like a wave, tumbling her emotions. With customary intensity he regarded her. Love—warm, unstinting, all-encompassing love—looked out at her through Charles Ramsay's eyes.

As plainly as if he had opened up his mouth to say, "I love you," she read the emotion. His love—and it was in no way a lustful, greedy, needful love—flowed over her like the turning of the tide. So completely did this man's openly expressed affection reach into the empty spaces of her heart, filling her, she felt as if she must overflow.

This was love. Not what she and Timothy had shared. Trust and truth stared her in the face. Timothy had needed her. His need had been desperate. Wanting to be needed, she had found him compelling. He had drawn her like a vortex, drawn her with his words, his hands, his lips, his need. Charles Ramsay drew her in a profoundly different manner. Like the sun, bright, warm and omnipresent, he drew her toward him as gently as the sun will draw a plant. She could feel herself stretching, growing, blossoming in his presence. She leaned toward the light.

They came together as naturally as the water washed up on the shore, as warm as the sun on their backs, as gently as the breeze that ran its fingers through their hair. There was nothing needy or clinging about their first kiss. It was an uncertain and gentle exploration. Ramsay's lips, like a wave receding, gently dampened the corner of her mouth, the curve of her cheek, the bone of her jaw. The tide of his lips washed up against hers again, gently shaping her mouth to his. She, like sand beneath the water's sway, felt lifted, stirred, and gently settled in a pattern new to her.

She gave herself completely to the sweep of emotion. It was, in the end, Ramsay who stopped the reshaping of their relationship.

"I have only kisses to offer you, dear Prudence," he whispered, turning his mouth away from hers. "It is not enough."

She had no opportunity to respond. He rose abruptly, distancing himself from her. His back to her, he stood looking out over the Channel.

"It is not nearly enough."

Chapter Twenty

Prudence felt as if she were floating when she breezed back into Mrs. Harris's boardinghouse, hat in hand, sand in her shoes, the heat of the sun baked into the cotton fabric of her dress. The heat of Charles Ramsay's kiss still warmed her lips, and the potential of his words hummed in her mind and heart. She felt prepared, even peaceful, about the prospect of confronting her cousin. There was something unreal about her happiness. The thought crossed her mind that this day was too splendid to be true.

And so it was.

The sight of her bags, piled unceremoniously against the wall in the hallway brought her abruptly back to earth. Prudence knew in an instant that Timothy was gone. She knew in her heart, and yet her head would not accept the truth of it. With a sinking feeling she rushed immediately up the stairs, fleeing down again when she found the doors to both hers and Mrs. Moore's rooms open to reveal strangers within, unpacking their bags and calling back and forth to each other, complaining about the accommodations. Fighting a rising tide of panic that threatened to drown her newly found sense of peace, Prudence went in search of Mrs. Harris.

"My bags . . ." she began.

Mrs. Harris looked her up and down with a puzzled expression, as if she had become a curiosity. "Yes, Miss Stanhope, did you see them as you came in?"

"Yes, but . . ."

"Your cousin informed me you were not to have the rooms anymore. I must say I was surprised that he and Mrs. Moore left without you to see them off. I had no idea you were to be leaving separately." Her interest in divining further details was blatant.

As Prudence was not forthcoming with any information to enlighten her, she went on briskly, "I have taken the liberty of packing up your things. I hope you do not mind, but we have had a sudden influx of visitors all clamoring for space on account of the races. The ladies who were given your room arrived early this afternoon and asked if they might not settle themselves in for the evening."

Prudence's mouth was dry, her head spinning. "My cousin," she managed to stammer, "when did he leave?"

Mrs. Harris patted at her pocket. "Just after noon, miss. How inconsiderate of him not to inform you as to his intentions. Perhaps all will be explained to your satisfaction in the letter he left you on payment of the bill."

"Letter?"

Mrs. Harris drew forth a handful of papers, among them the letter to Prudence.

The door bell jangled. "There it goes again." The missive was impatiently thrust in Pru's general direction. "People will not believe the fully occupied sign that stands in full view upon the step. I have turned away half a dozen or so already, all convinced I can conjure up another sleeping space if I will only try. Excuse me. I shall just go and send them away."

Prudence barely heard her. She was clutching the note from Timothy, her hands shaking, her legs stiff as pickets. While she had been frolicking on the beach, her entire world had been whisked out from under her feet.

Tim and Mrs. Moore were on their way back to Gillingham, the note said. The bills had been honored both here and at Mahomed's Baths. Folded in the letter was a handful of bank notes.

"You will need money," Tim wrote with cool finality.

The Ramsays will have none to spare no matter how highly you value their company. Please notify me as to your new address, so that your belongings may be forwarded to you. I will be happy to send them anywhere, so long as the address is not that of a Ramsay. You stand by your convictions. I must stand by mine. Perhaps cousin Tobias will take you in. I encourage you to write him with just such an appeal.

He closed the letter with a score of addresses, all of them Pru's distant relatives, all to whom she had already written. At the bottom of the page he had signed his name, but there were no parting words of affection, not a word of excuse or apology, not a word of regret or sorrow in their separation.

Prudence was stunned. All of her joy in the day fled in an instant. Guilt roared in her ears like the surge of a tide that threatened to sweep her off her feet. She had whiled away her security in far too carefree a manner. Where was she to go now? What was she to do?

The face of Charles Ramsay filled her thoughts. His voice whispered in her ear. "A state of repose, Miss Stanhope. I have found it in the midst of chaos." Her shoulders straightened. Closing her eyes, she concentrated on relaxing her neck. Again Ramsay seemed to whisper in her ear. "Strive for a state of repose. It will see you through the direst of circumstances."

She would go to him. He had asked her to rely on his assistance in just such an event. Surely, if any man might be trusted, it was Ramsay. He must, at the very least, be able to help her to find a room for the night. Bravely putting a mask of unworried repose on the face of her panic, Prudence informed Mrs. Harris she would return for her bags anon, and set out, on foot, for the house in which the Ramsays lodged.

The Ramsays were staying at a house in German Place, a street leading off the Marine Parade, no more than a few blocks away. Prudence set out on foot. She chose to go by way of St. James's, though it took her a little out of her way. There were shops along St. James's Street. A woman alone was less likely to be accosted among the shops than along the Marine Parade. She was glad she had thought to don her bonnet. Its brim shielded her from the occasional curious glances she received.

Prudence felt very strange walking alone—smaller somehow and oddly weightless, without her arm linked to Mrs. Moore or her cousin. Stranger still to be en route to a private residence with the intention of calling on an unmarried gentleman whose help she required—a gentleman she had known for no more than a few weeks—a gentleman she was not entirely convinced she could trust. The solitary clicking of her footsteps was a disturbingly hollow sound. She had no home. She had no home. She was alone, alone, alone. The strangeness of her circumstances brought tears to her eyes. She blinked them furiously away.

She was displaced. The thought increased the likelihood of tears. She resorted to her handkerchief, dabbing at the corners of her eyes. She did not belong here in Brighton. She no longer belonged in Gillingham. Where did she belong? She felt as if she floated a little above the walkway, tetherless. So unsettled was she by the impression, so distracted by sorting through her whirl of thoughts, that the sound of an approaching vehicle did not register in her ears as she came to the corner of German Place. She did not see it in the periphery of her vision as she stepped from the curb. Her bonnet blocked her view.

A man's voice called out urgently, "I say! Hallo there. Watch your step!"

A traveling chaise swept by her with a rattle of harness and a clatter of hooves. The blur of a man's face in the passing window frame swept by—dark hair, an expression of concern.

How strange! How disturbing! Prudence stood poised in the gutter, faced with her own foolishness. She had come very close to injury, perhaps even death, for no more reason than she had not been paying attention. She was alone. There was no one to look out for her but herself. She could not afford to be careless.

Her tear-blurred gaze followed the chaise. German Place was lined by attractive, bow-fronted, four-story buildings that were for the most part let out to visitors. What an ordinary place, what an ordinary way in which to be reminded of one's mortality! The strangeness of the moment was compounded, complicated by the fact that the chaise that had come close to killing her pulled to a halt in front of the address she meant to visit. From it descended the gentleman who had called out to warn her of her own imminent demise. Dark haired and fashionably attired, he went around the carriage to assist in the descent of a striking young woman who opened up her arms and cried out her pleasure as Grace and Rue and Charles came down the steps to greet her.

High spirits and carefree smiles so completely contradicted her own teary, rattled state that Prudence could not continue in her progress along the street. She could not thrust herself into this scene. The merriment of her carefree morning had become a time and a feeling so distanced by the afternoon's upset that it had almost faded from her realm of reality. She intruded, in coming here on an errand that must interfere with the happiness of her friends.

The impression that she arrived with the poorest of timing was compounded. The striking young woman hugged Grace. She kissed Rupert's cheek, but she threw herself most exuberantly into Ramsay's arms. He responded to her embrace with equal enthusiasm. He did, in fact, kiss her several times with unstinted ardor.

Who was this woman he held so freely? Who was this woman whose kisses he did not refuse? Doubts that had assailed her in the past came crowding back to trouble Pru. Was this the prior commitment Ramsay had referred to? Was this woman the reason he had nothing more to offer her than kisses?

Lessons came from hardship, Charles Ramsay had that afternoon professed to her. Lessons indeed! She had forgotten the most important lesson her hardships with Timothy had taught her. Men were not to be trusted. She had never imagined Ramsay led her on so masterfully. She had never dreamed he refused her kisses because he wished to lavish them on another's lips. She had believed his elaborate, cleverly plausible, all too tempting lies. He had played her for a fool all along, but never more masterfully than today.

There was only one among the glad party who noticed she stood indecisively shifting from one foot to the other at the corner of the road. The gentleman from the chaise turned to look in her direction. For a moment they stared at one another.

Men were not to be trusted. Not even this stranger who had, perhaps unwittingly, saved her from certain harm. Rash Ramsay was not to be trusted. He had proven that the first time they had met. Her mistake was in forgetting.

Prudence turned away. Fresh tears blurred her vision. The scene that played itself out before her eyes reminded her too vividly how vulnerable she was, how alone. She turned her back on the happy reunion. There was no one with open arms waiting to welcome her home. She no longer had a home, of any sort, to claim.

There was only one other person in Brighton to whom she felt she might turn. Hailing a passing cab, she directed the man to drive her at once to Rose Thurgood's address.

Endings, endings, endings the clop of the horse's hooves reminded her as she was jounced along the road to the cottage in Norfolk Street where Rose was staying while her house was being built. A maid greeted her at the door.

"Madame Rose," she said "is at the building site." She offered directions. It was not far.

Rose's new house was one of several being finished in Bedford Square. It had the distinction of being the first square to be built in Brighton, though ground had recently been broken on Belle Vue Field just down the seafront, on what was to be the second. Bedford was an attractive arrangement of over forty, four-storied houses grouped cheek by jowl on three streets facing what promised to be half an acre of garden. Many of the bow-fronted houses boasted Ionic pillars, ironwork balconies, and verandas. A number of the windows that opened onto the square were also afforded a view of the sea, which made up the fourth side of the square.

It was immediately apparent why Rose and her sister had planned to leave Brighton for foreign shores while the plastering and painting of her house was being finished. There was new construction all along the street. Indeed, the entire area was soon to be under development. There was talk of an Oriental

Garden going in nearby, with a conservatory and cultural center. Hard to imagine any of it coming to pass at this stage. Bedford Square sat in the midst of a great deal of nothing at this point.

One could not think about anything much, however, for the banging and sawing sounds. There were workmen everywhere, perched on scaffolding, hanging out of windows, scaling the raw framework of buildings just begun. They seemed happy at their work, laughing, singing, shouting out suggestive remarks to Prudence. An unattended female navigating the obstacle course of piled brick, dirt, and mortaring materials was considered fair game for lewd comment.

Despite such demeaning difficulties, Prudence reveled in the newness of Bedford Square. Here was not an ending, but a new beginning! It hung in the breeze in the odor peculiar to all construction sites: freshly cut wood, drying mortar, plaster, and recently spread paint. There was something exhilarating, even courageous, to be observed in the act of building something where there had once been nothing. To take an unknown—whether it was the unknown of an architect's dream or the unknown of declaring one's independence—to follow the necessary steps required to jump into that unknown, required vision. It required the ability to recognize potential. It required a leap of faith.

Some would have found it a noisy mess, but Prudence recognized that turmoil always accompanied the building of something new. She was comforted by the idea.

At number 39, Rose's house, a smocked workman was toting a ladder through the newly framed front door. "Help you, my dear?" he asked when Prudence hesitated at the bottom of the plaster-dusted steps.

"Is Mrs. Thurgood here?"

"Upstairs." he indicated the direction with a raised thumb.

Above them Rose herself leaned out of one of the unpainted windows, her face flushed with pleasure. "Miss Stanhope, is that you?" she called.

Prudence tipped back her head. "Yes."

"I have never been more pleased to see anyone in my entire life," Rose exclaimed. "I am in desperate need of another opinion with regard to the chimney-front tiles I am choosing. Don't stand there on the steps. Come up, come up."

To be welcomed so enthusiastically was a blessing. Prudence gladly went up.

The house was taking shape inside as much as it was taking shape without.

"How wonderful this place promises to be," Prudence said when Rose met her on stairs whose railings were in the process of being sanded.

"Do you think so?" Rose, a handkerchief guarding her nose from sawdust, gazed about her with a harried, doubt-filled expression. "It is all so raw and bare and unpainted. I have trouble imagining it will ever be finished, much less cozy. What luck you have come to see me. Ester was to have helped me with all of the decisions I am being hounded to make. Tiles for the fireplace, marble for the floors, and wood—wood for doors, wood for floors, wood for paneling and trim and cabinets—not to mention the draperies, wallpaper, and paint I must pick out. Doorknobs! Have you any concept of how many doorknobs there are to choose from? I pore over catalogs from morning till night. And all the while I am missing Ester. I am in fact, quite put out with her for dying when she did. She was to have seen me through all of this. She had a better eye for such things, an eye that did in a way see into the future. 'I see that on the wall,' she would say, or 'I can see what that will look like when it is finished.' I have no such ability to see."

And I see too much, Prudence thought. She had seen the potential of a future with Charles Ramsay when there was none. She took Rose's hand, stilling the flow of her thoughts. "Come," she said. "We shall have a look together. I am pleased to help in any way that I can, for I've a favor to ask of you in return."

A proud tour of the domicile was undertaken. Chimney tiles were decided upon. Doorknobs, draperies, and wallpaper were discussed. At last, Rose insisted they return to the cottage for refortification with tea and cake.

It was there, as the housemaid served up their tea, that Rose asked Prudence what favor she might do in exchange for smoothing her hectic day.

Prudence studied the leaves swirling in the bottom of her cup for a moment. Her voice seemed smaller than usual when she asked, "I wonder if you have reconsidered the prospect of hiring a personal companion. If you have, I should very much like to be considered for the position. If not, would you find it dreadfully inconvenient to put me up for the night?"

Rose laughed. "Inconvenient? Not in the least. Stay the night. Stay the week if you please. I have a whole host of decisions to make. It would be a great comfort not to make them all on my own. I have paneling to choose tomorrow, and wallpapers to look at. Come, I shall have Ester's bed made up." She sent the maid scurrying.

Arrangements were made to fetch Pru's bags from Mrs. Harris's boardinghouse.

It was only then that Rose responded to the rest of Pru's request. "Your cousin, my dear, will he not miss you if you become companion to me?"

Prudence laughed bitterly. "No, Rose. He will not miss me. He has, you see, washed his hands of me."

Chapter Twenty-one

They were a happy group, the carriage full of Ramsays, despite the flurry of traffic that they encountered due to the racing crowds, all in a hurry, all heading in the same direction toward the racing grounds located on the downs a little over a mile outside of Brighton. The weather was as bright, clear, and cloudless as their mood. Spirits were high. The entire company was buoyed by love and youth and the happiness that came with family reunion after an eventful separation.

There was, of course, an awkwardness between Charles Ramsay and his brother-in-law, Miles. How could there not be, given recent history? Miles now held in his possession all that Charles was to have called his own.

Charles knew that his every interaction with his new brother-in-law was observed with concern by his siblings.

"I am so pleased that the two of you have opportunity at last to meet," Grace had said with preternatural cheer on the previous afternoon when the Fletcher carriage had arrived and Charles and Miles stood warily regarding one another like dogs on the sniff.

"Best behavior," Rupert had whispered in his ear, "else I shall crack you over the head with my crutch."

"Best behavior," Charles agreed through gritted teeth. "My cheeks already ache with smiling."

"That's the spirit," Rupert approved. "This could be more of that kismet nonsense you are so keen on."

Kismet? Charles had to admit the thought never crossed his mind. For the moment he intended only to do his best to get through the next few days without saying or doing anything foolish to Miles Fletcher. He had thought his feelings were well

in hand, and had thought himself completely resigned to the fact
that the man who had married his sister now counted all of his
possessions as his own. The actual face to face with Miles
Fletcher when he was feeling thwarted in his pursuit of Prudence Stanhope because of the loss of his living, made the meeting more difficult than originally anticipated. It was all Charles
could do to shake the man's hand without squeezing too hard.

Looking far more radiant than Charles could ever recall,
Aurora pulled him aside to make plain to him her feelings.
"You *will* love him, Charles," she had insisted with desperate
fervor. "You must, for my sake."

"Love him? You ask too much, Aurora. I will be polite. I
will even tolerate the man. More than that you cannot ask of
me."

Fortunately, for all concerned, Miles Fletcher had little to
say in the matter of how he thought Charles should receive
him. The two managed to exchange good mornings pleasantly
enough. Charles even found it within himself to admit, "We
could not have asked for more comfortable racing seats."

The top of Miles's chaise was to be their vantage point, the
tiered seats in the racing stands having long since sold out.

"I am pleased it is to your taste," Miles said agreeably. "The
vehicle was my Uncle Lester's, a man blessed with complete
appreciation of creature comforts."

Charles realized that the uncle Miles referred to was the
very same uncle who had beat his brother at cards. He managed to smile through gritted teeth. He even went on to say,
"Our party is satisfactorily assembled in all ways but one."

"Yes, we must stop and ask Miss Stanhope if she will come
with us." Grace immediately guessed his meaning.

The others readily agreed, Rupert because he liked Prudence, Aurora because she had been told by Grace that
Charles was in love with the Stanhope woman, and Miles
Fletcher because he was intent on making himself agreeable in
all respects to the Ramsays, from whom he felt he had illicitly
gained a fortune.

A crowd of waiting carriages at the bottom of New Steine
Street delayed their progress. Eager both to see Prudence and

to distance himself from Miles Fletcher, Charles jumped down from the top of the chaise, where he had been sitting next to Rupert, who had been granted the privilege of driving.

"I shall stroll up to the boardinghouse," he called to the others. "By the time you get through this infernal mess, Miss Stanhope and I will be out on the steps, waiting for you."

New Steine was built on an incline. The walkway was busy. Charles briskly dodged his way through the milling people, all bound for the races. Breathless from his exertions, he rang the bell at Pru's boardinghouse. He was met, not by Mrs. Harris, the proprietress, but by a party of gentlemen on their way out. They politely held the door and allowed him to enter at will. Charles politely acknowledged their courtesy. Inside, he was faced with even more bustle and traffic than was to be found in the streets. Everyone, it seemed, was in a hurry. Everyone was preparing for a day at the races.

A tight-mouthed woman wearing an apron and carrying a tray full of steaming food spotted him as he came through the door. She dodged a crowd of ladies and gentlemen donning hats and cloaks in the hallway and called in an authoritative voice, "I've no rooms left to let if that's what you're here for, sir."

Sweeping through a swinging door to her right, she disappeared with her burden.

Charles held the front door for the departing crowd and headed for the swinging door. The woman with the tray, now empty, almost hit him in the face with it as she came swinging briskly through again.

"Oh dear, I thought you had gone," she said.

"It is not a room I am after, but one of your guests."

Grandly, she swept open the door at her rear. It opened on the crowded breakfast room. "Help yourself, sir. I've food getting cold."

Charles stepped into the room. A quick glance around, and it was clear Prudence numbered not among those who sat spooning food into their mouths. Neither, for that matter, were her cousin or her companion, Mrs. Moore, to be seen.

He swung back through the door again, his eye out for the

woman in the apron. She was soon back in the hallway, bearing another tray full of food. He fell in step in front of her, courteously holding the door to the breakfast room wide as he explained.

"It is Miss Prudence Stanhope I seek. Can you tell me if she or her cousin have come down to breakfast?"

"Stanhope?" She peered at him rather intently as she ladled stewed fruit into a chafing dish. "That one won't be coming down. Left yesterday, she did."

"Left? Miss Stanhope has gone?"

"Yes." Again she gave him the piercing look. "All three of them yesterday."

"But I spoke to her yesterday. She said nothing about leaving."

"It would appear you are not as much in her confidence as you supposed," she said tartly.

Her words stung. Charles was struck speechless. That Prudence Stanhope had gone was the last thing he had expected to hear. That she could leave with her cousin after the day they had spent together left him flabbergasted. He could not have been more stunned had the woman smacked him in the head with her tray.

She was impatient to return to her work. "I've breakfast to serve, sir. So, if you'll pardon me . . ."

He let her go, his mind a blank, his legs carrying him out the door to the sunny street where a chaise full of smiling, jesting family members stood waiting.

"Does she mean to come with us?" Grace called cheerfully from the window.

"No." he said, the word insensible to his ears. "She is gone."

"Gone?" Grace scoffed. "She cannot possibly be gone, Charles. She said nothing about leaving yesterday."

"Gillingham," he said flatly, all his joy in the day and the bright possibility of a future with Prudence Stanhope gone. "She has returned to Gillingham with her cousin."

Grace would not accept the truth. "This cannot be true. She meant to find another position. I am sure she did."

Charles grew weary of repeating himself. He did not want to be convinced himself that Prudence was gone. That he must now convince others made him irritable.

"She *is* gone," he said harshly. What else could he say?

"Makes no sense." Rupert looked baffled. "I thought the two of you . . . well, you know . . . had kismet working in your favor."

Charles sighed heavily. "I thought so, too," he admitted.

"Does the young lady sometimes wear an outdated Oldenburg bonnet trimmed in green ribbon?" Miles Fletcher leaned out of the coach to ask with lazy nonchalance.

"Why should you care whether her bonnet is outdated?" Anger, confusion, and the impatience he was feeling for stupid questions lashed out of Charles's mouth aimed at the most convenient of targets—Miles Fletcher.

"Charles! How rude you are!" Aurora scolded.

Charles frowned at Miles. "How do you know Miss Stanhope's bonnet?"

Fletcher shrugged, passing over Charles's rudeness as if it had never happened. "I saw her yesterday when we arrived at your accommodations. She came very close to being knocked down by our carriage as we turned into your street."

"Knocked down?" Grace gasped.

Charles saw red. Fletcher had come close to killing Prudence and mentioned the fact with no more feeling than had he mentioned the swatting of a fly! Charles wanted to grab Fletcher, to shake the man until his teeth rattled.

Aurora stayed his anger. "She was not watching at all where she was going. Had Miles not called out to her, I fear we might well have run her down."

Miles nodded. "Blinded by tears from the looks of it."

"She was crying?" The idea twisted at Charles's heart.

"Yes." Miles recalled the scene with touching sympathy. "Poor girl wept even harder after her near miss with our carriage. She was dabbing at her eyes in a most affecting manner as I was helping Aurora down. It was my intention to approach her, to see if she was all right, but no sooner did I take a step toward her than she set briskly off in the opposite direction."

"Perhaps she meant to say good-bye and could not collect herself enough to do so." Grace sounded as stunned as Charles felt.

"Shall we put off going to the races?" Aurora suggested.

"No. No." Charles waved Rupert onward. "There is no reason not to carry on and enjoy ourselves." He said the words with as much conviction as he could muster.

The others agreed that it would be a pity to waste such perfect weather. Only Rupert understood. Once the horses were in motion, he turned on his bench, his expression sympathetic. "What kind of kismet is this, Chaz?"

Charles shook his head, his heart as heavy as the day he had received word of Jack's fateful gambling losses. "The most unfortunate kind, I wager."

Chapter Twenty-two

I have begun to detest all wallpaper!" Rose exclaimed, clapping shut the book of samples she was perusing. She complained loudly enough that the clerk who had been waiting on them blinked like a frightened rabbit and scurried to the back of the store to hide himself away in the stockroom.

Prudence was wool-gathering. She had been woolgathering for more than a week now, thinking of Charles Ramsay, replaying every moment she had spent in his company, trying to figure out how she could have been so deceived by him. She thought of her cousin. Edith had responded to her letter with one of her own. "Come back," she had begged, "the children are devastated by your absence." Jane and Julia had sent pleas as well, carefully spelled out in their neatest copperplate. There had been no word from Timothy. Thank God for Rose!

She and Rose got along famously. Arrangements had been agreed upon to both their satisfaction as to Pru's position, her accommodations, her pay, her responsibilities. Woolgathering was not one of them. Thank God for wallpaper. She might have gone crawling back to Tim were it not for wallpaper.

She turned the page of the book she was examining. "What do you think of this?" She spread one of the samples in front of Rose. The paper was beautiful: roses, a trellis in the border, a trailing vine.

"Lovely, but not really a match for the items I have ordered from Lord Ramsay."

Ramsay again.

"No. Quite right."

Rose lowered her voice. "I've a good mind to cancel that order."

"Cancel it? Why?"

"Kissing another female! I thought he was such a nice young man. I *thought* he was quite smitten with you—the way he held your hand—the way he looked into your eyes."

"Yes." Prudence concentrated on not allowing her chin to wobble. "Be that as it may, your order has nothing to do with his kissing other females. I have no real claim on his affections—no promises to hold him to. My belief that he loved me was based entirely on supposition and inference. He did, in fact, show great restraint in his behavior toward me. On more than one occasion when I might have allowed a great deal of foolishness, he stopped me. I now know why."

Rose clasped her shoulders as warmly as a mother might. "We are a miserable pair, are we not? Shall we mope and suffer here together, Prudence?" She had a dangerous gleam in her eyes. "Or shall we forget all of our troubles—all men, all builders, all wallpapers—and make an opportunity out of our common misery?"

"I don't follow."

"Shall we pack up our bags as you once suggested and leave it all behind us?"

Prudence regarded her with wide-eyed disbelief. "Do you mean it?"

"Ester's trip. Shall we kick off the traces and go?"

"This is sudden."

"To the contrary. I have thought of little else since we last spoke of it at the bathhouse. The idea, once planted in my mind, has not stopped growing. I cannot seem to get China out of my head. I dream about it every night. Just how serious was your suggestion that we travel together?"

Prudence laughed with the first true feeling of joy experienced since she had seen Charles Ramsay kissing another woman. "Serious? Dearest Rose, I was completely serious. When shall we go?"

* * *

His smile, Charles decided, had begun to feel like a grimace—like the strange, red-lipped leer of the Oriental dragons that decorated the Chinese lanterns locked away in his shop full of goods. The dragon of his happiness had sprouted the wings of an evil he did not comprehend.

A week of races and being on his best behavior had given him a pounding headache that no Far Eastern palm pinching could cure, and the dragonlike feeling that he would breathe fire, given the slightest provocation. He could not really blame his mood on the races. The weather was beautiful. He had shaken a great many hands, pressing his business card into most of them. One of the horses Rupert placed a bet on had come in first. Even Miles Fletcher had not proved a problem. A good week by all accounts but one, and yet when he tried to find satisfaction within himself, he could not. He tried to adopt an attitude of repose. It eluded him. He sat unpaired atop the chaise trying to act cheerful when there was no cheer in him.

Unhappiness weighed him down, plaguing him with the oddest of notions as he watched the races. His thoughts, like the horses, ran endless circles, getting nowhere and leaving him lathered and jumpy. He imagined catching up one of the sleek Thoroughbreds to chase after Prudence Stanhope on these, the fastest horses money could buy. Problem was, he could not afford horses, fast or slow. Ironic that he sat atop the carriage of the man who had taken those fleet horses—the power to purchase them, the power to pursue Prudence—away from him.

His emotions raced. First he was stunned—numb to the laughter and color, noise and excitement that accompanied the racing event. Then he was angry. He had believed himself closer to Prudence Stanhope than to any woman he had ever bared his soul to. He had been certain she understood the depth of his feelings for her, and that she did in some way reciprocate those feelings. Doubts filled him. Had he misread her every word, her every gesture? What was it he was supposed to learn from his brief encounter with her? How could he reconcile all that had passed between them with her abrupt departure? Why had fate decreed she should leave without a word! Karma or kismet, whatever this was, seemed a cruel teacher. As cruel as the governess who had cut him to the quick. Sadness, regret, and helplessness gnawed at him. The well of peace he had grown accustomed to drawing on seemed to have run dry.

By the end of the week Charles could not subject himself to another day of sunshine, noise, horses, and crowds. He could not bear to spend another instant in the company of his family. The dragon within him needed space. He needed time alone. He needed to regain his sense of repose. Perhaps in solitude he could come to an understanding of Prudence Stanhope's rejection of the potential that blossomed like a lotus flower between them.

In order to avoid them, he lied to the others.

"I must spend the day at my place of business," he told them. "I expect a customer—a gentleman come down from London for the races. I mean to spend the day packing up Mrs. Thurgood's delivery while I wait for him."

"Oh no!" Grace moaned.

"What a bother," Aurora pronounced his imaginary customer. "I thought we might spend a quiet day at Donaldson's. They have a chamber orchestra scheduled to play a bit of Vivaldi."

"Need a bit of time to yourself, do you?" Rupert asked with perfect understanding when they had a moment alone.

"Exactly," Charles admitted. "The dragon returns to his lair to lick his wounds with the breath of fire. I want nothing more than to be left alone—alone to forget my heart is broken."

"Is it difficult to be around us because we are couples?"

"You have an uncanny understanding, Rupert. It does pain me. In witnessing your happiness I am reminded exactly what I had hoped for, imagined in fact I had within my grasp." Anger rose within him like a tide. "How could she go to Gillingham, Rue, to serve the needs of a man already blessed with a wife?"

Rupert shook his head. "I don't know, Chaz. I wish I did. I wish I could help."

Charles shook his head and tried to smile. "I just need some time alone." He could not articulate that his sense of peace, contentment, and order had deserted him. He could not explain that his steady assurance that things happened for a reason, that one might learn and grow from the encounter, was gone. What lesson might he learn in Prudence Stanhope's desertion other than to distrust his heart and to be wary of love? There was no great good he could fathom in their sudden separation.

"Would you mind terribly if I tag along today?" It was Miles Fletcher who politely placed an obstacle in the solitary pathway that led to his peace of mind. "I've no real desire to listen to Vivaldi when I might see instead this collection of items you brought back with you from overseas." He waited half a breath for some sort of response. He then suggested he knew one or two souls who would be interested in the items Charles had to offer.

Charles was too stunned to speak, too incapacitated by his thoughts about Prudence to formulate a suitable refusal.

That Miles Fletcher felt the need to offer him assistance in any way went decidedly against the grain. "You need not feel obliged in any way to make up for the foolishness of my brother for his losses to your uncle. I will not allow our strange history to come between myself and Aurora."

Miles listened politely before he said in his quiet and completely unobtrusive way, "There are one or two things I would have settled between us."

As much as he would have liked to, Charles could not refuse this blatant offering of the olive branch between them. With reluctance he said, "You are welcome to accompany me."

"Marvelous!" Miles said.

The parties went their separate ways. More than one set of eyes grew round with surprise that Charles and Miles planned to pair themselves off the way they had. Rupert even went so far as to try to dissuade Miles. With a gesture Charles stopped him.

"I am not the best of company today," Charles warned his brother-in-law as he unlocked the door to the narrow space that held his treasures.

"You need not be company to me at all," Miles said mildly. "We are after all, family, no matter how strange or undesirable it may seem. I am pleased you invited me to come here when you have every reason in the world to shun my company."

"You are not at all the man I expected my sister to marry," Charles said frankly, as he began to light lamps to illuminate the darkness they stepped into.

Miles laughed. "I am not at all the man Aurora planned to marry."

"Yes. I heard she had set her sights on Lord Walsh."

Miles nodded. "She had. But, as he was not at all the sort to keep her happy, I made a subtle point of getting in his way."

Charles wondered if he should have made a more obvious point of standing in Timothy Margrave's way.

"Why don't you chase after her?" Miles asked, as if he read his mind.

"What?"

"This Stanhope person. Why don't you go after her?" he asked in his deceptively mild manner, as if such a suggestion were no more out of the ordinary than the manner in which he began to study items in the crates on either side of him.

Charles was caught off guard. Welcoming Miles Fletcher to view his goods was one thing, welcoming him to view his innermost thoughts and feelings, quite another. They were not close enough to share confidences. "Is that how you lured Aurora away from Walsh? By chasing after her?"

Miles laughed. He had a pleasant laugh, a likeable laugh. As Charles did not particularly want to like Miles Fletcher, the laugh annoyed him. Fletcher had won too much that was his already. He would not so easily win Charles's friendship and respect.

Miles held a carved ivory piece to the light—a beautifully detailed elephant, trunk up. "Do you believe in fate, my lord?" he said.

Those words, of all the words Miles might have uttered, captured Charles's attention.

"Fate?' he repeated stupidly, completely unprepared for Fletcher, of all people, to throw fate in his face.

Miles tucked the elephant carefully into its nest of tissue. "Yes, fate. The reason I ask, is because I am convinced that nothing less than fate brings us together today."

Charles did not want to admit he and Miles might share so great a concept. Rather than admit therefore that he believed, he said with a trace of sarcasm, "I thought it was a deck of cards brought us together." Attempting to bring to earth their lofty discussion, he busied himself with the mundane task of packing up the items he intended to deliver to Rose Thurgood.

Miles continued to poke about among the crates. He seemed loath to let the subject drop. "I would argue that destiny had her hand in it. The deck of cards that brought Ramsays and Fletchers together determined our fortunes in more ways than one."

"I do not understand." Charles stopped what he was doing. He did not want to miss a word of this.

Miles ceased poking into the crates. "The very night Jack lost everything at cards to my Uncle Lester the old man entrusted me with what was to be his dying wish."

"Which was?"

"He wanted me to look after Aurora to see she did not suffer unduly for Jack's bad luck at cards. He knew I was on my way to the sheep shearing at Holkham Hall, where I was bound to encounter your sister, Aurora, for whom he had a fondness. He feared, quite rightly, that Jack's losses would leave her in an unenviable position."

"Does Aurora know all this?"

He shook his head. "I have never told her the whole story."

"Did you marry her then out of pity?"

Miles laughed smoothly. "Not at all. My intention was to fulfill her heart's desire."

"Walsh?"

He nodded. "Walsh. I did not count on falling in love. My Uncle Lester's winnings, therefore, proved both a blessing and a curse."

"I see." Charles did not really *see* at all. This man would have him believe that in having been bequeathed a fortune, *his fortune*, he was in some way a sympathetic creature. Truth was, he had no sympathy left in him for Miles Fletcher.

The sarcasm of his reply was not lost on Miles. He wound his way past the crates and boxes that separated them to stand at Charles's elbow.

"You must understand," he said. "I have offered the winnings to Aurora. She will not have them. I offer them now to you."

"What?" Charles gasped. "Why?"

"I would not have anything stand between Aurora and her happiness. If you and I cannot be friends, she is not happy."

Charles tried not to feel offended, and yet he could not help stiffening at the suggestion. It was insulting to have all that had once been his so casually offered up to him.

With more vigor than the task required he tied shut the box he had been packing, picked it up and moved purposefully away from Miles Fletcher, saying brusquely, "My inheritance was fairly lost and fairly gained. I could not in good faith accept what is no longer mine other than as charity, and I've no desire for charity, thank you."

Miles made no move to chase after him. His expression remained carefully urbane. "I am pleased you should say so. I do not think I could be business partners with a man afraid to stand on his principles."

"Business partners!" Charles fairly shouted. "Have you allowed Grace to fill your head with her odd notions?"

"Grace?" He evidenced confusion. "No! It is you I have been listening to these past few days. We have a great deal in common. It seems only logical that we should put the money I am uncomfortable in having won and you are doubtless uncomfortable in having lost, into a business together."

"A business!"

Miles had given the matter a great deal of thought. In his gently persuasive manner he outlined a grand plan involving warehouses and shopfronts with hired attendants to be established in both Brighton and in London. "We shall require a steady influx of new products from the sources you have already established. It will require a great deal of travel on both our parts," he said.

Before Charles could respond, they were interrupted by the abrupt entrance of Grace, who raced in the door, out of breath, her bonnet knocked askew, and her eyes fairly popping with excitement.

"Dear God, Charles! Can you believe it? She is off to China of all places."

"Who is off to China?" Miles inquired mildly.

Charles knew. "Prudence?"

Grace nodded enthusiastically, her eyes sparkling. "She did not go home to Gillingham at all as we supposed. I have just seen her at Donaldson's in the company of Rose Thurgood. They are booked on a clipper that leaves tomorrow."

"Not if I can help it." Charles vowed.

"Off on a business jaunt already are you, partner?" Miles asked quietly, as was his way.

"Partner?" Grace looked from Charles to Miles in confusion.

Charles considered Miles and all he so generously, so genially offered. And as he considered, Miles offered him one thing more. His hand.

Charles grasped it firmly. "Partners," he agreed.

Chapter Twenty-three

Prudence stood alone, the deck rocking beneath her feet, the sounds of a boat newly launched filling her ears: the flap, slap, flutter of sails, the creak of straining rope and wood and canvas, the strange, shouted lingo and piping whistles of the men who worked to put her adventure to sea from a London dockyard.

Change had Pru's whole body tingling. She was engaged in an ending here, an ending of her ignorance of what lay beyond the boundaries of England's shores, an ending of her innocence to the ways of the world, an ending to her dependence on family. The strings that bound her to the past, to England, had loosed their hold on her, one by one. She flew free, she realized, as free as the gulls that winged their way above the tossing water in their wake—as free, exhilarated, and lonely as embarking on a leap into the unknown could leave one. She was not prepared for the loneliness inherent with claiming one's independence. She had begun the adventure of a lifetime. She should be overjoyed. She should be satisfied. She should feel completely fulfilled, should she not, in the fulfillment of this, her lifelong dream? But she did not feel complete. Something was missing, something important. She had thought it was found in the company of Charles Ramsay. She had glimpsed it in his eyes. She had tasted its promise on his lips.

Her eyes had searched with an almost pained intensity the milling crowds along the pier. There was no loved one waving her away, wishing her well. No cheerful "Bon voyage, my dear. Come safely home to me!"

Charles Ramsay had not come. Too much to hope for, given the circumstances, to think he might follow her all the way to London. His absence pained her. Too late had she learned the truth. Too late had she learned to trust him. Too late, and now she was leaving behind more than England, more than her position as governess, more than her troubles with Timothy. She left behind as well, the beginnings of another dream, a dream that had begun in the arms of Charles Ramsay.

The faintly fishy, hemp, and pitch smell of the dock gave way to the fresh smell of the ocean as salt spray broke across their bow. Gulls dove and shrieked in the boiling water of their wake. Their frantic, greedy cries echoed the tenor of her thoughts. She was a little frantic, too, and more than a little greedy not to find satisfaction in her lot.

With the wrenching feeling that she had just been cut off from all that was familiar and loved, Prudence watched England grow small.

Chilled, she wrapped her arms about her shoulders. She had expected to enjoy this trip, every moment of it. To begin it in sadness, in regret, was surely wrong of her.

Endings, Pru thought. Her life, of late, seemed overwhelmed by endings. She had taken her leave of Grace Ramsay only the day before yesterday. She would miss Grace. Their friendship seemed nipped in the bud.

"Off to China?" Grace had exclaimed, wide-eyed, when they had run into one another in the crowd exiting Donaldson's after the Vivaldi concerto Rose Thurgood had insisted they make a point of catching. "Your ship leaves when? But Pru, we thought you had gone back to Gillingham. Have I found you, only to lose you again? Charles . . . well, Charles will be even more disappointed than I. He was deeply affected by your unexpected disappearance."

Prudence had found it difficult to listen to what she believed an embellished truth. Charles was sure to have found comfort in another woman's arms if her leaving had genuinely affected him as much as Grace would have her believe.

"Will you not be happy for me then, Grace?" she had asked

almost fiercely, her fervency born out of wounded pride. "This trip—my position as companion to Rose Thurgood—it is my dream come true. I can think of nothing that would make me happier."

Grace, caught off guard, latched onto the word as though it puzzled her. "Nothing? Are you sure? Not even—" She had been interrupted by Rupert, who had pegged his way out of the crowd in the company of a dapper gentleman and the young woman Charles Ramsay liked to kiss.

"Miss Stanhope! Is it really you? We thought you gone to Gillingham."

Prudence's stomach was in knots as the trio approached. Small wonder Charles Ramsay was attracted to this beauty. The young lady was striking. She had hair the fiery color of fox fur. Her eyes were pale, gray-green, almost the color of Charles's. The young lady was . . .

"Aurora Ramsay." She held out her hand politely. "So pleased to meet you at last. My brother was completely distraught the day he discovered you gone."

Aurora Ramsay! Dear God! She was Charles's sister. She had been jealous all this time of his sister! She had convinced herself he was not trustworthy over the love of a sibling.

The truth was almost as painful to bear as Pru's imaginings. Did he, in fact, really care for her? Was he trustworthy after all? She had nipped their promising relationship in the bud before ever it had chance to flower. She was going away tomorrow and might never see him again, might never know.

All of the endings she had suffered recently, Prudence had borne with a sense of the inevitable. They were endings she had anticipated and prepared herself for. She understood these endings. What she was not prepared for was this ignominious ending to her relationship with Charles Ramsay. It was tragic. The journey was ended before it had even begun. Why had she not trusted his words, the way he looked at her, his kisses?

She put a hand over her mouth. His kisses had been convincing. A tear, another drop of salty water in this ocean of salty water, slid down her cheek. Were the oceans made up, she wondered, of the tears of a millennia of men and women who had believed in love and been disappointed? How many, she wondered bitterly, were the tears of those who had captured love and then let it go, unwilling to take the leap of faith required to trust in it?

Resolutely, she wiped the tear from the edge of her chin. She would not add her bitter mite to the rolling waters that carried her away on the adventure she had dreamed of before she even knew there was a Charles Ramsay. She would not be sad. Her dream was come true. She was embarking on a journey that encompassed three continents. It was an adventure that she had planned from beginning to end in almost every detail. She had surprised herself at her own capacity to organize such an endeavor. The planning of this trip had been an adventure in itself. She had done a very competent job of it, too. One never knew what one was capable of until one tried.

She had every reason to be pleased with her lot, despite the ache of loneliness in her heart. She had just embarked on the trip of a lifetime. She was gainfully employed. She was blessed, the captain had informed her, with sea legs. Rose, poor, dear Rose, did not have sea legs.

"She'll probably be as right as rain in a few days," the captain had promised when Prudence had voiced concern for her friend's misery.

Rose had not been comforted by such blithe promises. "I hope," she said pitifully as she sat in their cabin with a basin between her knees, "the man knows what he is talking about."

So embarrassed was Mrs. Thurgood by her condition that she would not allow Prudence to remain belowdecks with her. "Go!" she instructed. "Take the air, enjoy the sunshine. I cannot bear that anyone should see me like this."

Prudence had obliged her after directing their cabin boy that additional basins should be brought down to Rose, along with a jug of fresh water and additional linens.

Another of the passengers came to stand behind her at the bow. England turned into little more than a memory on the fogbound horizon, as hard to make out as what it was that had convinced Pru Charles Ramsay had not meant to become a permanent part of her life.

Another tear slid quite contrarily down her cheek. She did not turn to greet her fellow passenger, unwilling to reveal her tearstained face.

"I have come to claim my twenty-four hours," the gentleman said softly in a familiar voice, the voice of the snake charmer, the voice of her beloved, the voice of Charles Ramsay.

"You!" she exclaimed, turning. "You are here!"

"Oh, so you remember me? I had begun to wonder if, after all your noble promises, you meant to cry craven on your debt to me."

"No," she said, her voice unsteady. She had not yet reconciled herself to the wonder of it that he stood before her as nonchalantly as if there were no other place in the world he should be. "How do you mean to spend the hours I owe you, sir?"

"Convincing you never to run away from me again, my dear. How else." He opened his arms to her.

As if it were the most natural thing in the world, Pru stepped into them. Her cheek met the fabric of his coat with the same feeling of embarking on adventure that she had felt as the ship had pulled away from the mouth of the Thames. His arms enfolded her with the exhilarating sensation that change was taking place, a profound change, a change of such magnitude that it colored everything she saw, heard, touched, or smelled. There was, too, inherent in their coming together, a feeling of peace that bloomed like a flame in the deepest part of her soul. Prudence leaned into Charles Ramsay's chest, listening to the drum of his heartbeat, and knew precisely what it meant to assume an attitude of repose.

He kissed her. Nose, chin, eyes, lips; there was no part of her, it seemed, he would not salute with his lips.

"Why did you not come to me?" His voice sounded strained when he stopped kissing her long enough to ask. "You promised that you would."

"I did come to you."

"And did you find me, or leave me word?"

"No. You were otherwise occupied."

"Occupied? In what way was I occupied?"

"You were occupied, sir, much as you are occupied now, in greeting a young lady. In kissing her almost as exuberantly as you kiss me. I thought you loved her, that she was the obstacle you mentioned on the beach, when you would not kiss me. I did not know she was your sister."

"Aurora!"

"Yes, I have suffered untold misery on behalf of your sister."

"Misery?"

"Yes. It did come nigh to breaking my heart that you might love another—that all that you had said and done to make me believe you sincere in your affections for me might be nothing but a hoax even more elaborate than the one you played when first we met."

"No hoax. I was afraid."

"Afraid?"

"Afraid to touch you. Afraid to kiss you. I knew that I would never let you go again if our lips did meet."

"Afraid to touch me?" she said, making no move to pull free from his hold on her. "Why afraid?"

His head bent close to hers. He whispered into her hair, "I had nothing to offer you and no solid prospects of any future to speak of. I was afraid that I could convince you to follow me into a most unhappy and uncertain future." He kissed her hair, her forehead, her nose. His hand rose from its clasp on her shoulder to tilt her chin, so that he might the more easily kiss her lips as well. These, too, he touched upon feather light, and once kissed, he pulled back his head to regard her expression, as if to verify she did not mind his advances.

Her eyes were closed, her mouth soft and lifted to his, waiting the next kiss. Her eyes flew open.

He smiled at her. "You do not mind then?"

She lowered her chin, suddenly bashful, and turned her head a little so that the hand upon her chin came into fuller contact with her face. Her lashes fluttered as her movement caused him to caress her, cheek and chin. "I have longed to feel your touch again, ever since that day in the bathhouse." She shivered as his fingers trailed along her jaw. Standing on tiptoe, she lifted her mouth to his and kissed him as gently as he had kissed her.

"We were fated to come together in the end, my dear."

"Fated?"

"Yes. It is just as Miles said. The very encounter that brought us together might have torn us apart. I might have lost you forever." He held her closer at the thought. "Will you set out on the adventure of a lifetime with me, my sweet—the adventure of marriage?"

"Yes," she whispered, but even as his lips descended to claim hers, she froze, gasping, "No. I cannot."

He backed away, surprised. "Cannot or will not?"

"I am promised to Mrs. Thurgood, Charles, for the duration of this journey. So good has she been to me, so much a support in my hour of need, that I could not in any way abandon her."

"Nor would I have it, Prudence. Are there any other obstacles in our way? Do any other doubts assail you?"

"We have no money, Charles. Will not a wife be too great a strain on already threadbare purse strings?"

He laughed. "Money should not stand in the way of true love, Prudence. I was foolish to let it come between us. You need not worry over money. It is no longer the obstacle I once judged it. I have gone into business with my brother-in-law, Miles Fletcher. We mean to be very rich men before we are done."

"Miles Fletcher? But is he not . . . ?"

"Yes, he is. If two such unlikely characters can see fit to

work together, surely you cannot deem us an unlikely couple in marriage.

"Will you kiss me again, sir? We must not waste your winnings. Twenty-four hours is it I owe you? What shall we do with twenty-four hours? I wonder?"

Charles laughed as he drew her close and set about making excellent use of the time remaining him.